W9-ATA-492

The silence was suddenly oppressive

All at once, Anne desperately needed the solid reassurance of Joshua's presence. She needed to hear him agree that this *was* the cabin where she'd been held captive.

"Joshua!" she yelled.

No answer. Why didn't he reply?

Because he's not here, a voice inside her skull answered. *You're still imprisoned in the cabin, and this is all a dream.*

"No! Damn it! I'm not dreaming!" She tore around the side of the cabin, lungs rasping, her mind churning.

There was no sign of Joshua in the front yard, but the Jeep was still there, exactly where they'd parked it. The pounding of her heart slowed fractionally at this evidence that she wasn't losing her mind. Joshua must be inside the cabin. But why hadn't he answered her shout? Anne raced across the grass and pushed open the front door.

Joshua lay facedown on the carpet, his body frighteningly still.

ABOUT THE AUTHOR

Born in Wales and educated in London,
Jasmine Cresswell now lives with assorted
members of her family in Solon, Ohio. She
and her husband are lucky enough to own a
small condo in Vail, Colorado, and Jasmine
fantasizes about the day when she will either
be so old and grouchy, or so rich and famous,
that her family will encourage her to retreat
there permanently.

Books by Jasmine Cresswell

HARLEQUIN INTRIGUE

51–UNDERCOVER
77–CHASE THE PAST
105–FREE FALL
124–CHARADES

HARLEQUIN PRESENTS

913–HUNTER'S PREY

HARLEQUIN HISTORICALS

6–THE MORETON SCANDAL

Don't miss any of our special offers. Write to us at the
following address for information on our newest releases.

Harlequin Reader Service
P.O. Box 1397, Buffalo, NY 14240
Canadian address: P.O. Box 603,
Fort Erie, Ont. L2A 5X3

House Guest

Jasmine Cresswell

Harlequin Books

TORONTO • NEW YORK • LONDON
AMSTERDAM • PARIS • SYDNEY • HAMBURG
STOCKHOLM • ATHENS • TOKYO • MILAN
MADRID • WARSAW • BUDAPEST • AUCKLAND

If you purchased this book without a cover you should be aware that this book is stolen property. It was reported as "unsold and destroyed" to the publisher, and neither the author nor the publisher has received any payment for this "stripped book."

To Kay Bergstrom, Lee Karr and
the Rocky Mountain Fiction Writers—
good friends, sorely missed

Harlequin Intrigue edition published March 1992

ISBN 0-373-22182-7

HOUSE GUEST

Copyright © 1992 Jasmine Cresswell. All rights reserved.
Except for use in any review, the reproduction or utilization of this work in whole or in part in any form by any electronic, mechanical or other means, now known or hereafter invented, including xerography, photocopying and recording, or in any information storage or retrieval system, is forbidden without the permission of the publisher, Harlequin Enterprises Limited, 225 Duncan Mill Road, Don Mills, Ontario, Canada M3B 3K9.

All the characters in this book have no existence outside the imagination of the author and have no relation whatsoever to anyone bearing the same name or names. They are not even distantly inspired by any individual known or unknown to the author, and all incidents are pure invention.

® are Trademarks registered in the United States Patent and Trademark Office and in other countries.

Printed in U.S.A.

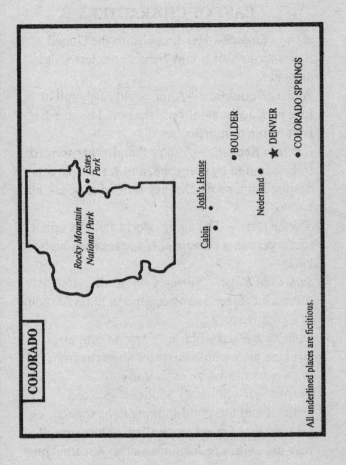

COLORADO

Rocky Mountain National Park

Estes Park •

Cabin
•

Josh's House
•

BOULDER •

Nederland •

★ DENVER

• COLORADO SPRINGS

All underlined places are fictitious.

CAST OF CHARACTERS

Anne Clarence—Her first visit to the United States looks as if it may become her last visit anywhere.

Joshua Donaldson—Anne could easily fall in love with Joshua—if only she could be sure he isn't trying to murder her.

Bertram Kennedy—Anne's grandfather seemed to be admired by everyone, and yet her parents despised him so much, they refused to speak his name.

Shirley Rossi—The aging, world-famous opera star is certainly eccentric. Is she crazy enough to kill?

Sebastian Rossi—Shirley's eldest son. His successful career as an accountant hides the soul of a creative artist.

Dominick Rossi—Shirley's second son, an airplane pilot whose frequent absences from town can't always be explained.

Carlo Rossi—Shirley's youngest son, too brilliant and too good-looking to be trusted.

Heather and Laurel Macmillan—The eighteen-year-old twins are Joshua's nieces. Are they just tiresome teenagers, or are they hiding adult secrets?

Prologue

The knock on the door came at precisely ten-thirty, five minutes after Anne walked into her hotel room. She sighed with relief. The bellman with her suitcases. She was exhausted by the long flight from London to Denver, and wanted only to stand under a hot shower and then tumble into bed. Her first trans-Atlantic flight had drained her of every drop of energy. To crown it all, the obnoxious Joshua Donaldson had been waiting at the gate when her plane landed at Stapleton airport. Coping with him—and his inexplicable hostility—had not improved her state of weariness.

"I'm coming!" she called, picking up the three dollar bills she had already set on the bedside table. Anne always liked to feel prepared. On the point of unlatching the door chain, she remembered Brian's dire warnings about violence in America and decided to exercise a little caution.

"Who is it?" she asked, squinting through the peephole and seeing only a maroon uniform.

"The bellman, Ms. Clarence. I have your luggage."

Anne slipped back the lock and opened the door. "Thank you," she said, smiling at the man, whose pleasant features were obscured by thick, horn-rimmed glasses. "Would you put the big case—"

The spray hit her full in the face. Eyes streaming, nostrils stinging, she gagged as she struggled to draw breath, doubling over with the effort of pulling air into her burning lungs. People—she wasn't sure how many—crowded into her room, propelling her backward. She tried to scream, but her frantic yells emerged as hoarse, inaudible grunts.

My God, are they going to rape me? Would they kill her if she resisted?

"Her purse is on the bed."

Maybe—please God—they just planned to rob her.

"I'll take care of the purse and the ransom note. You take care of her."

She felt a pricking sensation in her arm.

"Help me lift her onto the room service cart. For God's sake, Babe, move!"

"Oh gosh, I'm scared. Is she dead?"

"Of course not, you fool. Get your arm under her shoulders and shut up! I thought you'd be more help than this."

Someone must have switched out the lights, Anne decided. The hotel room was dark. And it seemed to be moving. The walls spun in sickening circles around her head. She felt the floor melt beneath her feet, and she toppled down onto her knees.

"You're sure she'll be out for the journey?"

"Much longer than that. Give her this shot when you get to the cabin, and she'll be out for eighteen hours, maybe more. She'll be free again before she even realizes she's been captured."

"You're sure she won't die? Promise me she's all right. She looks awful limp."

"I'm sure, damn it! I should never have brought you. We'll release her before the shot's worn off. I've explained this a dozen times. All we're going to do is keep her out of the way long enough to convince the old man to cough up half a million dollars. With all the money he has, he won't even notice a piddling half million. It's pocket change for him, but it makes all the difference to us."

Anne could feel herself dissolving, floating away at the edges until she couldn't distinguish where her body ended and the carpet began. Pain crashed over her in angry waves.She drifted onto the carpet. She tried to sit up.

Blackness.

Pain.

Nothing.

Chapter One

Through the bars sealing the window, Anne could see the sun beginning to set behind the mountains. The higher peaks reflected halos of pink clouds against the vastness of the sky. In another hour all trace of light would vanish, leaving the interior of the cabin shrouded in darkness.

Anne's hands tightened against the wooden sill, gripping the ledge with such force that her fingertips turned white. With an abrupt movement, she swung away from the window. Time to start making dinner. Time to mark another day off her calendar.

She reached into the drawer next to the chipped sink and pulled out a shard of window glass. With great care, she etched a small notch into the wall beneath the window ledge.

Anne knew without counting how many white marks she'd scratched into the faded yellow paint, but she counted them anyway, just to be sure. Three small notches to record three days of mind-numbing uncertainty, three days of desperate, futile attempts to find a way out.

She hurriedly switched the direction of her thoughts, and tugged open the door of her food cupboard. Six slices of stale bread, a lump of yellow cheese, a withered apple and a half-empty box of powdered milk stared back, mocking her in their sparsity.

The fear she had struggled to keep at bay clawed into her throat, choking off the faint stirrings of appetite. She had noticed these past few days that the less she ate, the less hungry she felt. It seemed as if her appetite had sunk into apathy along with her power to think and her will to escape. Her half brother would undoubtedly have devised some brilliant escape plan within hours of finding himself in captivity. But Anne could come up with no bright ideas on how to force her way out of the cabin when her only tool was a piece of glass.

For heaven's sake, Anne, don't you have any gumption? She could almost hear her mother's exasperated voice asking the question.

Not much, she acknowledged ruefully. Not much gumption and apparently no ingenuity.

Lord knows, your father wasn't very practical, but at least he was clever. Where's your ingenuity?

Anne shrugged her shoulders, shaking off the useless self-pity. Dusk was approaching, and she had established the rule of eating every night, just before sunset. She needed to keep to a rigid schedule to make sure that she didn't lose track of the days. Alone, walled into silence, it was all too easy to become disoriented. That was why she marked off her makeshift calendar at the precise moment the sun hit the top of the tallest mountain. She knew without doubt that it was three days since she had regained consciousness, curled painfully inside the cocoon of a big orange blanket. Three days since she had woken up, but how long had she been unconscious? Not only did she have no clue as to why she was here, but she didn't even know for sure how long she had been imprisoned.

Imprisoned.

The idea that anyone would abduct her from her hotel room and hold her captive was so absurd, so crazy, that even now Anne couldn't quite grasp the reality of it. She hadn't been tortured or molested or raped, so she could only conclude she was being held for ransom. But who did her captors expect to extort money from? Nobody Anne knew in the entire world, not even her mother or her stepfather, possessed a bank balance that was anything more than modest.

She was such an ordinary person to have ended up in this crazy situation. A boring, thirty-year-old schoolteacher who coped better with problem teenagers than she did with adults. Her unique claim to fame was the silver medal she had won in the All-England fencing contest when she was sixteen—the only moment in her life when her mother had *almost* approved of her.

Anne had toyed with the idea that she might be the victim of a group of political fanatics. But that made less sense than any other possibility. Apart from casting a vote in the elections, her political activity was limited to campaigning with Greenpeace to save the whales. She couldn't imagine even the most rabid of fanatics abducting her over that.

And her sex life certainly wasn't likely to provoke anyone's interest. She didn't have an oil sheikh, or a billionaire, or a member of the Mafia for her lover. In fact, if you discounted Brian—which, unfortunately, was all too easy—she'd never had a lover at all. Yet she had been grabbed from her hotel room in Denver, drugged, and abandoned in this isolated cabin, heaven knew how far into the wilderness.

And the terrifying truth was that she'd just about run out of ideas on how she might escape. She'd spent most of today and yesterday chipping away at the cabin's only door with a piece of broken glass, trying to cut around the bolt and handle, but when she'd finally broken through the inch-thick layer of wood, she'd discovered that the door had a solid metal core. Hours of dogged, patient work, and all she'd achieved was cut and bleeding hands.

Damn it! Anne slammed her fist onto the counter. She was behaving like the perfect victim, becoming an accomplice in her own destruction. There *had* to be a way out, some unbarred window, some tunnel, some possibility of freedom that she had overlooked.

She felt a wave of panic start to crest, and she fought it back. She was not going to waste any more time pounding against the solid walls, searching for an escape route that didn't exist. The floor was a concrete slab, and the windows were boarded. She knew all this. She'd spent hours in determined exploration.

Face it, Annie, there's no way out. You've tried everything. She closed her eyes, hugging her arms around her waist as she struggled to regain her calm.

When the urge to dash around the tiny cabin, clawing at cracks, had faded, she took two slices of bread from the shelf and broke off a piece of cheese. Dinnertime. Tomorrow morning would be soon enough to resume her dreary ritual of seeking an escape route. The cabin had electric power; she knew that, even though there were no lights and no appliances, because she could hear the hum of the generator. Tomorrow, in daylight, she would attempt the final, desperate ploy of trying to start an electrical fire. Since all else had failed, perhaps she could burn her way to freedom.

Anne banged the can of dried milk onto the counter, scooped powder into the cabin's single plastic cup, added cold water and stirred. The plastic spoon wasn't very efficient, and clots of powder floated to the surface. For a split second, she was afraid she might be sick. Hurriedly she leaned over the sink and took a gulp of cold water.

The nausea passed, although the dizziness, which was an almost constant companion, remained with her. She forced herself to replace the can on the shelf with brisk efficiency. *Milk is good for you, Annie. An excellent source of vitamins and protein. You're going to enjoy every mouthful of your meal.*

She carried her sparse meal into the tiny living room, which was devoid of furniture, and squatted down on the blanket. A wall of shelves stood bare of everything save dust. There was no television, no radio, no telephone—no method of contacting the outside world. No way to relieve the claustrophobia of endless days spent in solitary confinement. At least the cabin had a bathroom with functioning plumbing, although there was no hot water. Anne now understood why earlier generations had been so ambivalent about the value of personal cleanliness. Ice-cold showers were not for the fainthearted.

All the windows were boarded up, except for the barred one in the kitchen, so the cabin remained gloomy even at midday. This late in the evening, the living room was shrouded in darkness. Thank God for her view of the mountains, and for the grove of aspen trees that she spent hours watching for signs of wildlife. Sometimes Anne thought that the changing view from the kitchen window was all that stood between her and insanity.

She drank the milk, smoothed out her blanket and viewed her meal, grateful that she couldn't see too clearly what she was eating. Even so, after a few mouthfuls, the moldy cheese defeated her.

"Come along, now, you have to finish your supper. You need to keep up your strength." She spoke out loud, her voice rasping from lack of use.

"You're beginning to sound like the headmistress at boarding school," Anne told herself, giggling at the strangeness of hearing her own voice after days of silence. The walls of the living room were beginning to blur, as they often did after she had eaten. She spoke again. "You heard what I said. Eat up, Anne."

She crumbled a piece of bread between her fingers. "I can't eat this stuff, it's got green fluff growing over it. It'll probably give me food poisoning."

Nonsense. Mold isn't going to harm you. Or you can use your spoon to scrape off the green bits.

"It still looks disgusting. The cheese is curling at the edges. And the milk makes my head feel bobbly."

And why is that so terrible? What you need to do, my girl, is stop worrying about how your meal looks, and just be grateful you have something nourishing to put in your stomach.

"Huh! What I need to worry about, you miserable old thing, is the fact that I'm not only talking to myself, but I'm even beginning to answer back!"

Stricken, Anne registered the import of her own words. Dropping the lump of cheese onto the plate, she jumped to her feet. Time for a reality check, she thought frantically. Time to get another glimpse of the outside world. Tonight she would keep watch at the kitchen window until the moon had risen to its full height. The grove of aspen trees always looked particularly beautiful in the silver glow of moonlight. And maybe—if she was very lucky—she would see some deer.

She hurried into the kitchen and rinsed off her plastic plate and cup, leaving them on the counter to dry. Leaning against the grimy wall, she stared out of the barred and shattered window, letting the night breeze blow over her face while her fingers absently traced the three notches of her calendar. The sky darkened from purple to black. Stars shone in cold pinpoints of brilliance. The moon rose in silver silence.

For a while, Anne was able to lose herself in the majesty of the mountain night. But this high into the mountains, the August nights were chilly, and she eventually began to shiver. The silk blouse and linen pants she had worn on the plane were not ideal gear for camping. When her teeth started chattering, the prospect of wrapping herself in the big orange blanket began to seem appealing. Last night had been a torment of wakefulness. Maybe tonight she would manage to get a few hours of deep sleep.

Huddled inside the blanket, Anne welcomed the drowsiness that stole over her. She felt the tense, spring-tight muscles in her body gradually unwind as she slipped to the edge of oblivion. This is going to be a good night, she reassured herself. Tonight you're going to sleep all the way through until dawn.

The sounds coming from outside the cabin were so faint that at first they seemed part of her dreams. The drone of an engine. A skitter of shale rolling down the hillside. Then, when she heard the second twig snap, she jerked upright in bed, heart pounding.

"It's an animal," she told herself, then clapped her hand over her mouth as she realized that she was talking out loud once again.

Unwinding the blanket, she crept on silent feet to the kitchen window. Moonlight still bathed the familiar scene in silver. A puff of wind stirred the leaves on the aspens, setting them to a whispering, mysterious rustle. Somewhere far in the distance, she heard the muted call of an animal, or maybe a bird.

Her entire body strained with the effort to catch any unusual sound, but she heard no more snapped twigs, no more strange clicks. After a couple of minutes, her heart resumed its normal speed, and her palms stopped sweating.

"You're losing it, Annie," she told herself, not even caring that she spoke out loud. She rubbed angrily at her eyes, refusing to acknowledge their wetness. "You turned a prowling possum into a rescuer. And now you'll never get back to sleep."

The revving of an engine exploded against her ears.

My God! It's a car!

She rushed through the living room to the door, no longer trying to stop the flow of tears streaming down her cheeks.

"Don't go!" she screamed, pounding on the walls of the cabin, her mouth pressed against the damp glass of the boarded window. "Don't go, I'm here! I'll do whatever you want. My mother could get some money, I'm sure. Let me out!"

Above the noise of her screams, she heard the car driving down the mountain, the hum of its engine fading into the distance.

"Don't go," she babbled, crumpling against the cold, unyielding wall. "Please don't go... Don't leave me here alone."

Indifferent to her sobs, the night swallowed up her plea. The air inside the cabin pulsed with the pain of lost hope. Anne stopped crying. Silence returned, absolute, complete—and devastating.

A great cry of grief and despair tore from her throat, reverberating through the cramped cabin, echoing from the walls. Running to the door, she launched herself against it, beating the heavy wooden panels until her knuckles bled and her arms were too exhausted to beat any more. In a final flare of bitter frustration, she grabbed the door handle and shook it, jerking it violently from side to side.

The latch clicked.

For a split second, Anne's body froze into stillness, then she jumped back from the door as if she had been scalded. Slowly, holding her breath, she stretched her hand toward the door handle. She turned the knob and felt it move. She turned a little farther and pulled gently.

The door swung open. Pine-scented air rushed into the cabin. The breeze, no longer muted by walls and windows, soughed noisily in the trees.

With a shuddering gasp of relief, Anne drew a great gulp of fresh mountain air into her lungs. She wedged the door open with her blanket and stuffed her feet into her black leather pumps. Halfway out of the door, she remembered how cold it was going to be. She picked up the blanket and tossed it around her shoulders.

Common sense cut through her euphoria just long enough to give her pause. She hesitated on the threshold. What if this was just another trap?

The very air seemed to tell her that she was safe. Her imprisonment had been nothing more than a ghastly mistake, Anne decided. *They* had captured the wrong person, and now *they* were correcting their error and setting her free.

Abandoning the last vestiges of her caution, she stepped outside. The great outdoors welcomed her into the silvery darkness. A gust of wind blew softly through her hair, lifting it from her neck, cooling the sweat that had beaded there. An owl flew from one ponderosa pine to the next, then hooted to announce its move.

"I'm free!" she yelled, then yelled it again even louder, just for the pleasure of hearing the magic words. "I'm free, damn it, I'm free!"

The trees showed no interest in her news. She laughed and patted one of the trunks, her body aching with the weight of her happiness. She doubted if anyone had ever seen such beautiful ponderosas before. She had certainly never smelled such wonderful mountain air.

Without a backward glance, she tucked the blanket around her and strode out toward the twisting, moonlit path that would return her to civilization. Freedom, safety, everything that was familiar waited a few hundred yards down the mountain.

Joyfully Anne began her descent into the darkness of the valley.

Chapter Two

The road down the mountain was little more than a rock-strewn dirt path, but euphoria left Anne feeling bolder than Superwoman. Her feet marched to the fast drumbeat of exultation, and yet she managed not to trip over concealed boulders or the jutting branches of felled trees. She'd escaped! She was free!

See, mother, sometimes calm and patience bring greater rewards than dashing about madly just to prove you're doing something.

Anne's optimism was rewarded after less than an hour's walk. Through the trees lining the side of the road, she spotted the distant but unmistakable glow of electric lighting. A house! And probably a house with people inside, since several lights were on.

A narrow gravel driveway twisted through clusters of dark spruce and gray-trunked aspen toward the house. Without a moment's hesitation, Anne veered left onto the driveway, her pace picking up until she was running headlong toward the welcoming glow of light and the promise of human company. How wonderful it would be to talk to a real person again after days of solitary confinement.

The house could not have appeared more inviting. A delightful Victorian gingerbread, it nestled against a tree-rimmed clearing at the end of the driveway. Anne stopped running just long enough to admire the beautiful sight.

The moment her feet became still, her brain sprang into action. Her euphoria faded into uncertainty.

How do you know the people in that house are friendly?

Anne retreated on tiptoe to the cover of some nearby spruce trees and stared at the house. Perhaps her kidnappers were lined up in the hallway at this very minute, waiting for her to ring the doorbell. The more she thought about it, the stranger it seemed that the door to her prison had suddenly been unlocked. If she wasn't being set up for some horrible end, why had she been released from the cabin? Anne now realized how dangerous it would be to assume that her kidnapping had been a mistake and her release a kindly attempt to rectify the error.

She huddled behind the tree, considering how best to escape from the lighted yard without drawing attention to herself. Unfortunately she had run very close to the house before caution had stopped her. She realized that the aspen and spruce dotting the front yard were too sparse to offer any hope of long-term cover. If anyone looked out of an upstairs window, she would be seen.

The house itself appeared more sinister by the second. The pointed eaves and lacy wooden carvings no longer looked charming. Instead, they reminded Anne of the witch's house in Hansel and Gretel. The trellis around the porch loomed in ominous, secretive formation. The blank-eyed windows leered at her. The door seemed to hold its breath for her arrival, eager to spring its fatal trap.

Anne had watched enough police shows on television to know that this house was much too cozily inviting. The sooner she made a dash for it, the better off she would be. No point in worrying about the bright yard lights; she'd take her chances. She turned to run.

A heavy hand descended on her shoulder, and a steel-like arm closed around her waist. Anne screamed, a cry as much of frustration as of fear. Damn it! She'd been concentrating so intently on the house that she'd paid no attention to her rear. What's more, during all the time she had spent walking down the mountain, she hadn't been smart enough to pick up a stout branch to use as a club. She just didn't seem to be thinking very clearly these past few days, perhaps because her head always felt so aching and muzzy.

Weaponless or not, she wasn't going to be recaptured without a fight. Her legs were strong from years of fencing practice, and she kicked out with punishing force. But the blanket fell from her shoulders, hampering her movements, and her assailant was not only big; he fought with controlled, economical power. Within seconds, she had lost the unequal struggle. Her arms were grabbed and pulled roughly behind her back, then twisted with brutal expertise toward her shoulder blades so that any movement on her part meant instant dislocation of her shoulder. Or worse.

"If you're looking for easy money, kid, you've come to the wrong place." Cold steel pressed against the back of her head, and an ominous click interrupted the shallow pants of her breathing. "I have a gun, and the house is wired straight into the police station."

The cool, self-assured voice sounded familiar. Anne's heart pounded. She wasn't sure whether to feel relieved or more terrified. In a world turned topsy-turvy, familiarity no longer promised safety. Once she revealed who she was, would her captor pull the trigger?

"J-Joshua? Is that you?" Her voice came out as a humiliating squeak; her body shook with fright. "Joshua, it's me. Anne. You know, Anne Clarence, from England. We met at the airport, when I arrived in Denver." She held her breath, fearing the worst and praying for the best. "P-please would you put the safety catch back on the gun?"

The grip on her arms relaxed, and she was whirled around so fast a hank of hair ended up in her mouth. She found herself staring into a pair of hard, unfriendly gray eyes.

"The gun's not loaded. Where the hell have you been for the past five days?"

She pulled the hair out of her mouth so that she could speak. "Five days? I've been gone five days?"

He frowned, then reached out and pulled her eyelid up, staring into the pupils of her eyes. After a second or so, he pushed her away, gaze scornful. "What are you on, Anne? Is that why you ran away, because you were out of your skull at the time? I'd have thought you would manage to stay clean long enough to meet your grandfather."

"Ran away?" The nightmare seemed to be growing worse by the second. Joshua was speaking English, but she couldn't understand him. "I didn't run away, I was kidnapped," she said. "People came to the hotel and drugged me—"

"Oh, come on, Anne. Don't give me that." Joshua sounded impatient to the point of anger, and the injustice of it all hit Anne with overwhelming force. She wriggled her body from side to side, furious when she couldn't escape from his iron-fisted grip.

"I was kidnapped!" she yelled, putting all her frustration into one angry shout. "For your information, I've been held prisoner in a cabin with no light and almost no food—"

"And now you finally escaped. How clever of you!"

She couldn't understand the note of irony in Joshua's voice. What was he mocking her for? Because she'd taken five whole days to find a way out? Well, not everyone was trained to play Houdini. No doubt Joshua would have drilled a hole in the ceiling with his thumbnail, and leapt to freedom through the roof. Anne had realized within ten seconds of meeting him that he was precisely the kind of man who infuriated her. Confident, athletic, darkly handsome, he glowed with the aura of sexual power that always clung to men who attracted more women than they could handle. She had cordially disliked him at their first meeting. So far, nothing about this second encounter was making her like him any better.

It was tempting to claim she had dug through the concrete floor with a plastic spoon and tunneled her way to freedom. Cursed with an incurable honesty, she admitted the truth. "I didn't escape. I couldn't discover a way out, although I spent all the daylight hours searching."

"So how did you get here?"

"The kidnappers unlocked the door, and then I walked."

"Right. Typical behavior for kidnappers. I suppose you didn't happen to see who these mysterious kidnappers were? Before you started walking, of course."

"They came while I was asleep, and anyway, it was dark—"

"How did you find my house?"

"I didn't know this was your house."

"Ah, I see. You turned up here by happy coincidence."

Joshua no longer made the slightest attempt to conceal his sarcasm, and a fresh burst of anger fizzed through Anne's veins. "You know better than I do whether it's a coincidence," she said, throwing caution to the winds. "This was the first house I came to when I walked down the mountain. Which is amazing when you consider that you're about the only person I know in the whole of the United States." *Explain that one, you sarcastic pig.*

Joshua's expression sharpened into astonishment. "You're claiming you were imprisoned in Bertram's cabin on Smoke Top Ridge?"

"I don't know what the place is called. My kidnappers failed to provide me with an address." Anne pointed to indicate the direction of the road she had taken down the mountain. "There's a dirt trail over there. I followed it to your house from the cabin. It's scarcely an hour since someone came and unlocked the door." *Was it you who drove up there and set me free? If so, why did you do it?*

Joshua laughed without a trace of mirth. "Well, aren't we lucky to have found each other so soon after your daring escape?"

"Not especially," she said, irritated by his mocking, scornful attitude. "From my point of view, I'd much prefer to have met a stranger with better manners."

"I can certainly believe that. Planning to utilize those luscious baby blues, were you, Annie babe? I'll bet that kissable mouth and those quivering lashes have gotten you out of more trouble than you can remember."

"I don't know what you're—"

"Work on your assets, honey." Joshua sounded as angry as she felt. "A few pouts of that delectable lower lip, and any halfway decent lawyer will persuade the D.A. that there's no point in bringing charges."

Decent lawyer? *Charges?* Anne blinked. Joshua didn't look crazy, but he sounded more irrational by the moment. Anger faded to caution. Shouting at lunatics wasn't prudent. "It's not a crime to be the victim of a kidnapping," she ventured. Despite her best efforts, her voice shook. "I'd have expected you to be more sympathetic."

"Don't practice your tricks on me, honey. Vulnerability isn't my thing. I prefer competent women." Joshua picked up the orange blanket and shook off its coating of mulch, still keeping hold of her with one hand. "Here, take this. We'd better get you inside. Your body is turning into one huge goose bump. I don't want you claiming delirium and convenient loss of memory when the police arrive. I want to find out what you said that upset Bertram so badly."

Anne could never remember a time in her well-brought-up life when she had felt such an urgent need to deliver a hard kick to a man's rear end. Or a swift uppercut to his jaw would have definte appeal. But first things first. She needed to get away from Joshua. Needed to find some normal citizen who would offer help instead of making wild accusations. With a supreme effort, Anne swallowed her pride and took the blanket with downcast eyes.

"Thank you," she said, trying to sound humble and apprehensive instead of hopping mad. She folded the blanket and wrapped it high around her shoulders, out of the way of her legs. She still didn't have the faintest idea what was going on, but two things were perfectly clear: Joshua wasn't prepared to take her tale of kidnapping seriously, and she hadn't the remotest intention of following him into his house. She needed to get to a police station as fast as she could. Joshua might be crazy, or he might even be the leader of the gang that had kidnapped her, but whatever the situation, once she found a police station, she would be safe. Police officers in America were presumably like their British counterparts—anxious to help the victim of a brutal crime—and Americans took kidnapping very seriously.

Despite her sudden show of meekness, Joshua proved annoyingly alert. Anne wasn't tall, and her slender body appeared fragile. People who didn't know about her skill at fencing tended to assume she was a physical weakling. Unfortunately Joshua didn't make that mistake. He topped her by at least eight inches and sixty pounds, but he held her arm as tightly as if he expected her to make a dash for freedom at any moment. Which, of course, was exactly what she planned to do the second he relaxed his vigilance.

Her chance came when they were almost at the house. Anne pretended to stumble over a tree root. Joshua turned to help, and with a lightning adjustment of the balance of her weight, Anne managed to topple him forward. His hands swung out in an instinctive move to steady himself. She threw the blanket over his head and twisted out of his grasp, running for the cover of the trees with all the speed she could muster.

She might have succeeded in escaping if she'd been wearing sneakers, or if the stand of trees hadn't ended in a rockstrewn stream, swirling with foaming white water. In the ten seconds she wasted wondering whether to attempt a crossing or to run downstream along the slippery bank, Joshua caught up with her.

He yanked her arm behind her back in the same efficient wrestling lock he had used before, and marched her toward the house.

"Don't waste any more time running, Anne." He sounded almost weary, as if he didn't particularly enjoy chasing after her but felt it was his duty. "The first thing I'm going to do when we get inside the house is call the police and tell them you've finally resurfaced. If you think there are some mitigating circumstances in what you did, tell them. They aren't completely inhuman, you know. Neither am I. We all realize how scared you must have been."

Anne's stepfather was a dyed-in-the-wool British xenophobe. He had a theory, based on his occasional viewing of such imported television programs as *Dynasty* and *The Price Is Right,* that all Americans were brain damaged or crazy or both. After her experiences of the past few days and this encounter with Joshua, Anne was beginning to wonder if her stepfather might be right.

"For heaven's sake, Joshua, you're not being reasonable! I'd scarcely been at the hotel ten minutes before I was kidnapped! You're absolutely right, I was scared. How would you like to be locked up in a cabin, with almost no food and no idea why you're there or if you'll ever find a way out? I should certainly hope the police will think there are mitigating circumstances. Good grief, am I guilty of some terrible crime because it took me five days before I managed to escape?"

"Anne," he said softly. "Nobody's going to believe that story. My mother took the phone call from you, had you forgotten that?"

"What phone call are you talking about? I never phoned anyone. I didn't have time. The fake bellman came to my room five minutes after I left you in the lobby."

Joshua frowned. "Anne, things would go much more smoothly for you if you'd admit the truth of what happened to your grandfather that night. Dominick drove Bertram to the hotel and escorted him right upstairs to your room. Dom heard you say hello. He saw you greet Bertram. That was just before midnight, and the police pathologist estimates Bertram died somewhere between midnight and one. If you hadn't run away, Anne, people would have been completely sympathetic. Your grandfather had high blood pressure—a stroke could have killed him any time. He should never have been out that night. Nobody's accusing you of murder, just negligence. And selfishness, too, I guess."

Grandfather dead. The words danced around inside Anne's head, making no sense at all.

"Grandfather?" The whispered word was a question, all she could manage through lips and throat too dry for long speeches.

"The funeral was yesterday, so you avoided that, too, don't worry. It was a splendid turnout. Here, let's go in." Joshua opened the prettily carved door to the gingerbread house, and Anne hobbled over the threshold in his wake. Joshua no longer held her arm, but all thought of escape had vanished from her mind.

Her grandfather—dead before she'd ever had the chance to talk to him. Before she could ask him why he'd ignored her existence for thirty years. Before she could ask him what he'd done that was so terrible her father had rarely mentioned his name and her mother hadn't even known where he lived.

A middle-aged woman, wearing a dressing gown, waited just inside the front door. "Oh, good heavens! What's happened? I saw you dash outside a few minutes ago, Josh. Who is this?"

"It's Anne Clarence."

"Anne Clarence!" The woman looked at Anne as if she expected her to sprout horns and a tail.

"You can imagine how surprised I was to find her roaming around in the front yard," Joshua said. "I'm going to take her into the living room and ask her a few questions before I call the police. And actually, if you're feeling generous, she looks as if she could use a cup of hot tea."

"You're asking me to make tea for *that woman?*"

"Please, Bree. If you could."

"Well, it's your house, and your tea. If you feel we must..."

"Thanks, Bree. We don't want her keeling over before the police get a chance to question her."

"Huh, I'm not sure I care whether she keels over or not. After the way she left poor Bertram... My God, who knows? Maybe with prompt medical attention, he could have survived."

"We've been over all this," Joshua said, his voice containing no trace of the harshness Anne had grown accustomed to hearing. "Let's not torment ourselves with maybes, okay?" He turned to Anne, his voice resuming its usual briskness. "Anne, by the way, this is my sister, Bree Macmillan."

Thirty years of training overcame Anne's numbness. "How do you do?" she inquired politely, holding out her hand.

The woman shrank back as if contact with Anne's fingertips would be contaminating. "I'll be in the kitchen, Josh. Let me know...what she says. You know, about Bertram. How it ended, and everything."

"Of course." Joshua gave the woman a quick hug. "Are the twins okay?"

"They're in their room, sleeping. Although I can't imagine how. You made quite a lot of noise thrashing around in the undergrowth."

"Teenagers can sleep through hurricanes and World War III. Only the smell of pizza revives them. You should know that by now."

"We're not sleeping." A young, soft voice spoke from the top of the stairs. Anne, still dazed, glanced up and blinked, convinced she was seeing double. She rubbed her eyes, but the duplicate images remained: two identically tall, curly-haired, brown-eyed girls, somewhere in their late teens. With great difficulty, Anne's buffeted brain came up with a logical explanation. Twins. She wasn't seeing double; she was looking at identical twins wearing the standard teenage sleeping uniform of oversize T-shirts. The twin on the left spoke.

"We saw you chasing her, Josh. What's up? Was she trying to steal something? Shall we call the police?"

The older woman hurried forward before Joshua could answer. "No, Heather, I'm afraid it's not that simple. This woman isn't a thief." She lowered her voice as if mentioning something too vulgar for polite company. "This is—er—this is Anne Clarence. Now, girls, I think you should go back to bed and let Joshua deal with her."

"Anne Clarence!"

Her name certainly seemed to produce a startling reaction in everyone who heard it, Anne reflected ruefully.

Heather and the other twin looked at her with the sort of fascination normally reserved for a serpent, or possibly a large black rat. Heather spoke again. "Oh, Mom, for heaven's sake, we're nearly nineteen years old, you know, not ten. We can stay up and help Josh guard her."

The second twin spoke for the first time. "Maybe Mom's right, Heather. Perhaps we should go to bed. Remember, we've got to get up early tomorrow." She emphasized the last few words, and Heather seemed to capitulate.

"Oh, all right." Heather shrugged and swung around in the direction of the narrow upstairs hallway. "See you tomorrow, Anne. G'night, Mom. Don't be too mean to her, Uncle Josh."

"I'll try not to be," he said, sounding indulgent. "Scoot, kids."

Anne's brain had expanded until it felt too big to fit inside her skull, and the pain was excruciating. Nevertheless, she knew there were questions that needed to be asked. Important questions. She swung around to confront Joshua, turning her back on Bree Macmillan and the retreating twins.

"Joshua, what did you mean?" She swallowed hard. "Are you telling me something has happened to my grandfather?"

"Oh, good lord, she's sickening! I'm going to call the police." Anne scarcely heard Bree's disgusted exclamation. She kept her gaze fixed on Joshua's mouth, as if by watching him form the words, she might somehow manage to grasp their meaning.

Joshua stared at her almost as intently as she stared at him, then moved abruptly. "Here, sit down. You don't look too good."

She felt the prickle of upholstery beneath her knees and realized he must have led her to a chair or a sofa. A glass of water appeared in her hand.

"My grandfather," she repeated. An aching hollow opened deep inside her, a sense of loss so acute that she could hardly bear to acknowledge it. She took a sip of water. "What happened to my grandfather?"

"Anne, if you really don't know, if you've somehow blanked it out of your mind, I'm sorry. But the fact is, Bertram is dead. He died last Monday in your hotel room."

With supreme care, Anne set her glass onto the coffee table. She folded her hands in her lap and stared straight ahead, unblinking. If she blinked, she would cry, and she had no intention of crying. Not in front of Joshua. She never cried in front of other people, not since her father's Red Cross plane crashed in the Vietnamese jungle, and her mother told her to dry her tears because now she could live in a big house in the country with a nice new English daddy and her very own pony.

Joshua laid his hand on her arm. Oddly enough, the warmth of his touch was rather comforting. She turned to look at him.

"How did he die?"

"He had a stroke, which precipitated a heart attack. He was dead by the time Dominick Rossi found him."

"I've heard the name, but don't remember who Dominick Rossi is."

"Dom is . . . was . . . Bertram's nephew. His sister's son. That makes him some sort of cousin to you, I guess."

Anne was silent for a moment. "You say my grandfather had a stroke. Could he have been saved if he'd had immediate medical help?"

Joshua hesitated. "It's possible, but we can't be sure."

His voice sounded grim, and Anne finally understood why everyone had been so hostile toward her. She stared up at Joshua, shock cushioning her from the full horror of his unspoken accusation. "You think I ran away and left my grandfather in the throes of a heart attack. You believe I'm capable of leaving an old man alone to die."

Joshua said nothing. Anne felt her hands tighten on the arms of the chair. "Joshua, I wasn't there. I'd already been taken from my hotel room. I didn't leave my grandfather. I could never have done such a thing. What reason would anyone have for leaving him to suffer alone?"

"He was eight-two years old," Joshua said, not answering her directly. "He would probably have died even with the best of medical care. That's what we keep telling my mother, anyway. As you can imagine, she's taking this very hard. She and Bertram had been happily married for nearly thirty years."

Anne felt her throat tighten in sympathy with the bereaved woman. Joshua's mother was also her stepgrandmother. Then a fresh horror occurred to her. "Your sister went to call the police. Are they going to charge me with criminal negligence or something?"

"That depends on a number of technical factors, I'm sure. And I'm not a lawyer. I can't answer that question."

With a supreme effort, Anne controlled the dizzying spin of her emotions. "Joshua, I feel like some character who's wandered out of the real world and into wonderland. I feel as if I flew across the Atlantic and the world suddenly went crazy."

Joshua spoke with more gentleness than he'd ever used with her. "Anne, discounting for a minute all the evidence that you were with Bertram that night, why would anyone want to kidnap you—"

He broke off abruptly. "Of course," he murmured, almost to himself. "The most obvious reason of all. Ransom money. Everyone knew Bertram was longing to meet you."

Much as she disliked to discourage this promising line of thought, Anne felt compelled to point out the flaw in Joshua's logic. "Unfortunately nobody in my family is rich enough to pay a worthwhile ransom," she acknowledged. "My stepfather's comfortably off, but all his money is tied up in the house and land—"

"Spare me the naive disclaimers. Obviously your kidnappers expected Bertram to pay the ransom money."

"My grandfather? He was poor as a church mouse!"

"A quaint cliché. But your grandfather would best be described as a fat cat, not a thin mouse. A very fat and prosperous cat. Why else did you suddenly decide to get in touch with him?''

"How could my grandfather be rich?" Anne found this piece of information almost more extraordinary than everything else she'd heard. "My mother always claimed he and my father were a matched pair. Shortsighted scientists who could never see anything beyond the end of their test tubes."

"Bertram stopped his scientific research back in the midsixties. He took out a series of patents on some fertilizers and pesticides he'd developed, and set up his own company to market them. He eventually sold out to Agricon about ten years ago, and made himself a comfortable little fortune."

How furious her mother would be that she had never managed to dig out this interesting piece of information about Bertram Kennedy! Julia Clarence *always* knew when people possessed money. She had a nose that scented wealth as efficiently as a terrier scented foxes. And she pursued her prey with equal determination. Her father must have been so closemouthed about Bertram Kennedy that, for once, Julia's sensitive nose failed her. If Julia had known Bertram Kennedy had money, Anne's mother would have made sure that he met his grandchild years ago.

"If you really don't know the truth," Joshua interrupted her thoughts, "your grandfather has been a multimillionaire for at least twenty years. At last count, his net worth was assessed in the neighborhood of sixty-five million dollars. Give or take a few million, of course. It's difficult to be precise at that level."

Give or take a few million. Anne choked off a gurgle of laughter. If she ever made it safely home to England, she would have to drop that phrase into a conversation with her mother. Julia would be furious to know that Bertram Kennedy had been inconsiderate enough to die before he could be stripped of any of his assets. Julia was not greedy, merely obsessed. As far as she was concerned, nothing in the world deserved money as much as her second husband's ancestral mansion. Clarence Towers sprawled, twenty-seven chilly bedrooms wide, on the edge of the Yorkshire moors. From the thirteenth-century tapestries in the great hall to the linenfold ceiling in the tiny private chapel, Julia was determined to restore every inch of the old house to pristine, authentic glory. She genuinely didn't understand why Anne chose to live in London and work as a high school guidance counselor when she could have lived in the family home and acted as unpaid house servant.

"I got through to the local police station." Bree Macmillan returned to the living room. "They notified the Denver police, and Detective Goodine would like us to take Anne to his office for an interview at ten o'clock tomorrow morning."

"We're supposed to keep her here as our houseguest for the rest of the night?"

"It sounds crazy, doesn't it? But how else can you be sure that she'll be around tomorrow morning? Personally I hope they find some grounds to arrest her."

"I'll have to call Sebastian and ask him to find one of his partners to act as her lawyer. After all, she's in a foreign country. She's going to need counsel."

Bree looked at Anne with undisguised hostility. "Why should you or Sebastian show her any special concern? She didn't show any consideration to our stepfather. Or to the people who loved him."

Anne was tired of hearing herself discussed as if she were a worm that deserved squishing. "There are a couple of rather important points you seem to have overlooked."

"Nothing that we need to discuss until the police are listening," Bree snapped.

"Are you sure? Why aren't you willing to consider the possibility that I'm telling the truth? If I was kidnapped and locked up for five days in my grandfather's cabin, who abducted me? Bertram's close friends and family are the only ones who knew I was coming to the States. They're also the most likely people to know about Bertram's cabin. So it seems highly probable that whoever kidnapped me is someone in the family."

"Impossible," Bree spluttered.

"Go on," said Josh.

"If the kidnappers hoped to raise ransom money from my grandfather, their plan failed. Which probably means that you, or someone in your immediate circle, is desperately short of money. Are you sure you don't want to consider who that might be and what they might do next?"

Bree muttered and Joshua shoved one hand through his thick, unruly hair. He looked at Anne with a speculative gaze. "If you were abducted, according to your own reasoning, my sister and I are the most likely kidnappers. Isn't it rather dangerous to tell us your suspicions?"

"Very dangerous, but if you're the kidnappers, I haven't a hope anyway. I've walked straight into your trap. And if you're not the kidnappers, I *must* persuade you to listen to me."

Joshua hooked a chair with his heel and sat down so close she could feel his breath brushing her cheek. "Okay, I'm listening. Tell me what happened in your hotel room the night you arrived in Denver."

Chapter Three

Bree snorted. "If you want to stay and listen to this drivel, that's your business, Josh. Personally I'm too tired to waste the energy. I'm going to call Mother and let her know Anne Clarence has turned up. I guess she'd like to be kept up-to-date. Shirley ought to be told, as well."

"You're right." Josh smiled at his sister. "Tell Mom I'll be in touch tomorrow morning, will you?"

She nodded. "And keep that woman locked up somewhere, Josh. I don't want her free to wander around during the night. Who knows what she might do or say to the twins."

"I'll see she doesn't get up to any mischief," Josh promised.

"She's already gotten up to enough mischief for a lifetime," Bree commented dourly. "And I don't suppose she'll pay any price for what she's done, not even a guilty conscience. Her sort always gets away with murder." Bree stomped out of the room, her shoulders hunched in a way that reminded Josh his sister was forty years old and fast sinking into a dispirited middle age.

What a miserable pair we are, he reflected wryly. *Neither of us able to keep our marriages together, and both of us determined to blame everyone except ourselves.*

Josh was startled by this insight into his own psyche. Until this moment, he hadn't realized that the messy end of his

marriage to Merrilee had given him a knee-jerk dislike of
women who appeared frail or vulnerable.

Still, it was more than prejudice causing him to suspect
the motives behind Anne Clarence's sudden trip to the
States. Her desire to be reunited with Bertram Kennedy had
followed hard on the heels of an article in the *Wall Street
Journal* about the ten wealthiest men in Colorado—one of
whom was Bertram Kennedy. From the moment Anne
greeted Josh at the airport, her translucent skin turning rosy
with pseudoshyness and her plummy British voice sounding breathless with uncertainty, his doubts about her motives in seeking out Bertram Kennedy had deepened. Her
flight from the scene of Bertram's death had simply confirmed his low opinion of her.

"Why does your sister dislike me so much?" Anne's quiet
question interrupted Josh's thoughts.

He shrugged. "Bree doesn't like anyone very much at the
moment. She's just gone through a messy divorce."

"I'm sorry." Anne sounded genuinely sympathetic. "But
you don't have any special reason to dislike me, so would
you please listen to my version of what happened the night
I arrived here in Colorado?"

No special reason to dislike her? Josh glanced down and
found himself staring into her eyes. Dark blue, fringed with
unexpectedly thick gray lashes, they sparkled in the lamp-
light with a soft sheen of tears. Merrilee had mastered the
identical wounded-fawn look and exploited it to the ut-
most, right up to the end. Josh turned his gaze away, hating the reflexive tightening of his stomach muscles. Why the
devil was he cursed with a set of male hormones that propelled him into a protective *Me Tarzan, You Jane* mode
every time a female squeezed out a few tears? At thirty-five,
he ought to be past such teenage bursts of misjudgment.

"I've agreed to hear you out," he said, voice curt. "But
be warned. I'm not in the mood for fairy stories."

Anne put her water down on the side table, and the glass
rattled on the coaster. She started speaking quickly, her
voice low and husky. "I was only in the hotel room for

about ten minutes before a knock came at the door. When I asked who it was, a man's voice answered, saying he was the bellman with my luggage. I opened the door. A youngish man in a maroon uniform was standing outside, with my suitcases on a cart. He looked like a perfectly normal hotel employee, so I swung the door wider to let him bring the luggage inside. Suddenly he lunged forward and grabbed my arms. He forced me back into the room until I toppled over on the bed. They held me down and stuck a needle into my arm.'' She drew in a tight little breath, as if forcing the fear out of her voice before continuing. ''Whatever drug they used was very fast acting. Within a few seconds, the room started to spin, my sense of time and place became distorted, and I had this crazy conviction I was being swallowed by a piece of carpet.''

''By a *carpet?*'' The image was so bizarre that Josh was startled into speech.

Anne flushed. ''Well, I know it sounds silly. But I suppose the kidnappers rolled me up inside a blanket or something so that I couldn't see. Anyway, my drug-addled brain became convinced I'd been consumed by a carpet and that everyone was walking on top of me. It was pretty painful. I remember feeling a whole new sympathy for carpets.''

Josh had been convinced Anne was lying; now he wasn't so certain. For the first time he began to consider the staggering implications of what she was saying. If Anne really had been kidnapped, then Bertram Kennedy must have been the intended ransomer. Which meant that Bertram's death had left behind some very angry and frustrated kidnappers. How frustrated? he wondered. Frustrated enough to plot further harm?

''You say *they* held you down on the bed. How many men were there? And would you recognize them again?''

Anne must have sensed the lessening of his hostility almost before he was aware of it himself. He hadn't realized how brittle with tension she had been until he saw her body slump back against the sofa cushions.

"It all happened so fast," she explained. "At the time, I felt surrounded, but when I thought about it afterward, I realized I heard only two voices."

"Can you remember what they said?"

She grimaced. "'Don't forget her purse. Carry her here.' That sort of thing."

"Nothing that would give us a real clue as to their identity?"

"No, although I think one of them may have been a woman. The bellman's voice was deep and definitely masculine. But I think the other voice I heard was a woman's. She sounded panicky—afraid they'd given me too big a dose of the drug." Anne stopped, her forehead wrinkling in concentration.

"What is it?" Josh asked.

"Something's niggling at me. Something the woman said. Or something about the way she said it."

"Maybe they called each other by name?"

She frowned again. "The harder I chase the memory, the more elusive it becomes. But I think something about the kidnappers reminded me of England, of the school where I work."

"Did they speak with English accents?" Josh suggested.

Anne sighed. "I don't think so, but my memories are all so dreamlike. It's almost as if I'm *seeing* the kidnappers speak, instead of *hearing* them."

"Unfortunately that's the way dreams are. There's never any soundtrack on dreams."

"If I'm confusing drug-induced fantasy with reality, there may not have been a woman in my room at all. I never actually saw her face-to-face, she was always in the periphery of my vision."

"But you're sure about the bellman? You'd recognize him again?"

"I expect so. Unless he was heavily disguised. He wore thick, horn-rimmed glasses, I remember."

She looked so forlorn that Josh experienced a strong urge to put his arm around her shoulders and comfort her. With a mental shake, he resisted the urge. Deciding that Anne Clarence was telling the truth about being kidnapped didn't mean that he needed to sink into a state of maudlin sympathy. The hard facts were that, having ignored her grandfather for thirty years, she had turned up in Denver at precisely the moment Bertram Kennedy's precarious state of health and glowing state of wealth became common knowledge. She could be a kidnap victim *and* a grasping relative hoping to get her hands on some of Bertram's hard-earned money.

"At least it's easy to guess why the kidnappers grabbed you," he said. "No mystery there. Obviously they knew my stepfather was looking forward to meeting you, and they planned to make him pay for the privilege. I wonder how much ransom they planned to demand from him?"

Anne looked up. "Do you think the kidnappers got as far as making their ransom demand, Joshua? If so, the shock of hearing from the kidnappers may have been the trigger for the stroke that killed my grandfather."

"My God," Josh murmured, wondering how he could have overlooked such an obvious fact. "You're probably right. No wonder the kidnappers ran without attempting to get medical help."

"You say 'the kidnappers' as if these people were total strangers. But surely the kidnappers are likely to be members of your family, Joshua."

"I don't follow your logic," he said, angry with her for making the suggestion and even angrier with himself for fearing that she might be right. "Half the population of Colorado knew my stepfather was rich and therefore the ideal man to hold to ransom."

"But nobody outside the Kennedy family circle knew I was coming to America."

"Nobody except a few dozen airline employees, the entire staff of the hotel and the thousands of people who read the local newspaper. The *Suburban Press* ran an article about your arrival. Long-lost Granddaughter From England To Be Reunited With Multimillionaire Grandfather. It was their lead story last week."

"How would any of those people have gained access to my grandfather to make their ransom demands? It must have been close to eleven when I was abducted. How could an airline employee or some other stranger arrange an appointment with my grandfather in the hotel in the middle of the night?" She stopped suddenly. "Come to think of it, what in the world brought my grandfather to my hotel room that late?'

"Bertram received a phone call, supposedly from you, saying that you needed to speak to him right away. My mother took the phone call herself. Dominick Rossi, one of his nephews—"

"You mentioned him a while ago. He's my cousin, isn't he?"

"I guess so, a few times removed. Anyway, Dom agreed to drive my stepfather to the hotel where you were staying..." Josh's voice tailed into an abrupt silence as he remembered the crucial reason why he hadn't believed Anne Clarence's kidnap story.

"What is it?" Anne asked.

"I just remembered something important. Dom saw you, Anne. He says he left Bertram alone with you, in your hotel room, at your insistence."

"Then he's lying," Anne said fiercely. "I never met my grandfather, I swear it. What's more, I've never set eyes on this Dominick person."

"But Dom only went downstairs to the lobby after he'd met you and made sure Bertram was comfortably settled. He told us Bertram had tears in his eyes with the emotion of meeting you. Maybe the drug has blurred your memories—"

"No," Anne said with absolute conviction. "I know I never met my grandfather. Dominick's lying, he must be."

Could she be right? Josh wondered. If so, Dom had a hell of a lot to explain. He heaved a huge sigh of relief when he realized what must have happened. "We're forgetting something important. Dom didn't come to the airport to meet your plane, so he had no idea what you really look like."

He saw comprehension dawn in her eyes. "So any woman could have been waiting in my room, claiming to be me, and Dom would never have known the difference. Is that what you mean?"

"Right. And you already mentioned that you thought one of the kidnappers was a woman. Perhaps she impersonated you. After all, since Dom had never met you, that wouldn't be too difficult."

"She'd have to speak with an English accent."

"But only well enough to deceive Dom, who's never visited England, and your grandfather, who was probably too excited to notice."

"The kidnappers seem to have set up an incredibly complex scheme, and then my grandfather died before they managed to squeeze any money out of him. I wonder how they plan to get their money now?"

"Not from Bertram's estate, that's for sure," Josh said. "His affairs will take months to settle, and no probate court is going to pay out a ransom. So you're safe, Anne. The kidnappers aren't going to try again."

"Let's hope they're making their plans on the basis of the same information as you."

"Even the dumbest kidnapper must know you can't hold a probate court to ransom. And these people don't seem stupid. What's more, we know they're not vicious because otherwise they wouldn't have let you go. They'd have killed the only witness to their crime."

"'Vicious' is a relative term," she said. "During those days I was locked up, there were moments when I'd have preferred to be dead."

Josh sat down on the sofa, wrapping his arm around her thin shoulders in an instinctive offer of comfort. "Don't let the kidnappers win," he said softly. "Don't let the memory of what happened control what you choose to do in the future."

"You're full of good advice, Joshua. Or are you just anxious about what I might tell the police?"

His brief moment of sympathy vanished in a flash of renewed anger. "What are you accusing me of, Anne?"

"Nothing," she said quickly.

Too quickly. She was afraid of him, Josh realized, afraid that he might be physically violent again. The realization sickened him. She'd endured enough over the past few days; she didn't need to spend the night hours wondering if she was sleeping in the same house as her kidnapper.

"Let's make a deal," he suggested quietly. "You take it on faith that my sister and I didn't kidnap you, even though this house is so conveniently near Bertram's cabin. And I'll take it on faith that you weren't planning to wheedle your grandfather out of millions of dollars, even though you turned up at such a suspicious time."

Anne smiled without a trace of humor. "How uncomfortable for both of us—having to trust someone we so cordially dislike."

Josh astonished himself by laughing. "Do you know how British you sounded just then? Anyway, is it a deal?"

"I suppose so." She extended her hand, her back straighter than the proverbial poker. Josh found himself thinking that despite the trembling eyelashes and shy blushes, perhaps she wasn't very much like Merrilee after all. The thought was strangely disturbing.

"At least we won't have to tolerate each other's company for long," he said, expressing his relief out loud. "Once the police have finished their interview tomorrow, I'm sure you'll be anxious to get back to England."

"You're right. At the moment, my own flat, some friendly faces and the prospect of a good English pot of tea has an almost magic appeal."

"I'm sorry, I didn't think. You must be hungry."

"Some soup would be wonderful. Although what I want most in the whole world is a hot shower and some clean clothes. I feel dirty right down to my bones."

"Food first. Come into the kitchen, and I'll make you a bowl of Campbell's best. You can tell me the rest of your kidnap story while the soup heats."

She followed him into the kitchen, the exhaustion she had been fighting now plainly written on her pale features. Curling up in one of the chairs, she accepted a cup of tea and sipped it slowly as she described her five long days of captivity. She made no attempt to be dramatic, but the careful flatness of her monotone couldn't conceal the terror she had experienced locked away in totally unknown surroundings, in a country that was alien to her and thousands of miles away from home. Josh's lingering suspicion that she might have been a party to her own kidnapping withered away. Nobody could act well enough to fake the goose bumps that rose on her arms or the sheen of sweat that dampened her face as she described the suffocating totality of her isolation.

Anne accepted the soup and accompanying toast politely, but without much interest. It wasn't until she had taken a couple of tentative spoonfuls that her appetite returned and she began to eat with ravenous enthusiasm.

Josh watched her in silence. "More?" he asked quietly when she finally put down her spoon and swallowed the last bite of toast. "I have plenty of other cans."

"No, thanks, I think my digestive system has taken on enough for now." She smiled. "But that was delicious. You're obviously an experienced cook."

"King of the can openers, that's me. I'm also great with a microwave."

"I'm more ambitious than you. I have a shelf full of gourmet cookbooks, but so far, I've never made it past the lesson on *choux* pastry." She smiled again, her delicate features springing into vivid life. She pushed the bowl toward the center of the table and yawned: a giant, childlike yawn that swamped her too-thin body. She stretched in the chair, eyes sleepy. "Can you tell me where the bathroom is before I fall asleep where I'm sitting?"

"Top of the stairs, second door on your right. I'll get you one of my shirts to sleep in. And I'll find something of the twins for you to wear tomorrow. You're about their height."

"Thanks." She yawned again, carrying her soup bowl over to the sink before making for the stairs. She was half-way to the second floor when she stopped and swung around to look at Josh. "I forgot. Where shall I sleep?"

He'd promised Bree that he'd lock Anne up somewhere, but having heard her harrowing account of the past five days, Josh knew he couldn't be cruel enough to shut her into the gloomy basement, the only room that possessed a functioning lock. Which left him with no choice other than to take her into his own bedroom. Into his bed. Despite her soft blue eyes—or maybe because of them—he didn't trust her enough to offer her the living-room sofa. She'd disappeared once at a crucial moment. He didn't intend to leave her free to wander out into the night.

Josh cleared his throat. It was amazingly difficult to tell Anne she would have to sleep in his room. "This house only has three bedrooms," he said finally. "Bree and the twins are using two of them, so you'll have to sleep with me. But my bed is king-size, so there'll be plenty of room."

"That's all right, Joshua, I understand." Anne's smile actually seemed a touch mischievous as she turned and continued to walk up the stairs. She spoke over her shoulder. "Don't worry. Even if we happen to touch, I promise not to ravish you during the night."

Josh still hadn't found a suitable reply by the time she went into the bathroom and quietly closed the door.

JOSHUA'S BATHROOM contained fluffy towels, shampoo, scented soap, talcum powder and endless hot water. Anne soaped herself under the pounding spray of the shower until her hair squeaked, her skin withered and her toes turned invisible beneath clouds of steam. When she finally pushed aside the shower curtain and reached for a towel, she was dizzy from the heady combination of cleanliness and lack of oxygen.

She was almost dry when a knock came on the door, followed by Joshua's voice. "Anne, I have a comb and a new toothbrush if you'd like them."

"Yes, I would, thank you." She anchored the towel beneath her arms and opened the door. Joshua, barefoot and wearing a short dark robe, handed her a small plastic bag and a cotton shirt.

"I think you'll find everything you need in there." He gestured to the bag. "And the shirt should be comfortable."

"Thank you," Anne said, not at all surprised to see how well prepared he was for impromptu visitors. No doubt when Bree and the twins weren't acting as chaperones, Joshua enjoyed a constant stream of female houseguests. She could guess exactly the sort of woman Joshua liked to entertain. Luscious, long legged and balloon breasted, they would be equally spectacular in bed and in the office. Anne normally felt inferior just thinking about such talented women, but tonight she was too exhausted to worry about her own inadequacies.

"Five minutes to clean my teeth, and I'll be through," she said, and smiled simply because her body felt warm and well nourished after days of deprivation.

Joshua blinked. "No rush," he said after a moment. "I already took a shower in the other bathroom. By the way, I've put a sleeping bag on top of my bed for you. I'll sleep under the covers. We'll be quite separate."

"I'm sure we won't have any problems." Not quite sure why she confessed her failing to Joshua of all people, she admitted the truth. "To be honest, I'm rather glad to be spending the night in your room. After those days in the cabin, it may be a while before I enjoy my own company again."

Joshua didn't mock her cowardice, thank heaven. He simply touched her cheek in a gesture that was oddly reassuring. "Your hair's gone all curly," he said.

Anne grimaced. "It's the steam. Usually I manage to blow it dry before the curls get too bad."

"They're nice. Sort of soft and bouncy looking."
Abruptly Joshua's hand fell to his side, and he stepped back.
"Good night, Anne," he said, sounding somewhere between brisk and curt. "Switch off the bedside light when
you're ready for sleep, will you?"

When she came out of the bathroom, he was lying with
his back toward her, his tall body squashed into less than a
third of the giant bed. Anne climbed into the sleeping bag
and zipped herself in, taking care to leave a healthy eighteen inches of space between herself and the hump of Joshua's body. She'd never shared a bed with any man except
Brian, and she wondered if the strangeness of the situation
would keep her awake.

She needn't have worried. Anne barely remembered
stretching across to switch off the lamp before exhaustion
overtook her and she fell asleep.

BABE TOSSED restlessly between the cool white sheets, her
skin feeling hot and prickly. Tonight the wakefulness
wouldn't go away, although normally she fell asleep the
moment her head touched the pillow. For a while, she was
content to stare at the ceiling and fantasize about her lover.
Then the worries began to crowd in. Who had set Anne
Clarence free? Babe wished that she could call her lover and
get some answers to her questions, but of course that was
impossible.

She felt a little bit sick, and her stomach refused to un-
knot. The image of Anne's pale, exhausted features kept
returning to haunt her, making her head ache. She was glad
Anne hadn't been hurt, but she wished she hadn't come
back right this minute. Babe didn't know exactly what had
happened the night Bertram died, but she suspected a lot,
and it was all too possible that Anne Clarence knew even
more. Enough to cause trouble?

Babe tossed and turned on the bed, twisting the covers
until the sheet was as tightly knotted as her stomach. Her
lover was more talented than anyone she had ever known,
and he was soon going to be famous. So why did she have

this creepy fear that something terrible was about to happen? That her life was about to become unraveled? The Kennedy family had too many secrets, and Babe was afraid that one of them might explode and shatter her world. Damn Bertram for dying when he did! He'd lived for eighty-two years; couldn't he have managed to stay alive for another couple of months? Her lover needed Bertram's money.

Babe cradled her stomach in her arms. The painful knot eased slightly. There was no need for her to worry. She was in love with a wonderful man, who loved her in return. Her lover would make everything come right. She could rely on him absolutely.

Couldn't she?

Chapter Four

During the night, Anne's arms became entangled in the puffy folds of the sleeping bag, so that when she rolled over, the fabric tightened around her like a rope. Every time she moved, the grip became tighter, until her dreamless sleep degenerated into a vivid nightmare of bondage and captivity. For a few horrifying moments, she was once again a captive, tied up in the suffocating prison of the mountain cabin. Sweat broke out in a cold dew across her face, and her body stiffened. Even her vocal chords seemed paralyzed, so that she couldn't vent her terror by screaming.

It was the sound of Joshua speaking that finally pulled her out of sleep into reality. "Are you okay?" he asked quietly. "Did you have a bad dream?"

"Yes, awful." She couldn't quite control the shake in her voice. "I dreamed I was back in the cabin."

"You're safe in my house." Joshua sat up and switched on the bedside lamp. Soft light flooded the corners of the room, revealing Joshua's pleasant, masculine bedroom with its overstuffed armchair and tallboy piled high with magazines. The image of a stark log cabin faded from Anne's mind, leaving only faint tendrils of her nightmare.

Joshua took her hand and held it in a loose clasp. "You're not a prisoner," he said gently. "The door to my room isn't even shut. You're free to walk anywhere you please."

"I can see that now." Anne scrunched down in her sleeping bag, embarrassed to have made a fool of herself, especially in front of such a self-assured man. Joshua didn't look as if he'd ever had a nightmare in his entire life. She forced a smile. "Silly of me to get so worked up over nothing. I'm sorry to have woken you."

"You didn't wake me. I never managed to get to sleep."

It was nice of him to lie, and she smiled again, this time with unconcealed gratitude. He squeezed her hand once more before reaching toward the light switch, flicking the room back into darkness.

"Ready to try for another few hours' sleep?" he asked. "Or would you rather talk for a while?"

Sleep seemed light years away. "If you're not sleepy, I'd rather talk," Anne admitted.

Joshua stretched out his arm. "Lean back and get comfortable," he suggested.

Anne resisted for a second or two, then—succumbing to the lure of human contact after days of isolation—she lay back against his chest, allowing herself to soak up the comfort of his strong arms and the soap-scented smell of his warm, sleepy skin. Unlike Brian, who would have seized the opportunity to lecture her on the stupidity of insomnia, Joshua simply said, "Tell me about your father, Paul Kennedy. I've always wondered about him."

She was delighted to oblige. She didn't get nearly enough chances to talk about her father. "You knew he was an agricultural chemist working at Cambridge University?"

Joshua nodded. "That's about all I do know. I'm not even sure what Paul looked like as a grown man. Bertram didn't have any photos."

"He was slim, with thick brown hair and strong, competent hands. He loved silly practical jokes and inventing word puzzles. He used to dress up as a clown for all my birthday parties, complete with a red rubber nose that made honking noises." She smiled in the darkness. "Once the students at his college put on a pantomime to raise funds for famine relief, and he played the rear end of a horse. At the time, I couldn't understand why my mother was so cross."

Joshua laughed. "Did he play his part well?"

"I thought he was super. Of course, I may have been a bit prejudiced."

"Sounds like he enjoyed taking time off from his test tubes to have fun."

"When I remember him, I always think of laughter and happiness," Anne agreed. Quelling a moment of wistfulness, she looked up at Joshua. "Good grief, I've just realized you and my father were stepbrothers, which makes you my step-uncle!"

"I don't feel in the least avuncular toward you," Joshua said at last, his voice dry. "You might be smart to remember that. What else can you tell me about Paul?"

"Dozens of things."

"Tell me some of them."

"We used to spend Sunday afternoons exploring the countryside around Cambridge. Dad was a keen amateur naturalist, and I still have the book of pressed wildflowers we collected together."

"He was working on some new sort of pesticide at Cambridge University when he met your mother, wasn't he? Bertram told me that much on one of the rare occasions he talked about your father."

"Dad never talked about my grandfather, either. They seem to have had one row after another ever since my father started college. And yet my father was an easygoing sort of man."

"So was Bertram. And they were both research scientists, too. The pair of them ought to have had a lot in common."

"I don't know about that," Anne said doubtfully. "The research scientists I've met usually seem incapable of agreeing about the time of day, let alone the details of their research."

Joshua chuckled. "You have a point. But it's a shame Paul didn't live long enough to share in your grandfather's commercial success. Bertram's company didn't really start to be profitable until after your father died."

"My dad wouldn't have cared much about the profits of the company, but I've always thought that the split with my grandfather bothered him a lot."

"Do you know why he volunteered to serve in Vietnam?"

"I think he felt the need to do something healing in the midst of all that destruction, so he joined the Red Cross as a medical orderly. I was only eight when he died, but even I vaguely understood that he was furious about the chemical defoliants the Americans were using to flush the enemy out of the jungles."

"I guess for a scientist who was trying to increase the world's food production, defoliation must have seemed particularly evil."

"He was only scheduled to stay in Vietnam for three months. And then he died two weeks before he was due home."

"It must have been devastating for you." Joshua linked his hands around her, pulling her deeper into the comforting circle of his arms. "Bertram and my mother were already married when word came that Paul was dead, so I heard the reports firsthand. His plane was shot down by a stray missile, wasn't it?"

"Yes, an American missile. It's ironic to think my father was probably killed by a frightened American teenager who fired first and saw the Red Cross symbol afterward."

"Does it bother you that an American serviceman may have taken your father's life?"

"It did once. Now I just feel sorry for all the people caught up in the war. I realize my father was one victim among thousands, and not all the victims came home in coffins."

"In a way, your grandfather was one of those victims. He lost not only his son, but also his granddaughter because of the war. Your mother refused to answer his phone calls and letters, then once she remarried, Bertram never could trace her. Or you."

"My mother believed Bertram Kennedy and his entire family were dreadful, dishonest people. After Dad died, she tore up every scrap of correspondence with Grandfather Kennedy's name on it. I'd never have been able to trace him if Dad's college at Cambridge hadn't started remodeling. They cleaned out a roomful of old filing cabinets, and found a stack of my father's research papers. They sent them on to my mother, who gave them to me."

"And that's how you traced Bertram?"

"Yes. There were a couple of my grandfather's letters in among the research papers, complete with an old address. After that, it was easy to track down his current whereabouts."

"It's curious, you know. Nobody seems to have any clue as to what Bertram and Paul argued about. Does your mother know?"

"About scientific principle, or so she claimed."

"Families usually fight about money."

"Not in this case, I'm sure. My dad was pretty unworldly. According to my mother, he was so obsessed with finding some way to feed the hungry masses of the world that his own wife and child could have starved to death right under his nose and he'd never have noticed."

In the semidarkness, she saw the white gleam of Joshua's smile. "Do you think she's right?"

"I'm sure Dad would have noticed if we were starving. But I have the impression he wouldn't have cared in the least if my mother hocked her wedding ring in order to buy food."

"Is your mother equally unworldly?"

Anne laughed. "Good heavens, no! My mother believes that everything and everyone in the world has a price, and that the more money you have, the easier it is to buy happiness."

"She and your father certainly sound like the oddest of Odd Couples."

One of her feet was getting pins and needles, and Anne shifted inside her sleeping bag. As she moved, the hair on

Joshua's chest prickled through the thin cotton of her nightshirt, and a flush of sensual awareness heated her skin. Usually she would have been embarrassed by this evidence of her own sexuality, but in the anonymity of the darkened bedroom, her feelings seemed permissible, just as it seemed all right to talk about subjects that were normally off-limits. Anne relaxed against Joshua's chest and considered her parents' marriage from an outsider's perspective, something she'd never really done before.

"Perhaps my mother isn't the same person now as she was when she married my father. Or perhaps they fell so passionately in love that the differences didn't matter. I don't think they married in haste and repented at leisure. Our household was too happy."

Joshua's fingers brushed lightly across her hair, and Anne tensed, wondering if he felt the same tug of desire as she did. "Your mother married again very quickly after Paul's death, didn't she?" Joshua asked.

"Six months later. But I'm not sure that proves anything about her feelings for my father. I think she may have been so devastated by his death that she married the first sensible, practical man who presented himself."

Now, where in the world did that insight come from? Anne asked herself. Until tonight, she'd never realized that she understood so much about her mother's motives for marrying the worthy but dull Harold Clarence.

Joshua stopped stroking her hair, and she heard him yawn. "The experts say that people who are alike enjoy the happiest marriages, but I guess most of us have a sneaking suspicion that the flaming love matches are always between opposites."

"Mmm," Anne agreed. The sound of his yawn made her feel drowsy, and she didn't protest when Joshua eased down in the bed, taking her with him. They were still chastely separated by the sleeping bag and layers of covers, a fact that didn't please Anne as much as it should have done.

"Ready for a couple of hours' sleep?" Joshua asked softly.

"Mmm." Her eyes were beginning to close, and her body felt heavy with fatigue. Which had to be why she allowed herself to fall asleep with her head still nestled against Joshua's chest and his arm circled possessively around her shoulders.

ANNE WAS EATING cereal and drinking coffee under Bree's disapproving gaze when the phone rang the next morning. Bree picked up the phone. "Hello."

From her seat at the kitchen table, ten feet away from the phone, Anne could hear the babble of semihysterical words gusting out of the receiver. Bree tried without success to interject questions and comments. When Joshua came into the kitchen and mouthed "Who is it?" she held out the receiver to her brother. "It's our dear Aunt Shirley," she said. "Some major disaster, but I can't make out what."

The lavalike flow of words continued at the other end of the phone. Joshua grinned, not bothering to listen. "The cat threw up on her new cashmere sweater?" he suggested.

Bree grinned back, looking suddenly years younger and almost attractive. "At least. I'd call this eruption an eight on the Shirley-scale of cosmic disaster."

Joshua took the phone. "Shirley," he said. "This is Josh. Shut up."

The babble of sound ceased as if by magic. "What's happened, Shirley?" Joshua asked into the silence. "Start from the beginning, please. And no phony Italian accent. Bree and I both know damn well you were born in Milwaukee."

The laughter faded from Joshua's face as his step-aunt launched into another, more coherent account of her problem. "When did you last see him?" he asked.

Shirley's answer seemed to reassure him. "Well, then, he hasn't even been missing for twenty-four hours. He's a grown man, Shirley, and entitled to take off without giving an account of his movements to his mother—"

This comment apparently provoked a spate of hysteria that even Joshua couldn't control. "Let me talk to Sebastian," he said wearily when he managed to get a word in edgewise.

Shirley must have handed the phone over to Sebastian, for the conversation immediately became calmer and less one-sided. Joshua asked a few more questions, his worried frown lifting.

"I'll come around to the house as soon as I get through taking Anne Clarence to the police station," Joshua said finally. "Although one of these days it would be nice if I could put in a couple of hours at the office. My staff are beginning to think I'm the new Invisible Man."

Whatever Sebastian said brought a faint smile to Joshua's lips. "Yeah, well, I know it's Saturday, but we workaholics like to keep in training, you know. I'll see you around noon. Try to stop your mother notifying the media that Dom's been murdered, will you?"

One of the twins—Anne had no idea which—came into the kitchen just in time to hear Joshua's final remark. She stopped abruptly in the doorway and pressed her hand against her heart.

"Oh, heavens," the twin said, her voice squeaky with emotion. "What's happened to Dom? Surely...don't tell me he's been *murdered?*"

Joshua hung up the phone while Bree hurried over to the door. "Don't worry, Laurel sweetie," Bree said, taking her daughter's hand and guiding her to the table. "It's just Aunt Shirley overdramatizing again."

Anne, who was being ignored by everyone, sat up straighter in her chair and stared intently at Laurel. Anne had spent the past six years working as a guidance counselor in schools all over south London, and by now there wasn't a trick in the teenage repertoire that she hadn't seen. She might not be much good at understanding adult behavior, but she was very good at psyching out teenagers, and she was willing to stake her excellent professional reputation on the fact that Laurel Macmillan was acting her adolescent heart out. The girl didn't have a smidgen of worry about the missing Dominick Rossi, Anne would swear to it.

Interesting, she thought. *Is that because Laurel doesn't care about him? Or is it because she knows darn well he's safe?*

Neither Bree nor Joshua seemed to share Anne's cool assessment of the situation. Joshua came and sat next to Laurel, patting her hand soothingly. "There's nothing to worry about, honey, but Dom didn't keep a dinner date with Aunt Shirley last night, so she went around to his apartment first thing this morning and discovered some of his things were missing from the closet. You know what your great-aunt is like, she immediately decided some terrible disaster had occurred."

"Shirley's never happy unless she's turning everything into a grand drama," Bree said, her voice thick with disapproval.

"She's an opera singer," Laurel said. "Isn't that what opera singers are supposed to be like?"

Joshua smiled. "Maybe. But sometimes I wish Shirley would stop believing her own publicity agent. Dom is a grown man. How old is he? Thirty something?"

"Thirty-two," a voice supplied from the doorway. Anne looked quickly across the room and saw the other twin had arrived. What was her name? Heather.

Joshua, Bree and Laurel all greeted the newcomer, then Laurel broke the important news. "Guess what! Dom's disappeared from his apartment."

"Oh, wow! Has he been kidnapped, too? Like Anne?" Heather's pretty, immature face flushed with anxiety. Or was it anxiety? Anne wondered. Why did she get such a strong feeling that the twins weren't in the least surprised to hear of Dom's disappearance?

"I'm sure nothing bad has happened to Dom," Joshua said reassuringly. "Sebastian has already checked out the apartment, and he says there's no sign of robbery or foul play. I expect Dom just wanted a weekend away and forgot about last night's dinner date with his mother."

"Who's Sebastian?" Anne asked.

Four pairs of shocked eyes turned to stare at her. Obviously they had all forgotten she was in the kitchen. She smiled wryly. So much for her moment of glory. Last night she had been treated as more dangerous than the Devil incarnate. This morning she was returning to her usual role of being totally overlooked by everyone. "Who's Sebastian?" she repeated.

"I keep forgetting that you don't know anyone in the family," Joshua said, pushing an impatient hand through his hair. "Sebastian Rossi is Shirley Rossi's older son, Dominick's brother. Dominick is the middle son. He has a younger brother, Carlo, who's a musician."

"And Shirley Rossi is Grandpa Bertram's sister," Heather added helpfully. "She's a famous opera singer. Or at least she used to be, before she got old. She lives in Italy because she's married to an Italian count, but once upon a time she sang all over the world."

"I've heard of Shirley Rossi, of course," Anne said. "Her recording of *Faust* with Bernardo Batelli is one of the best." How odd to think that such a famous singer was her great-aunt, and she'd never known it.

The twins looked impressed by this evidence of Anne's cultural knowledge. "Do you go to operas and things, then?" Laurel asked.

"I'm afraid I do. I even think Gounod and Verdi write better music than Prince and Phil Collins."

The twins looked blank, either from shock that anyone could be considered superior to a genius like Phil Collins, or because they had never heard of Gounod.

"You two aren't going to make it to the police station by ten o'clock," Bree interjected almost as if she were jealous of Anne's conversation with her daughters. "The traffic into Denver is dreadful at this time of the morning."

"It is Saturday," Joshua pointed out.

"That doesn't seem to make any difference. You'd better leave now unless you want to keep the detective waiting."

"I'm ready," Anne said, standing up. "Ready, and anxious to get this interview over with."

DETECTIVE GOODINE listened politely to Anne's tale of kidnapping and imprisonment. His expression gave no clue as to whether or not he believed her, and from the number of times they were interrupted by phone calls and uniformed cops bringing in messages, Anne thought it would be a miracle if his scribbled notes conveyed any coherent account of what she was saying. However, she wasn't about to complain. Detective Goodine's harried state carried with it a distinct advantage: it was less work for him to accept her story than to attempt to disprove it, which meant that she was in no danger of being arrested for leaving the scene of Bertram Kennedy's death. Anne was willing to be thankful for such small mercies.

"We'll do all we can to find out who abducted you," he said when she finished her story. "Of course, kidnapping's a federal offense, so we'll have to make a report to the FBI."

"Will the FBI want to interview me?" Anne asked.

"I expect so."

"Is that really necessary?" Joshua asked. "You've taken an extremely detailed statement. Naturally, after all the trauma Anne has been through, she's anxious to get back to England."

Not half as anxious as you are to ship me off, Anne thought ruefully.

"I'm afraid it's not that easy for Ms. Clarence to leave," the detective said. "Ms. Clarence lost her purse and her luggage and all her papers, including her passport, so right now, technically speaking, she's an undocumented alien."

Detective Goodine was beginning to sound more than a touch pompous, which Anne considered a bad sign. "What happens to undocumented aliens?" she asked.

"If we go by the book, we're supposed to lock you up and wait for the INS—that's Immigration and Naturalization—to take over," the detective said with a cheerful smile. "That's just the letter of the law, of course. We'll be happy to release you into Mr. Donaldson's custody. I guess you're willing to take responsibility for your—um—relative until she can get a new set of papers together, right Mr. Donaldson?''

"Oh, right. Fine." Joshua sounded about as enthusiastic as a union leader volunteering for unpaid overtime.

"But this is ridiculous!" Anne exclaimed. "Please, Detective Goodine, can't you sign a form for the immigration people, explaining what happened, so they'll let me out of the country?''

"Sorry, miss, but there's no such form. Besides, as of now, we don't exactly know what happened, do we? We only know what you've stated. Which doesn't agree at all with the story we were told a few days ago by Mr....'' Detective Goodine searched among his papers. "Ah, yes, here it is. By Mr. Dominick Rossi.''

"Anne has just gotten through explaining that Dominick never met her," Joshua interjected curtly. "Obviously the kidnappers relied on that fact in making their plans. Dom was tricked.''

"As you say, Mr. Donaldson. I dare say he was. Pity he's not here to give us his version of the events, isn't it? But I'll be sure to pass your views along to the folks over at the bureau. I expect they'll want to take statements from you and Mr. Rossi, as well as from Ms. Clarence.''

Even though it was nice to see Joshua put in his place, Anne didn't much like the direction the interview was taking. She was almost relieved when a uniformed police officer rushed into the tiny office and tossed a file onto Detective Goodine's desk.

"Hutton's been picked up," the police officer said. "He's already called his lawyer. They need you in interrogation, Goody. Room 4. Lickety-split.''

Detective Goodine rose to his feet. "Sorry I have to run," he said. "Seems they've caught a slippery character I've been after for six months. Tax evader. Drug dealer." He shook hands with Anne. "Don't leave town without telling me where you're going, will you?''

"Er...no.''

The detective treated Joshua to another of his cheerful smiles. "Been nice seeing you again, Mr. Donaldson. Glad Ms. Clarence turned up safe and sound. Show her something of Colorado, why don't you? It's a beautiful state." He nodded toward the uniformed officer. "Show them out, will you, Ted?"

JOSHUA, OBVIOUSLY NOT happy about his new role as Anne's legal keeper, didn't talk much during the fifteen-minute drive from the police station to his stepfather's house.

"We're here," he said, turning into a sweeping circular driveway on a street of imposing, mock-Tudor houses. "This is Cherry Hills." Cherry Hills, Anne concluded, was a very expensive part of the city.

The scene that greeted their arrival was a surrealistic mixture of tragedy and farce. Ellen Donaldson Kennedy, Joshua's mother and Bertram's second wife, greeted Anne with barely concealed dislike. Like Bree, she obviously didn't believe a word of Anne's kidnapping story, and only years of social training prevented her from saying so outright.

Shirley Rossi, a plump, pigeon-breasted woman with totally unbelievable russet hair and sequins on her glasses, didn't waste any time introducing herself to Anne, but simply launched straight into the last act of her personal drama. Hurling herself into Joshua's arms, she announced between copious tears her conviction that "dearest Dom" had been brutally murdered. She produced no evidence for this startling assertion other than the fact that Dom has missed his dinner date with her, "and the terrible ache in this mother's heart of mine." This last statement was delivered in a thick Italian accent.

Anne studied Shirley Rossi with unabashed fascination. Since Shirley and Ellen were both ignoring her, Sebastian had no difficulty in drawing Anne to one side and introducing himself. He was a sensible-looking man in his mid-thirties, neatly dressed in tailored slacks and a cotton-knit shirt. He reminded Anne of her English schoolteacher colleagues, and she heaved a mental sigh of relief at meeting someone so normal. Her American relations were turning out to be a bit more eccentric than she'd bargained for.

"I'm glad you're finally here," Sebastian said, giving her hand a firm shake. "I only wish you could have managed to meet up with Uncle Bertram before he died. He was so excited when he heard from you last month. He carried your letters around with him everywhere."

"Did he?" Anne flushed with pleasure at the news. "Thanks for telling me that. Before I go back to England, I'd love to have a chat with you about our mutual relative. I know so little about him."

"He was an interesting ma—" At this point Sebastian's voice was drowned out as Shirley Rossi's wails rose to an agonized crescendo. Sebastian glanced toward his mother, then winced in humorous resignation. "Well, I guess this isn't quite the moment to sit down for a quiet chat about the good old days. But you're right, we must get together some time soon. I need to talk to you about Bertram's will—"

The poor man seemed destined never to finish a sentence. Ellen Donaldson sailed regally over to the corner where they were sitting. "Sorry to interrupt, Sebastian, but I need to have a word with this young woman." She glared at Anne. "Josh tells me that you can't go home because you don't have your passport."

Anne lifted her chin slightly to meet the clear challenge in Ellen's words. "That's right. My passport was stolen, along with everything else I'd brought to the States. At the moment, I'm a real charity case. I've no money, no credit cards and no papers."

"Very unfortunate," Ellen said ambiguously. "Perhaps you'd like to make a phone call to your parents to see if they can arrange for whatever duplicate documents you need."

"Thank you. I'd like to make a call to England. I can certainly arrange for someone to wire me some cash, if nothing else."

"No need for that," Sebastian said quickly. "We can loan—"

"There's a phone in the kitchen," Ellen said, her voice sweeping over Sebastian's offer before he could complete it. "You're welcome to use it. Follow me, please."

When they arrived in the kitchen, a tall, startlingly good-looking man was just walking out. Anne had never seen such an exquisite specimen of male beauty. "Carlo," Ellen said sharply. She tapped him on the shoulder. "Carlo, this is Anne Clarence."

The young man directed a smile at her that positively dazzled in its white-toothed perfection. "Hello," he said. "So nice to meet you again."

"We've never met," Anne said.

"I've missed you, too," Carlo murmured. He took her hand and carried it to his lips. "Goodbye, beautiful Madonna." He drifted from the room.

Anne realized that her mouth was hanging open. She snapped it shut. "Carlo is a musician," Ellen said curtly, as if that explained everything. "At the moment, he's composing a symphony and he's not totally connected to reality."

That, Anne thought, was something of an understatement. After twenty years of enduring her stepfather's relatives, who thought wild eccentricity consisted of taking afternoon tea at four-thirty instead of at four, she found the Rossi family rather entertaining. Carlo was so good to look at, it almost didn't matter whether or not he made sense when he spoke. She wondered if he could actually write music, or whether that was simply a pose.

Ellen indicated the phone and left the kitchen. Anne dialed England direct, but she couldn't reach her mother, so she called Brian and explained to him what had happened and why she wasn't able to return to England right away. Brian was horrified, more by the indignity of Anne's being held in custody by her American relatives than by the trauma of what she'd been through.

"I'll call your stepfather and ask his help in getting you a new passport. He knows a few chaps in the Foreign Office. And Anne, as soon as you have the papers, make sure you get the next plane back to London. I knew you should never have gone to America. It's not at all the right sort of place for a sweet, innocent girl like you."

"I rather like it here," Anne said, surprised to realize she was speaking the truth. In the hours since she had escaped from the cabin, her life had been more interesting than anything she ever experienced in London. "Besides," she said, surprising herself again, "I need to stay here until I find out why I was abducted."

Brian's irritated response that she'd been kidnapped because all Americans were gangsters failed to dissuade Anne from her conviction that she had a right to search for a more specific answer, and a right to want the people who'd deprived her of a reunion with her grandfather to go to jail.

"You don't sound at all yourself," Brian complained. "You almost sound like one of those horrible women's libbers."

The old-fashioned term made Anne smile. "I feel like one," she said. "It must be something in the Colorado air. Goodbye, Brian." She hung up before he could launch into a lecture on the dangers of mental sickness induced by high-altitude climates.

Miracles had been achieved in the living room by the time Anne returned. Sebastian had left. Carlo was seated in front of the piano, occasionally pecking at middle C with his forefinger, then scribbling in a staved music book. He gave no indication that he was aware of anyone else in the room.

Shirley, flaming hair still askew but otherwise noticeably calmer, was chatting amiably to her sister-in-law and to Joshua. She rose to her feet as Anne entered the room.

"The victim of the dastardly abduction is safe!" she exclaimed, flinging her arms wide.

"Er... yes, thank you. Quite safe." Anne advanced cautiously and extended her hand. "How do you do, Ms. Rossi. It's a great honor to meet you. I've admired your work for ye—'' A warning frown from Joshua stopped her just in time. "I've admired your work for some time."

Shirley lowered her outflung arms and placed her hand graciously inside Anne's, a queen acknowledging her subject. "You have endured much, according to Josh," Shirley announced. Her Italian accent changed from gangster-movie thickness to a mere hint of international princess. "I am sorry that you did not meet my brother before he died. He wished very much to right old wrongs with you, to settle old feuds."

"I'm sorry, too, that we didn't meet."

"He had no soul for music, but his heart was kind." Shirley narrowed her eyes and inspected Anne with unabashed thoroughness. "You look exactly like Katrina."

"I'm afraid I don't know who Katrina is."

"Was. She was your grandmother, Paul's mother and Bertram's first wife. She died of leukemia when Paul was still a young boy. She was from Sweden and exquisitely beautiful. Your hair and skin are just like hers."

"Thank you for a lovely compliment, Ms. Rossi."

"For heaven's sake, I'm your aunt. Call me Shirley. Why are you wearing those awful clothes? They look as if you borrowed them from the twins."

"Actually that's just what I did. My own things were stolen."

"Good lord, how positively *frightful!* Is that why you don't have on any makeup?"

"Yes, all my luggage was stolen when I was kidnapped."

Shirley's hair vibrated with outraged sympathy. "But what is everyone thinking of?" she demanded. "Why haven't you taken this poor girl shopping, Joshua? Have you no sensitivity to a woman's most basic needs?"

"Apparently not," Joshua said. "Although I'm not quite sure where we'd have gone shopping between ten o'clock last night and nine this morning."

Shirley dismissed this trifling practicality with a wave of her beringed fingers. "There are shops in Denver, I daresay. Even in this outpost of civilization, they must have some of the basic necessities. Perfume, silk underwear, lipstick.'' She reflected for a moment. ''Since it is August, I suppose that you will not need a fur.''

Anne was intrigued by Shirley Rossi's definition of *necessities*. She glanced at Joshua and saw that he was smiling at his step-aunt, his gaze exasperated but affectionate.

''I'll make a deal with you, Shirley. I'll take Anne to buy the silk underwear you're so keen on, if you'll stop making a fuss about Dom.''

Shirley rose to her feet, eyes flashing. ''How can you so lightly dismiss the terrible disappearance of my son?''

Joshua spoke lightly. ''Dominick's a grown man, Shirley. If you'd stop treating him like a child, maybe he'd stop acting like one and take the time to tell people where he's going.''

Shirley sank back into her chair. ''I guess guilt makes fools of us all,'' she said, losing the last trace of her phony accent. She looked across at Carlo, still pecking away at middle C. ''My career took me away from the boys so much while they were growing up, I like to kid myself I can make it up to them now.''

Ellen Kennedy crossed the room and gave her sister-in-law a sympathetic pat on the shoulder. ''Shirley, my dear, if mothers allowed themselves to feel guilty about the way they raised their children, every priest in the church would spend twenty-four hours a day hearing confessions. Your voice is a gift from God, it deserves the widest audience you can find.''

''You don't think I neglected them?''

''I think you made the choices your career demanded,'' Ellen said. When she wanted to be, Josh's mother was obviously a skillful diplomat.

''On which note,'' Joshua said, kissing his mother and his step-aunt, ''I'm going to say goodbye.'' He raised his voice. ''Goodbye, Carlo.''

The piano erupted in a trill of liquid melody, proving that Carlo could play considerably more than middle C.

"Goodbye, Josh," he said in an amazingly normal voice. "How about some fishing next weekend?"

"Sounds great," Josh said. "Will the symphony be ready by then?"

Carlo's hands crashed into a triumphant cord. "It will be ready," he said.

"What a relief!" Josh tucked Anne's hand into the crook of his arm. "Coming, Anne? It seems we have a date to go shopping."

Chapter Five

They stopped for lunch at McDonald's, and Anne discovered that Big Macs tasted exactly the same in Denver as they did in south London. A quick shopping spree in the local May Company department store equipped her with makeup, underclothes, T-shirts, a pair of jeans and a cotton dress. Not exactly the luxury wardrobe Shirley Rossi had intended, perhaps, but after a week of wearing the same outfit, Anne loved every crisp, new item.

"Thank you for the loan of your credit card," she told Joshua as they carried the packages to his car. She was already comfortably clothed in the new jeans and a mint green T-shirt. "I'll repay you as soon as I can."

"Don't worry, my credit's good." He smiled. "Just make sure Aunt Shirley doesn't think I chose any of your new clothes, or she'll accuse me of being the world's greatest cheapskate. She doesn't understand price tags that read less than a hundred dollars."

Anne laughed. "How lucky she's a famous singer and can afford to indulge herself!"

"Yes, I guess so." Joshua frowned, or perhaps he merely squinted against the sun. "What are your plans for the afternoon? I could take you back to my town house here in Denver while I go to the office—"

"No, thank you." Anne drew in a deep breath. "Josh, I need your help. I want to go up into the mountains," she said. "Back to your stepfather's cabin."

Joshua looked genuinely startled. "Whatever for?"

"To search for clues," she said, which was at least partly true. The more important truth was that until she inspected the cabin in the bright light of day, until she walked through that steel-lined front door and emerged again unharmed, she would have no hope of banishing the suffocating fear the memory of the cabin produced.

Joshua would clearly have preferred to go to his office. But—either because he felt guilty for having doubted her kidnap story, or else because he still doubted it and hoped to catch her in some inconsistency—he agreed to spend his afternoon driving her back to the cabin.

They took the road north out of town, traveling through Estes Park. Anne found the view of spruce-clad mountains, foaming white water and wide blue sky so spectacular that she almost forgot the ultimate purpose of their journey. Coming from England, with its misty island climate, it was a revelation to see that sky could be this high and the horizon this vast.

Dark clouds drifted across the sun just as Joshua put the Jeep into four-wheel drive and started the climb up the rutted gravel road to the cabin. Anne heard the distant rumble of thunder and, within seconds, rain skittered over the windshield. She shivered, although it wasn't cold, and immediately Joshua glanced toward her. She'd forgotten how sensitive he was to her changes of mood.

"This rain will soon pass," he said. "Twenty minutes and it'll be over. Afternoon showers are common in the mountains during summer."

She nodded, accepting—at least intellectually—that there was nothing sinister in the appearance of a few rain clouds. But the closer they drove to the cabin, the harder it became to cling to reason, and the more she felt herself retreating into a protective shell of silence.

"My house where you stayed last night is to the left," Joshua said. "You can see it through the trees. I bought it two years ago, when my divorce from Merrilee became final. Merrilee was my wife," he added. "She didn't like country living, so I guess buying this house was my way of telling myself the marriage was finally over."

Anne couldn't speak, not even to mumble *Nice house,* or *Sorry about your wife.* She clenched her teeth and stared straight ahead, waiting for the cabin to appear in view.

"The town house I have in Denver is tiny," Joshua continued. "Two bedrooms upstairs, small living room and a cubicle for a kitchen, you know the sort of thing. At least it's better than a hotel, and the bathrooms are great."

"That's nice," Anne said. Good grief, how could she ever have thought this unfeeling brute of a man was sensitive? How could he chatter on about his stupid living arrangements when at any moment they would arrive at the cabin? Anne closed her eyes, cutting off the frightening image. A few moments later, she felt the Jeep draw to a halt.

The warmth of Joshua's hand on her arm penetrated the clammy chill of her skin. "We've arrived."

Reluctantly she opened her eyes and faced her enemy. The cabin. It squatted in the overgrown yard, the door closed and its windows shuttered. Logically she knew its rough-hewn log exterior looked rustic and appealing amid the setting of evergreens and silvery aspens, with delicate wild-flowers outlining the path to the door in splashes of summer color. But all Anne could feel was a strong sense of menace.

Joshua opened the door of the Jeep. "Rain's stopped," he said. "Ready to go inside?"

Never. But she couldn't admit as much to him, of course. She could imagine his scorn if she told him she was scared witless at the mere thought of stepping back into the cabin. She made the first excuse that came into her head. "We can't go in. We forgot to bring the key."

Joshua reached over into the well of the Jeep and pulled up a cotton zippered jacket. He patted one of the pockets. "I have keys in here," he said. "But do we need them? You didn't lock the door when you left last night, did you?"

Anne stared at the cabin door, registering the fact that it was closed tight, and her stomach knotted. "I didn't even shut it," she whispered. "Just dashed out and ran down the mountain. Someone must have been here since I left."

"More likely the wind blew the door shut," Joshua said. "There's quite a breeze this afternoon. Coming?" he asked again, and jumped down from the Jeep without waiting for her reply.

Anne scrambled out of her seat and tagged along behind him, although she could feel her legs starting to shake. She swallowed hard, striving for control.

Joshua's hand reached for the doorknob. "Wait!" Anne said, knowing she couldn't go in. Joshua looked over his shoulder.

"Er...I'm just going round to the back of the cabin," she said. "I'm...um...there's something important I want to check on outside the kitchen window."

"Okay," Joshua said. He sounded patient and understanding, which had the perverse effect of irritating Anne almost beyond endurance. She hated the thought of Joshua patronizing her. No doubt he had chalked her up as one more tiresome step-relative he needed to cope with, less eccentric than Carlo and Shirley Rossi, but also less interesting. Thank heaven he didn't offer to come to search for clues with her. At least she would be able to conquer her panic attack in private.

"I'll check out the inside of the cabin," he volunteered. "You do the outside. What are we looking for, by the way?"

"Clues about anyone who's been here," Anne suggested. "You know, cigarette stubs and things. And I'd like to take a sample of the milk powder from the kitchen, I think it was drugged."

She sprinted to the back of the cabin before he could ask any more awkward questions, then leaned against the rough bark wall and closed her eyes, soaking up the sun. After a few minutes, the chills stopped chasing over her skin, and her breathing steadied. Eventually she worked up enough courage to open her eyes.

She was standing directly outside the kitchen, on a little concrete patio, and the familiar view of aspens, mountains and blue sky greeted her. Now that her panic was under control, she felt ashamed of her cowardice. She'd come up here in order to conquer her fear of the cabin. But her nightmares would never go away unless she screwed up her courage and walked through that threatening front door, joining Joshua in the claustrophobic darkness of the living room. She scuffed her toes along a crack in the patio, summoning courage. Sunlight danced off the panes of kitchen window glass, and she glanced up at the window, remembering—

Anne's breathing stopped so abruptly she almost choked. Dear God, she'd smashed this window in one of her earliest efforts to escape. How could the pane be in place again?

Inching her hand through the iron bars that had frustrated her escape attempts, she ran her fingers over the cement that held the pane of glass in place. It felt perfectly hard, as if it had been there for years. And the dust looked as if it had taken months to accumulate.

The silence was suddenly oppressive, heightening Anne's sense of unreality. All at once, she desperately needed the solid reassurance of Joshua's presence. She needed to hear him agree that this *was* the cabin where she'd been held captive. She *had* smashed this kitchen window three days earlier.

"Joshua!" she yelled. "Come here, please!"

No answer, except the echo of her own voice on the afternoon breeze. Why didn't he reply?

Because he's not here, a voice inside her skull answered. *You're still imprisoned in the cabin, and this is all a dream.*

"No! Damn it! I'm not dreaming!" She tore around the side of the cabin, lungs rasping, her mind churning.

There was no sign of Joshua in the front yard, but the Jeep was still there, exactly where they'd parked it. The pounding of her heart slowed fractionally at this evidence that she wasn't losing her mind. Joshua must be inside the cabin. But why hadn't he answered her shout? Why couldn't she hear him moving around? Anne raced across the rough grass and pushed open the cabin door.

Joshua lay facedown on the floor, his body frighteningly still, his legs sprawled wide. With frantic, fumbling speed, Anne wedged the cabin door open with a small rock and entered the living room. Kneeling beside Joshua, she searched for his pulse. When she felt its strong, steady throb against her fingertips, she rocked back against her heels, drawing in lungfuls of air. Thank God! With such a strong pulse, he couldn't be fatally injured.

Her training as a school guidance counselor required some knowledge of first aid, and the correct procedures seemed to come automatically. She made sure nothing blocked the passage of air into his nose or mouth, then ran her hands over his head, searching for injuries. She soon found the bump on the side of his skull, a huge lump sticky with a thin layer of congealed blood.

When she was satisfied that the head wound was his only significant injury, she ran into the kitchen and flung open the cupboard door, reaching blindly for the plastic cup she had used. It was still there, on its familiar shelf, although the moldy remnants of her food supply had disappeared. She filled the cup with water and hurried back to the living room. She rolled Joshua over and eased his head onto her lap. When she was sure his breathing remained regular and his pulse steady, she sprinkled a few drops of the cold water over his forehead.

He didn't speak, but his tongue flicked out to lick at the trickle of drops. Disturbing him as little as she could, Anne cradled his head in the crook of her arm.

He groaned.

"You've been hurt," she said softly. "If you drink some water, it might help." She put the plastic cup against his lips. Joshua sipped at the water trickling into his mouth, and after a few swallows, he opened his eyes.

For a split second his gaze was blank and unfocused, then recognition dawned. He gave her a lopsided grin. "Anne Clarence, the long-lost granddaughter from England. Fancy meeting you here." He closed his eyes and nuzzled his cheek against her breast. "Mmm. You feel good. You've got fantastic boobs, did you know that?'' He sighed. ''This is very comfortable.''

You're wrong, Anne thought. It isn't in the least comfortable. But she had no desire for the disturbing sensations to end.

Joshua opened his eyes again, and this time the vague recognition sharpened immediately into full awareness. He elbowed himself into a sitting position, scowling as he probed the lump beside his ear. His gaze fell on her breasts, and he reddened.

''Good lord, if I said what I think I said, I owe you an apology, Anne.''

''Don't worry about it,'' she said. ''Every woman likes to think she has great . . . um . . . attractive breasts.''

''Well, you sure do. They're a great pair—'' Joshua shook his head. ''I'm still not functioning right. I'm sorry, let's start over. Did you see what happened? Did you see anyone running away?''

''No. I came around from the rear of the cabin and found you lying here, unconscious. Somebody must have been waiting for you.''

''Behind the door.'' He grimaced. ''I can't believe I was jumped so easily. The oldest trick in the book, and I fell for it. I walked in, didn't look to left or right and—zappo—next thing I know, I look up and discover you playing ministering angel.''

''You don't believe that I—''

''Of course not. You could never have entered the cabin without me seeing you. Besides, my attacker was a man.''

''Did you get a good look at him?''

''Not really. I have this almost subliminal impression of a hairy masculine arm reaching out to hit me. *Damn!* It's my own fault.''

''I don't see how you could have anticipated some maniac would be waiting behind the door.''

Joshua was silent for a moment. ''I'd have exercised a bit more caution if I'd truly believed your story,'' he admitted. ''The truth is, I was discounting a lot of what you told me.''

"Wow, I'd never have guessed that," she said with heavy sarcasm.

Joshua sighed. "I must have seemed cold and unwelcoming to you, Anne, but try to understand. Our family spent the past week grieving for Bertram and venting our anger by disliking you. It's hard to switch our emotions over into accepting that you've been more victimized than anyone else. Does it help if I say I'm very sorry and that I no longer have any doubts?"

"At least I'll know how to win your sympathy in the future," Anne said dryly. "Hitting you over the head with a two-by-four is obviously the way to do the trick."

Joshua's gray eyes warmed with laughter. "Hey, I'm a quick study. Next time a brisk rap on the knuckles will be enough to get my attention."

Her stomach responded to his smile with a curious little lurch of pleasure. She moistened lips that suddenly felt dry. "You need to splash some cold water on your face," she said. "Don't you have a headache?"

"Among other problems." With a brusque movement, Joshua turned away. Refusing Anne's help, he struggled to his feet and walked in a fairly straight line to the kitchen. He poured another cup of water and drank thirstily, leaning against the counter as he drank. "This is a miserable place now all the furniture's been removed," he said, glancing around.

"It made a very efficient prison."

Joshua muttered something beneath his breath that expressed both sympathy and exasperation. "I wish I could promise that the FBI will find out who was behind your kidnapping," he said. "The reality is that no law enforcement agency is going to waste time and manpower chasing down kidnappers who didn't make any ransom demands and whose victim emerged from captivity in perfectly good health."

"Perhaps I can track them myself."

"Amateur detectives only triumph in TV shows." Joshua crossed to the window and looked out. "Did you find whatever it was you were searching for on the patio?"

Anne took a few seconds to realize what he was talking about. "Actually I wasn't looking for anything," she admitted ruefully. "I ran away because I was too frightened to go with you into the cabin. I'm not what you'd call a courageous person."

"Feeling fear doesn't mean you're a coward," Joshua said. "You had a terrifying experience. It's rational to feel afraid. I take it you didn't find anything that might help us track these kidnappers down?"

She hesitated. "Probably not, although maybe there is one thing. Take a look at the window frame, would you?"

"This window here?"

She nodded. "Joshua, I swear I smashed that glass to smithereens days ago when I was trying to escape, but there are no shards of glass on the patio outside, and the cement holding the pane in place seems rock hard. Could somebody have replaced it since last night?"

Joshua felt carefully around the window frame. Then he bent down and sniffed. "This cement hasn't been here long," he said finally. "But whether it's a few weeks old, or a few hours old, I can't say. Some of these new silicone fillers dry rock hard within a couple of hours."

"But why would kidnappers take the risk of coming up here simply to replace a pane of glass?"

"To cast doubt on your story, I expect. Think about it, Anne. If we'd arrived here fifteen minutes later, the cabin would have been empty. And from my point of view, with that glass replaced, there isn't a single piece of hard evidence that anyone has actually been imprisoned up here. Same thing holds true for the police and the FBI."

"What about my fingerprints?" Anne said.

"The counter and the cabinets presumably have been wiped clean. Everywhere else is too rough to hold a print."

"You can still see the notches I made beneath the kitchen windowsill. The kidnappers didn't attempt to obliterate those."

"Notches?"

"Bend down and you'll see them," she instructed him. "I gouged out three notches in the plaster to mark off each day I was imprisoned here. I didn't count Monday, when I was captured, and apparently I slept through Tuesday. Every other day I made a notch in the plaster so that I wouldn't lose track of the time."

Joshua ran his fingers slowly across the three small holes. "Now you've pointed them out to me, they're very noticeable," he said. "But the paint in here isn't new, and I doubt if the kidnapper saw them. He'd think that with the counters wiped, the food gone and the broken window replaced, he'd done everything he needed to discredit your story."

Anne shuddered. "But why doesn't he want people to know I was kidnapped? Why should he care now that my grandfather's dead and his ransom scheme has fallen through?"

"I don't know," Joshua admitted. "But then, nothing that's happened since Bertram died seems to make much sense."

Annie frowned in frustration. "I have the impression that it would all make perfect sense if only we could find the right thread to start unraveling the mystery."

"Well, we don't seem to be finding any threads in here. Let's get back to Denver, shall we?"

Joshua paused in the doorway to cast one last look around the cabin. He put his arm around Anne's shoulder. "Try to imagine this room full of good friends, spicy hot food and cold beer," he said. "Bertram and I had some great weekends up here, years ago."

"I'll take your word for it," Anne said, waiting for Joshua to lock the door.

"This key's sticking," he said. "The lock must have rusted."

Anne stared at the grime-encrusted lock. "It's not rusted," she said abruptly. "Someone's changed the backplate, and the keyhole isn't quite in alignment. That must be what the kidnapper was doing behind the door when we arrived."

Joshua frowned. "He's gone to all the trouble of changing the backplate? That's even crazier than replacing the window glass."

"Not really. I'd chipped away at the wood surrounding the lock when I tried to break out of the cabin. This new plate is bigger than the old one. It covers up all the little pieces of wood I'd chipped out."

"But anyone who takes off the plate will see the damage you inflicted."

"From the kidnapper's point of view, who did he expect to take off the plate? He obviously didn't expect me to come back, and you said yourself that the police and the FBI are only going to give this case the most superficial investigation. As long as everything seems all right on the surface, who's going to probe deeper?"

Joshua pocketed the front-door key, his expression thoughtful. "Our arrival here this afternoon must have given the kidnapper a nasty surprise."

"Yes," Anne agreed. "Bopping you on the head was probably a panic reflex."

Joshua rubbed the egg-sized bump behind his ear. "In the future, I shall try to avoid surprising these guys." He eased himself into the Jeep, taking care not to bang his head. In answer to Anne's queries, he insisted that he felt fine and perfectly capable of driving back to Denver.

As soon as the cabin disappeared from sight, Anne heaved a sigh of relief. "Why didn't my grandfather ever sell that place?" she asked.

"Bertram couldn't bring himself to admit he was too old and too frail to use it again. And in his financial position, the upkeep and property taxes on a simple cabin were negligible. In fact, until last summer the place was in pretty good shape. Dom only cleared the furniture out this spring."

Anne felt her entire body snap to attention. "Dom?" she said. "Dom cleared out the furniture? Is that the same Dominick Rossi who claims to have seen me in the hotel room with my grandfather?"

"Well, yes, but I don't see what—"

"Was Dom the person taking care of this cabin for my grandfather?" she demanded.

"Officially I'm in charge. Since my house is just down the road, I come up to the cabin every month or so. But this spring I was away a lot, partly on business and partly helping my sister clear up the wreckage from her divorce. Dom volunteered to check out the cabin for me. When he reported that a family of mice had died inside the sofa bed, we hired a trash collector to haul the furniture away. So as it happens, I guess Dom was the last person from the family to come up here. But that's sheer coincidence, I'm sure."

"Don't you find it a very suspicious coincidence that the member of Bertram's family who's been taking care of this cabin is also the only person who claims to have seen me with my grandfather? And the person who would be most likely to think of hiding someone here?"

"If you're accusing Dom of kidnapping you, Anne, you're way off base. He was escorting my stepfather to the hotel at precisely the same time your kidnappers must have been driving you up here into the mountains."

Anne could think of several ways around that difficulty, and she assumed Dominick Rossi could have thought of them, too. The hotel was a scant ten-minute drive from Bertram Kennedy's house. Dom could have been abducting Anne one moment and offering to chauffeur her grandfather fifteen minutes later. All he needed was somewhere to stash her inert body. But she didn't think Joshua was ready to listen to such speculation, so she changed her approach.

"I must say I'm very interested in meeting this missing cousin of mine. When do you think he's likely to turn up at his apartment again?"

Joshua chuckled. "I'd guess whenever his latest girlfriend gives up hope of getting his signature on a marriage license. Dom hasn't quite accepted that commitment and faithfulness are the key words for the nineties."

"You seem so certain nothing's wrong with him."

"Anne, he's a pilot for a small commuter airline, and his schedule is erratic. He often takes off on trips where he flies his girl of the month to somewhere like Las Vegas or Disneyland. In fact, I've noticed he does a disappearing act whenever his mother stays in town for more than a couple of weeks."

"Shirley Rossi doesn't live in Denver?"

"No. She's married to an Italian count who's the owner of a crumbling castle on the shores of Lake Como. The plumbing and electrical wiring work about two days out of seven, but the views are magnificent. Whenever Aunt Shirley gets tired of playing countess, she comes to Denver and attempts to reorganize her sons' lives." Joshua grinned. "You spent an hour in Aunt Shirley's company this morning. Do you blame Dom for deciding he needs the occasional weekend to himself? Frankly I think Dom's disappearance is less surprising than the fact that Carlo didn't take off for New York the moment Bertram's funeral was over."

"Then you think Dom has simply gone out of town on holiday?" Anne asked, feeling deflated. Joshua obviously didn't share her sense of urgency, but she was convinced that if they could catch up with Dom, many puzzles would seem less puzzling.

"Not necessarily. He may be hiding out somewhere in Denver, enjoying a cozy few hours with a new girlfriend." Joshua glanced at his watch. "It's going to be six o'clock before we get back to my town house. If you like, we could check out some of the nightclubs where he usually spends Saturday night. It's just possible we might catch up with him."

During her university years, Anne had been too busy training for England's Olympic fencing team to have much of a social life. Since leaving college, her only boyfriend had been Brian Cochran. Brian was a serious-minded man of high cultural pursuits. His definition of an exciting Saturday night out was attending a poetry reading at the local college library. Anne was quite fond of poetry, but she suddenly thought what fun it would be to spend an entire evening chasing a mysterious, missing cousin through various exotic nightclubs. Somehow she was quite sure Joshua would be an excellent guide to Denver nightlife.

"I really think we need to speak with Dom as soon as we possibly can," she said.

Joshua nodded. "Then let's go get him."

Chapter Six

Joshua's town house was much as he'd described it, functional but not especially inviting, except for the bathrooms, which verged on the luxurious. Having grown up in an English country house that boasted twenty rooms but only one Victorian bathroom—and no showers—Anne found it extraordinary to have two tubs, two showers, two sets of double sinks and two wall-to-wall mirrors in a condo that was clearly intended to house a maximum of one childless couple.

Bathing in such pleasant surroundings could quickly become addictive, Anne discovered, pulling herself from a sea of scented bubbles and grabbing a towel. Not wanting to keep Joshua waiting, she quickly put on the paisley cotton dress she'd bought that morning, noticing with pleased surprise that the Colorado sun had already tinted her pale face with a sheen of rosy color.

By the time she added a dash of eye shadow and smoothed on some of her new lip gloss, she hardly recognized the vibrant, colorful woman staring back from the fancy bathroom mirror. Unused to feeling so aware of her own body, Anne smoothed her skirt nervously as she walked out of the spare bedroom into the condo's small living area.

At first, Joshua didn't notice her. He stood behind his desk, flipping through the pages of a leather-bound diary. The rays of early-evening sun streaming through the window revealed a hint of pallor beneath his tan. The blow to his head was causing him more pain than he cared to admit, Anne realized.

"We don't have to go out tonight if you don't feel up to it," she said. "It'll probably be a wild-goose chase anyway."

He looked up, and his mouth quirked into a smile. "But we can have fun during the chase," he said. "I called Dom just to make sure he wasn't back, but there's no answer from his apartment, and my mother says they still haven't heard a word from him."

"How is Aunt Shirley doing?"

"She's gone out to dinner with Sebastian. He always has a calming effect on her, so my mother is hoping Shirley will behave more reasonably when she gets back."

"Do you have any idea where we should start looking for Dom?"

"We're in luck. I picked Dom up at his girlfriend's apartment three or four months ago, and I've just found the address in my diary. Her name's Jolene Wright and she lives about ten minutes' drive away from here, on a street called Monaco. Shall we go and see what she knows, if anything?"

Jolene, an attractive blonde in her late twenties, certainly knew something. She knew that she was furious with Dominick Rossi, who had dumped her cold early in the summer. "That louse promised to fly me to Reno for the weekend. I'm so dumb, I thought the guy was actually talking marriage. Then two hours before we were due to take off, this delivery boy arrives with a dozen red roses and a kiss-off note from Dom. He didn't even have the courage to tell me himself, the jerk."

"Did he say why he was calling off your—um—relationship?" Anne asked.

"Which cabbage leaf did they find you under, kid? He was dumping me for another woman, of course. What else? Dom's attention span is about ten minutes in bed and five minutes outside it." Jolene smiled cynically, not quite covering her hurt. "I told Dom I wanted to have kids one day. Scared the hell out of him. I should have known better."

"Do you know who his new girlfriend is?" Joshua asked.

"No idea," Jolene said, her mask of careless indifference once again firmly in place. "Try the Mile High Cavern. His flying buddies hang out at the bar, and he usually takes his women there at least once before he dumps them."

"My cousin Dom doesn't sound like a very nice person," Anne ventured when they were once again back in Joshua's car, a Toyota this time, instead of the Jeep.

"He's immature in his relationships with women, but he's irrestibly charming when you meet him in person. Wait until we catch up with him, you'll see. There's nobody like Dom for making you laugh and convincing you you're having a great time."

Her lunchtime Big Mac now seemed a very distant memory, and Anne was delighted to discover that the Mile High Cavern served a dish called *nachos grande* along with foaming mugs of beer and various lethal drinks disguised by such exotic names as Miner's Ruin, Sky Flight, and Fool's Gold. Nachos, according to Josh, were a favorite snack food along the Mexican-Texas border, and a staple of something he called Tex-Mex cuisine. Anne had never seen such a bizarre mixture of ingredients as appeared on her plate, but the spicy melted cheese and crunchy corn chips actually tasted rather good. Although she suspected that the cherry-topped Sky Flight that appeared alongside her plate of nachos was potent enough to make arsenic taste delicious.

Sipping her drink, she stared wistfully at the undulating bodies on the strobe-lit dance floor, and wondered if across the Atlantic Brian was at this very moment enjoying an earnest conversation with a half-baked poet. How very glad she was to be in a Denver nightclub, Anne decided. And how nice it was to be sitting next to a man who probably thought meters were something you parked near rather than the essence of literary civilization. Why in the world had she spent the past two years going out with a man who bored her to tears?

She drank the last of her Sky Flight, wondering what it would be like to dance with Josh. Fencing had enhanced her natural sense of rhythm and made her agile on her feet, so that dancing had always been one of her greatest pleasures. And Josh had the coordinated sort of body that would no doubt move with stunning grace around a dance floor....

She jumped when the real Joshua intruded on her fantasy by leaning across the table and suggesting they should make for the bar and order a refill. "Good excuse to chat with the barman," he explained. "So far, I don't see anyone I recognize, but of course, I don't know all Dom's friends. There may be several people here who could help us."

With some difficulty, Anne refocused her thoughts on the evening's true objective. Feeling guilty about her daydreaming, she jumped up and marched briskly to the bar.

"Yes, honey, what'll it be?" asked the young barman. He wore a ruffled shirt and fringed buckskin waistcoat, giving him the appearance of a nineteenth-century cowboy.

Anne smiled, delighted at this picturesque evidence that she really was four thousand miles from home, in a foreign country where the natives just happened to speak English. Sort of. "Could I have a small dry sherry, please?"

The barman stared at her. "You from England?" he asked, reaching behind him for the sherry bottle. "I like your accent, it's real cute."

"Thank you. I'm a schoolteacher from London, and I just arrived here last week."

"Wish my teachers had looked like you," the barman said, pushing an overflowing glass toward Anne. "Are you on vacation? You picked a nice time of year to come. That's three bucks, honey."

He poured four beers and stacked them on a waitress's tray, scarcely pausing in his conversation with Anne. "My gran was born in London, and I've always wanted to go over there. She's dead now, but I'd kinda like to check out my long-lost relatives. See if they're all as stubborn as she was, you know."

"That's just what we're doing," Joshua said, putting a five-dollar bill on the counter to pay for Anne's sherry. "We're looking for a lost relative. Do you know a guy called Dominick Rossi? We wondered if he's been in here the past couple of nights."

The barman pocketed the five dollars, his friendly smile changing to a suspicious frown. He made no attempt to produce any change. "Hey, man, I got smart years ago. I don't know nothin' about nobody. Never heard of anybody called Dominick Rossi."

Joshua placed another five dollars on the counter. For lack of anything better to do, Anne took a sip of the sherry and winced at the biting taste. The barman seemed to mistake her puckered lips for a grimace of despair. He picked up the extra five dollars and jerked his head in the direction of a tall blond man gyrating on the dance floor. "That's Trent O'Toole," he said. "He might be able to tell you something. Talk to him."

Trent O'Toole seemed to be dancing with two women at once, and he saw no reason to abandon his budding harem just because Joshua wanted to ask him questions about Dom.

"Sure I know Dom, but he's not here tonight. Join us," he added. "This is a great song. Man, the Bully Boys are just great, aren't they?"

"Terrific," Joshua agreed, flashing Anne a look that made her giggle. Josh drew her onto the dance floor, wrapped his arms around her and pulled her close. "Sorry," he murmured into her ear. "But we'd better dance, or Trent is going to close up like a clam. I'd say he's had lots of experience fending off angry women chasing Dom."

"It's no problem, I like to dance."

"Here goes, then." Joshua loosened his hold on Anne's waist, snapped his fingers and executed a few pelvic wriggles that confirmed every one of her earlier fantasies. The rhythm of the music pulsed in her veins, and her body responded with instinctive movement. Soon she couldn't resist letting rip with a couple of swirling leaps.

Trent was impressed. "Hey, babe, you're great! You're a great dancer, babe." Trent was obviously a man of limited vocabulary. Perhaps he was used to having his hips say it all. He abandoned his two partners and positioned himself squarely in front of Anne. With a murmured "I'll leave him to you, Annie," Joshua began dancing between Trent's two neglected women.

Trent was an excellent dancer, and he was positively ecstatic about Anne's skills. "You're just great, babe," he repeated when the deejay accidentally allowed thirty seconds of silence to descend over the dance floor. "Where did you learn to dance?"

"In England."

"Great place, England. You a friend of Dom's?"

"I'm his cousin from London," she yelled. The music had resumed at its previous level of megadecibels. "I need to see him, Trent. Do you know where he's gone this weekend?"

"From London, hey? London's a great place. Man, I hope to fly there one day. Yes, babe, I want that to be my route."

"Are you a pilot?"

"Yeah. I work with Dom for Alliance Air. He's been off this week, though, his grandfather died or something."

"His uncle," Anne suppled. "We haven't seen him since Thursday, and I need to talk to him."

"Hey, your accent's great, you know that?"

"Do you know Jolene Wright?" Anne tried another tack. Could Trent really be as dumb as he seemed, she wondered, or was he being deliberately obstructive? "Jolene used to be Dom's girlfriend."

"I know Jolene. She's not a bad sort. Not great, but not bad. She and Dom split up."

"She says Dom found a new girlfriend a few weeks ago."

"I guess he did. Dom's always finding new women."

"Have you seen his new girlfriend?" Anne asked, developing a whole new respect for policemen. Gathering information wasn't as easy as the TV detective shows made it appear.

"Maybe I have seen her," Trent said amiably. "She's a ditzy little thing. Cute body, though. I told Dom she was too y—" he stopped abruptly. "Hey, this music is great, isn't it? Really great."

"The music is very nice," Anne said. "Dom's new girl-friend," she persisted. "Do you know her name? Or where she lives?"

"Dom just called her *babe*, you know." Trent shrugged. "You should quit worrying about Dom and his women. They'll make out fine, you'll see." He delivered a couple of blatant pelvic thrusts as the music crescendoed in a rattle of bass drums. "Great dancing with you, babe." He eyed her speculatively, then shrugged. "Hey, if you're dead set on finding Dom, maybe you and your man should try the Hot Spot, in Boulder. Dom often goes there on a Saturday night and this new ki—this new girlfriend of his likes it a lot. Or you could try Kelly's, up on Colfax. Great beer at Kelly's."

Outside in the parking lot, Joshua shook his head. "My eardrums are still vibrating. Did you find out anything useful? All I learned was that I'm not man enough to keep two women satisfied on the dance floor."

Anne laughed. "I've no doubt Trent would be happy to give you some pointers on how to improve your stamina."

"Like never waste brainpower searching for a new word when *great* will do?"

Anne's smile faded. "Do you think he was putting on an act, Joshua?"

"I don't think he had any interest in helping us find Dom, that's for sure. He and Dom are probably old hands at running cover for each other."

Joshua unlocked the car, and they got in. "Trent told me Dom often goes to a bar called the Hot Spot, in a place called Boulder," Anne said, latching her seat belt. "Is that far from here?"

"Far enough. Boulder's a college town about an hour's drive north. Did Trent mention anywhere else that Dom might be?"

"A placed called Kelly's on a street called Colfax. Which apparently has great beer."

"Not to mention topless dancers," Joshua commented dryly. "We can go there if you like, but I have a suspicion Trent just steered us toward two places where he's fairly sure Dom won't be found."

Anne glanced down at her wrist, then remembered her watch had been stolen along with everything else. "What time is it?" she asked.

"Not quite ten."

"It's still early. Let's try Kelly's and see if we can get one of the patrons there to tell us a bit more about Dom's new girlfriend. Perhaps she's at the root of his sudden disappearance."

Joshua drove out of the parking lot. "What did Trent have to say about the new girlfriend?"

"She has a cute body, and Dom calls her *babe*."

"He calls all his women 'babe,'" Joshua said. "That way, he can't slip up and call them by the wrong name at a crucial moment. Most of them have cute bodies, too."

"How very practical," Anne said, her voice tart.

"Only if you view your women as interchangeable commodities," Joshua replied quietly. "And that was all Trent said? No other clues?"

"Nothing direct. But I had the impression that Trent disapproved of this new girlfriend."

"She must be absolutely dreadful for Trent to disapprove!"

"I think he felt she was too young for Dom."

"Good lord, if Trent thought that, the kid must still be in high school. He's not the sort of guy to worry about a five or six-year age gap." Joshua frowned. "To be honest, Dom's irresponsible, but I can't imagine him getting involved with a really young woman. He likes his women friends to know the score. Jolene is typical of the type who attract him.''

Kelly's, or what Anne could see of it through the haze of cigarette smoke, looked like the setting for a pickup joint in a bad movie. The dance area was much smaller than at the Mile High Cavern, the bar much longer. A spotlight illuminated a bored-looking woman with waist-length hair who seemed to be trying to make love to a sequined, floor-to-ceiling pole. If this was the sort of place Dom's new girlfriend enjoyed, Anne didn't think much of her taste.

Encouraged by a ten-dollar tip, the barman managed to recall that he had seen Dom a couple of weeks earlier. "He had this young girl with him," the barman said. "Short curly hair, sort of slim, bouncy figure. Looked like she was a high-school cheerleader, you know the type.''

"Did Dom say where he'd met her?'' Anne asked.

"Lady, that's not the sort of question I ask my customers.''

"Well, did Dom mention her name?''

"He called her 'babe.' Dom calls all his women 'babe.'" The bartender gave Joshua a sly, man-to-man nudge. "Saves trouble in the long run, you know what I mean?''

"Yeah, I know what you mean.'' Joshua held out his hand. "Ready to leave, *Anne*, honey?''

"More than ready.''

They were making their way through the crowd when Josh suddenly stopped. "Sebastian!'' he exclaimed. "What in the world are you doing here?''

Sebastian turned around. "Same thing as you, I expect. Looking for my wretched brother. My dear mother spent the entire dinner hour having hysterics over the lobster thermidor. Finally I couldn't stand it. I told her I'd find Dom if I had to spend all night searching.'' He smiled ruefully at Anne. "It's bad enough that I have to waste my time, but why in the world has Josh dragged you to a dump like this? You ought to be at home catching up on your sleep. Or at least eating a leisurely meal somewhere civilized.''

"I'm the person who persuaded Joshua to come here," Anne explained. "I'm really anxious to meet my cousin."

Sebastian looked surprised. "Rumors of his fatal charm have preceded him?"

"Not exactly," Anne said. "Although everybody says your brother is very charming. But I'm trying to find out who kidnapped me, and I think Dom could answer some of my questions."

Sebastian patted her arm. "I can understand how anxious you must be. That kidnapping is a complete mystery, isn't it? But don't worry, Anne. Dom will turn up in his own sweet time, although whether he'll be able to give you any worthwhile information is another matter. I can't think what's gotten into my mother," he added. "Dom flies out of town and disappears for two days as routinely as other people go to church or visit their dentist. He'll be back in town soon, with some breezy story of meeting up with a pal and flying down to Vegas."

"Sebastian's right, you know," Joshua commented to Anne. "I've been telling you exactly the same thing, haven't I?"

"You have indeed," she acknowledged.

Sebastian sidestepped to avoid being trampled by a waitress carrying a tray loaded with beers. "This is a grim place, isn't it?" he remarked. "I can't think why Dom likes it. Where are you two going now?"

"Somewhere less noisy, where they don't smoke," Josh said.

"Sounds wonderful. I guess since I promised my mother, I'd better try one more club, then I'm calling it a night. This chasing around town is ridiculous. Dom's scheduled to fly to Durango on Monday, and we all know he'll be back home in time for that. My brother isn't too reliable about most things, but he never screws up on his work assignments."

"That's true," Joshua agreed again. "Dom is a first-rate pilot. Anne, do you think we could get out of here?"

Sebastian looked at him sharply, then cleared a path to the door. "What's up, Josh? You're looking dreadful."

Once outside, Joshua drew in gulps of fresh air with obvious relief. "Anne and I drove up to Bertram's cabin this afternoon. There was an intruder inside the cabin, and he hit me over the head on his way out."

"Good lord, how terrible. Have you seen a doctor?"

"I'm not hurt—"

"That lovely shade of pea green is just your usual color," Anne interjected.

Josh almost managed a smile. "I guess I'm not as thick skulled as everyone claims. The smoke and noise in Kelly's made me feel pretty bad. But I'm okay now."

"We should get you to your car," Sebastian said, concerned. "Did you see who hit you?

"Not a glimpse."

"I hope you reported the attack. Was there any damage to the cabin, or were you the only victim?"

"No, we didn't report it. Detective Goodine already suspects our entire family is crazy, and there's no point in confirming his suspicions. There's not much up at the cabin to damage, and certainly nothing to steal."

"I wouldn't say that. What about Bertram's fishing tackle? He had some pretty expensive stuff, as I recall."

"That was all cleared out a couple of years ago, remember? And the furniture was taken out this spring."

"That's right, I'd forgotten. Are you sure you're okay to drive?" Sebastian asked as they stopped beside Josh's Toyota.

"I'm fine. Really." Josh held out his hands. "See? Steady as a rock."

"All right. But drive carefully." Sebastian waited for them to get into the car. "You know, I haven't been up to the cabin in years. I'd almost forgotten about it. You and I will have to get on top of all this administrative stuff, Josh, since we're the executors of Bertram's will. It's going to be a hell of a task making an inventory of all Bertram's property. He has real estate holdings scattered in twenty states."

"Give me a couple of weeks," Josh asked. "When I have things at my office back on track, I'll give you some serious help."

"I'll hold you to that," Sebastian said. He turned to Anne with a pleasant smile. "Maybe you and I could get together for dinner tomorrow night. There's a great deal we need to explain to you in regard to Bertram's estate, and if Josh is too busy, I'll be happy to take over."

"But my grandfather's estate has nothing to do with me," Anne said. "Unfortunately he died before we even said hello."

"You may not have met, but he was your grandfather, and you were his only direct descendant," Sebastian explained. "As soon as you got in touch with him, he wrote a letter to his lawyers expressing his intention of making provision for you in his will. On the basis of those facts alone, you have every right to sue for a substantial share of Bertram's assets. And if you sue, the estate could be held up in litigation for years."

"But I would never dream of going to court," Anne protested.

"Any lawyer would tell you not to make foolish statements," Sebastian said. "The money's there, and you won't bring Bertram back by refusing to touch it. As executors, Josh and I have a responsibility to see that Bertram's wishes are carried out. The letter Bertram wrote to his lawyers clearly indicates that he intended you to benefit from his wealth. As executors of Bertram's estate, Joshua and I are obligated to make some settlement of your legitimate claims. I would simply prefer to make that settlement out of court, if at all possible."

Joshua's smile was a touch weary. "Sebastian's an accountant, Anne, which is why he's sounding so pompous. He gets like this whenever he talks about money."

"I'm afraid we accountants do tend to get a little earnest when we talk about a sixty-five million dollar estate," Sebastian acknowledged stiffly.

"Sixty-five million dollars is enough to make anyone pompous!" Anne exlaimed. "I feel uncomfortable even thinking about such huge sums of money."

"It wouldn't feel so strange if you'd known your grandfather and grown accustomed to the idea of his wealth," Sebastian said.

Anne smiled wryly. "I must have inherited more of my father's social conscience than I thought. Somehow it seems all wrong for me to become rich just because I'm related to a man my parents wouldn't even speak to."

"Don't worry," Joshua said, his voice hard. "The whole sixty-five million isn't going to be yours. Do you think your conscience can bear the burden of a mere three or four million dollars?"

Anne was surprised at how much Josh's renewed burst of cynicism hurt. "I'm not a fool or a hypocrite, Joshua. Of course I can see the benefits of inheriting a large sum of money. But there are negatives, too, you know."

"I think we're all a bit overtired," Sebastian interjected soothingly. "Time for us to get some sleep. I'll look forward to seeing you for dinner tomorrow evening, Anne. Does seven sound good?" She nodded, and he clapped Josh affectionately on the arm. "'Night, Josh. Take care of that headache, okay?"

They drove without speaking through several dark, almost empty streets, and Anne made no attempt to break the silence.

"Hell, Anne, I'm sorry for snapping at you like an ornery bear," Josh said finally. "I was way out of line. But my ex-wife is one of those women who grabs money from every source she can, all the time assuring people that she really has no interest in money at all. She sobbed prettily in divorce court and won a settlement that would have bankrupted my business if we hadn't gotten it overturned on appeal." He broke off abruptly. "I meant to apologize, not bore you with a load of ancient history."

"I'm not bored," Anne said. "And your apology is accepted. What sort of business do you run, Joshua?"

"I have a company that makes timing devices for machinery. It sounds simple, but actually we produce crucial controls for the operation of everything from refrigerators to huge factory production lines. Bertram loaned me the money to get started, but we've built a reputation for accuracy, and the business is expanding every year. I'm really glad my stepfather lived long enough to see a return on his investment, because when he made the initial loan there wasn't a reason in the world to think I'd make good on the debt." He spoke reflectively. "Maybe that's why I'm so tolerant towards Dom. I was one of those kids who spent my college years majoring in basketball, with a minor in midweek parties. I scraped through engineering school with a bare passing grade. Bertram literally gave me the chance to be a success."

"It's amazing how much power money gives people, isn't it?" Anne said. "To do good things, as well as bad." She stared out of the car window at the distant shadow of the mountains, thinking about the ironies of life. At this moment she had no passport, virtually no possessions, not even a handful of loose change. If Joshua refused to foot the bill, she couldn't afford breakfast or a bed for the night. And yet it seemed she was an heiress.

In many ways she was already a different person from the naive, trusting woman who'd left London a week ago. Since arriving in Colorado, a whole new dimension had been added to her life. Fear.

Maybe all rich people felt afraid, she reflected. Afraid that their wealth would disappear. Afraid that people liked them only for their money. Afraid that someone would try to rob or cheat them.

Anne didn't think like a rich person, not yet. Her fear was more basic, more simple. She realized as Joshua drove the car through the quiet, clean streets of Denver that she was afraid for her safety. The slightly sick feeling, the knot in her stomach that never went away, was the fear of dying. With an instinct for self-preservation that went beyond logic, she knew that her life was at risk until her kidnappers were identified. Her escape from Bertram's cabin didn't mark the end of a strange incident; it marked the beginning of a potent new threat.

Being an heiress was a dangerous business.

BABE COULDN'T SLEEP. Again. She had wasted another entire day trying to get in touch with her lover. He didn't answer his phone, and she hadn't been able to track him down in any of his favorite hiding places. Her lover was smart, much too smart to be in trouble, but Babe felt frightened. What had gone wrong? They had never spent two whole days without communicating before. And this was an especially important time to be in touch.

Anne Clarence was at the root of the trouble; Babe was sure of it. The kidnapping hadn't turned out the way it should have. Anne shouldn't have been kept captive so long. She was supposed to be on her way home to England by now. Instead, she was still in Colorado, chasing around town with Josh, poking her nose into things that weren't her concern.

Anne was still here because she'd lost all her documents. If she had her passport and her luggage, she would go home. Back to England and her boring life as a schoolteacher. Yuk, why would anyone choose to become a teacher? Babe knew where the cases were, knew where they'd been taken after the kidnapping, because her lover had given her the responsibility of hiding them. Maybe she could find some way to return them to Anne. Then Ms. Schoolteacher Clarence would take herself off to London, and everything would work out the way it should have done. Babe's lover would have time to pay attention to her once again.

Babe smiled in the darkness. She was much smarter than her lover thought. All by herself, she'd worked out that the suitcases were the key that would make everything come right again. Quietly, on soundless feet, Babe got out of bed.

She was going to return the suitcases.

Chapter Seven

When they got back to his town house, Josh helped Anne make up the bed in the spare bedroom. Pride kept her from admitting that she would have felt safer sleeping in his room. Pride and a lingering suspicion that safety wasn't what she truly sought in his bed or in his arms.

After a night filled with bad dreams, she was still dozing fitfully when Josh knocked on her door the next morning. "Detective Goodine just called. He'd like to speak to you."

Anne sat up and reached for the bedside phone. "Hello, this is Anne Clarence."

"Sorry to interrupt your Sunday morning, Ms. Clarence, but we had a rather interesting delivery at the police station last night. A pair of suitcases."

"Suitcases!" Anne said. "My luggage, you mean?"

"Would you describe your suitcases for me, Ms. Clarence?"

"They're brand-new, a matching pair in gray tweed fabric."

"That's what we have, all right. Complete with your name and London address on the tags."

"Thank goodness! How about all my documents? Did the kidnappers steal them?"

"It seems as if whoever took this luggage has returned your belongings untouched," the detective said. "Including a purse with your passport and a wallet containing two hundred dollars. Would you come down to the station and identify your belongings, Ms. Clarence?''

"I'll be there as soon as possible," Anne said. "In about an hour, I should think."

Joshua was as perplexed as she was by this unexpected turn of events. They discussed and discarded a dozen different explanations for the return of the suitcases as they drove to police headquarters in downtown Denver. Nothing they could think of made the slightest sense.

Detective Goodine greeted them with the same uncomfortable mixture of politeness and suspicion that had marked their last interview. "Can't say I've ever known stolen property to be returned right to the police doorstep," he said, conducting them to a shelf-lined room piled high with television sets, stereo equipment and miscellaneous items that ran the gamut from one odd ski boot to a purple polka-dot raincoat. "Can you point out your missing property, please, miss?"

By the time she'd finished signing forms and papers and was handed her suitcases, Anne felt as if she'd stormed the citadel. "Whew!" she said as she and Josh escaped to the parking lot. "Detective Goodine certainly knows how to make a person feel guilty!"

Josh grinned. "Do you think he practices that polite sneer in front of a mirror? Still, at least you have your cases again, that's the important thing. Do you want to go back to my place and check them out?"

"Now that I'm a documented person again, I can move into a hotel if you'd prefer it."

"Hotels are lonely places," Josh said. "Why don't we go home, and I'll cook you breakfast while you check that all your belongings really are safe and sound."

Anne discovered that Joshua's repertoire as a cook extended far beyond heating canned soup. He poured foaming glasses of orange juice, whipped up a package of blueberry muffins that filled the kitchen with a wonderful smell while they baked and made two fluffy cheese omelets. Anne found the combination of sweet, cakelike muffins and savory omelet very odd, but after yesterday's experience with the nachos, she had already decided that American food was much stranger to English tastes than she'd anticipated. Americans and English might speak more or less the same language, but they ate quite different food.

After breakfast, she and Josh went through the suitcases together. Her clothes had obviously been taken out and then repacked, but nothing seemed to be missing. She was grateful when Josh showed her a small washing machine and suggested she might want to launder some of her clothes.

"Thanks," she said. "The thought of putting on things that my kidnappers had pawed through wasn't very appealing."

While they waited for the laundry cycle to finish, Anne leafed through her father's working papers, which had been returned along with everything else inside the suitcases. "This is what my father was working on before he left for Vietnam," she said, handing a heavy ring binder to Joshua. "My grandfather asked me to bring over everything the people at Cambridge University sent me. I can't understand why, really, unless he wanted to see what my dad was researching in the last year of his life."

Joshua glanced at the neat, closely written pages interspersed with entire lines of chemical formulae. "My undergraduate courses in chemistry aren't up to understanding this. Can you make head or tail of it?"

"Only enough to see that Dad was working on some sort of fungicide that would increase crop yield." Anne grinned. "And that's because I knew that already. Plus he was kind enough to head one section of graphs Fungicide Test Data." She turned to the middle of the book, flipped through a few pages, then stopped.

"That's strange," she said. "The page with that heading seems to be missing." She began to turn the pages more carefully, searching for the elusive test data. After ten minutes of intense reading, she looked up at Joshua, eyes blank with bewilderment. "Joshua, I think pages are missing throughout this folder."

"They can't be. We'd have found them loose in your cases. May I?" Josh took the binder and studied a few pages with frowning concentration. "It makes no sense, but I believe you're right. This page is a fairly simple chart of crop yields—it stops in the middle without reaching any conclusions. And these pages deal with the toxic effects of some chemical on immature rice crops. They're incomplete."

"Josh, I hate to sound melodramatic, but I'd say whoever kidnapped me and stole my luggage has gone through these files and removed just enough pages to make this record of my father's research project meaningless."

"While at the same time, enough papers remain that nobody is likely to notice anything wrong," Josh suggested.

"That's true. I would never have noticed pages were missing if I hadn't started searching for that specific sheet of test data."

"I suppose you don't have any copies of this material?"

"No, it never occurred to me I'd need a copy. There are hundreds of pages here, and none of them has anything more than sentimental value." Anne paused, then added, "At least I assumed they only had sentimental value."

They looked at each other across the stack of folders. It was Josh who broke the small silence. "Anne, your father died over twenty years ago. Surely nothing in this project could have any commercial value nowadays?"

"I wouldn't think so. Agriculture has progressed by leaps and bounds in the last decade, and chemical fungicides are completely out of fashion. They do too much harm to the environment, for one thing. Besides, the university declared these papers as without current scientific interest before they released them to my mother."

"You're sure he wasn't doing any related research in the field of bioengineering?"

"I'm sure. Dad's work was strictly chemical, almost old-fashioned by today's standards. He was looking for a substance you could spray on rice crops to kill harmful fungi."

"We need someone to tell us more precisely what his experiments were all about, and what pages are missing."

"We need a chemist for that. Do you know any of the chemists in my grandfather's company?"

Josh shook his head. "Not really. Since Bertram sold out, the research headquarters have been moved to Nebraska. But I have a college friend who was a chemistry major. Richard Durbin. He teaches at Denver Univeristy. Shall we take this stuff over to him and see what he can come up with?"

"Please." Anne sighed. "You'd better call first to make sure he's home. The way our luck's running recently, he's probably left town to give a seminar in Timbuktu."

But Richard was in town and willing to help. "I'll expect you before lunch," he said.

They had scarcely hung up the phone when the doorbell rang. Josh answered the door, and a smiling Carlo was revealed jogging from foot to foot on the other side.

"Hi, Josh! I've come to invite you out to brunch." Carlo walked in without waiting to be asked. He wore shocking pink shorts and a lime green shirt that would have looked tacky on any normal mortal. On Carlo, it looked gorgeous. His headband seemed designed more to emphasize the noble height of his forehead than to mop up sweat. He strode into the living room, the muscles in his bronzed legs rippling, his broad shoulders exuding sex appeal.

"Why, hello," he said to Anne, noticing her with a start of surprise. The pleasant smile he had given Josh turned into a high-wattage instrument of seduction. He took her hand and gazed down at her in rapt wonder. "Haven't we met somewhere before? Although I can't believe I'd ever forget such a wonderful Botticelli face."

Anne retrieved her hand. "We met yesterday," she said dryly. "I'm Anne Clarence, your cousin from England."

"Ah! the long-lost relative, of course. I did not remember you because yesterday I was working. What I did yesterday is a total blank in my mind. Except, of course, for my symphony."

Showing no sign of embarrassment at his lack of memory, Carlo sat down and helped himself to a leftover blueberry muffin. "These are very good, Josh," he said without a trace of his previous Italian accent. "You'll make decent house-husband material yet."

Josh snorted, but his gaze was affectionate as he watched Carlo consume the muffin with the air of a man saved from starvation. "I'm not in the matrimonial market. How's the symphony? As if I didn't know."

"The first movement's finished," Carlo acknowledged. He licked his fingers with a triumphant flourish, then turned to Anne, his beautiful face crumpling into an expression of mingled wonder and regret. "Do you know that Mozart composed most of his symphonies while he slept? He would wake up after a restless night and find the entire symphony stored in his brain, in its entirety. His task for the day was then merely to write down the music he had already perfected in his mind, the various instrument parts already scored, everything."

"That's amazing."

Carlo sighed, and for a moment it seemed that the weight of the weary world had descended onto his splendid shoulders. "It's depressing," he said gloomily. "Would you believe that it has taken me a whole month to complete the first movement of my symphony?"

Anne was surprised to find herself feeling genuine sympathy for Carlo. "We can't all be Mozarts," she suggested. "There's room in the world of music for people whose talent isn't quite so monumental."

"You speak with the voice of reason. Such cool logic rarely appeases the creative soul." Carlo's stunning blue eyes darkened with a touch of wry humor. "For a musician who longs to soar with the power of an eagle, it is disconcerting to discover that his talent may be just sufficient to enable him to hop with the skill of a sparrow."

Josh gave Carlo a brisk, encouraging thump on the shoulder. "I can't believe what I'm hearing. What's brought on this unusual attack of self-doubt? Two weeks ago in this very room, you told me the world hasn't seen a genius like you for a generation."

Carlo sprang to his feet and stretched his arms skyward in a gesture that on anyone else would have seemed absurd. On him, it merely seemed a natural way to reduce tension. "It must be lack of food," he said. "Or too big a dose of my mother's artistic temperament. Or maybe it was the lecture I just received from brother Sebastian on the disgraceful state of my checkbook. Who knows? Are you two going to come out to brunch and relieve my misery?"

"We just ate," Josh said. "Besides, we have an appointment at the university with a chemistry professor. We need to leave right now or we'll be late."

"Why do you wish to see a most boring chemistry professor when you could spend the morning with me?"

"Because we need to ask him some questions about the project Anne's father was working on when he died."

Carlo looked at Anne, clearly mystified. "But your father is Paul, my cousin. He died many years ago, didn't he? Of what interest is this project he worked on nowadays?"

"That's what we're hoping to find out," Anne said. "Someone seems to have been interested enough to steal several pages of his test data."

Carlo shrugged. "I do not understand science," he said. His tone of voice implied that the subject was too dull to be worthy of attracting his attention. With another of his startling reversions to full-blooded American, he turned to Josh. "Hey, old buddy, give me a ride to Dom's apartment, will you? I promised my mother I would stop by and pick up his address book."

"What does she want that for?"

He grinned. "So that she can start calling his girlfriends and demanding to know where Dom is hiding."

"I guess that's a relatively harmless way to keep her occupied until he comes back. Don't you have a car?"

"I walked over here." Carlo flexed his muscles to demonstrate. "Now I will ride in your car and talk with Anne."

Behind Carlo's back, Josh's gaze met Anne's, and they smiled in perfect, mutual understanding. "You'll have to come with us to Richard's house first, or else he'll wonder what's happened to us."

"That is okay," Carlo said magnanimously. "I am not in a hurry."

Richard was waiting for them when they arrived at his house, close to the D.U. campus. He took the heavy ring binder and flipped through the closely written pages. "It's going to take me a few hours to come up with anything worthwhile," he said. "Do you want to call me later this afternoon?"

"How about giving me a report over dinner? You choose the restaurant, and I'll pay." Josh shook his friend's hand gratefully. "I owe you one, Richard."

"You sure do. One dinner isn't gonna get you off the hook."

They emerged from the hallway of Richard's house, blinking in the bright sun. "Now to Dom's apartment," said Carlo. He was leaning against the hood of Josh's car, seemingly oblivious to the amazed and admiring gazes he was eliciting from every woman who passed by.

Anne was delighted to have the chance to see the inside of the elusive Dominick Rossi's apartment. She was frustratingly aware that her search for the kidnappers was going nowhere, and she clung to the belief that Dom—if they could ever find him—would provide the lead she needed.

Dom's apartment had the same aura of beige neutrality as Josh's town house, but it was overflowing with knick-knacks and mementos, not to mention a fair amount of straightforward mess.

"How in the world am I supposed to find his address book among all this garbage?" Carlo demanded. He poked along the sofa and extracted two grubby white socks, four flying magazines and an empty champagne bottle. Scowling, he deposited his finds on the coffee table. "This is going to be a long job," he said. "And already I am faint with hunger."

Josh searched the bedroom, and Anne volunteered to help Carlo in the living room. After half an hour, the house was marginally tidier, but the address book was nowhere to be found.

"If Aunt Shirley or my mother want to poke around in the back of Dom's drawers and closets, they'll have to come themselves," Josh said. "Dom's entitled to some privacy. Good grief, he's thirty-two years old! He pays for this apartment. He's entitled to come and go without alerting us to his schedule."

Carlo shrugged. "He knows our mother. If he wants privacy, he shouldn't leave town when he's made a dinner date with her. You know how she worries. Beneath all that sound and fury, she's genuinely panic-stricken. She believes something dreadful has happened to him."

"We might as well check the kitchen before we leave," Anne suggested. "Just so that you can tell your mother you looked in every room."

She saw the address book as soon as they entered the kitchen. It lay on the counter, right next to a copy of the local Yellow Pages. Picking up the address book, Anne noticed that the phone directory lay open at a page headed Physicians And Surgeons. Could Dom be sick? she wondered. Had he left town in search of urgent medical treatment and didn't want to tell his mother?

Carlo pounced on the address book. "Triumph!" he exclaimed, kissing Anne soundly on the cheek. "You are a woman of brilliance. I knew it in the first instant that I saw you."

"Except that you forgot me the moment after we were introduced."

He didn't deign to give such an irritating remark any reply. "I'm going to take this home right now to my mother," he said. "Then we shall have an entire afternoon of peace while she calls all these poor, unsuspecting females who have allowed their names to be written in Dom's book."

"You don't want a ride?" Josh asked.

"I shall walk. I feel the melody of my second movement start to take shape. It is to be in A sharp, an interesting key.

But the theme for the coda is worrying." Carlo left the room without saying goodbye.

"Will he make it home safely?" Anne asked.

"Don't worry. He seems to have some instinct for self-preservation that stops him walking out in front of moving vehicles."

"Is he . . . er . . ."

"Is he as crazy as he seems?" Josh smiled. "On the contrary, he's a certified genius. He graduated from high school with honors when he was thirteen, and finished college two years later."

"Good heavens! Can he really compose symphonies, too?"

"Far better than you'd think from the way he carries on. He won the Leningrad Prize for Conducting when he was eighteen, and he's a virtuoso violinist, although he prefers to concentrate on composing."

"All that talent, and slightly better looking than the average Greek god. I'm surprised some enterprising woman hasn't snapped him up."

"They keep trying," Josh said, closing the phone book. He stopped as a scrap of paper attached itself to his fingers. Yellow, like the pages of the directory, neither he nor Anne had noticed it before. "Do you think it's worth calling this number?" he asked, showing the sticky note to Anne. "It might be the last number Dom dialed, in which case it could give us a clue as to where he's disappeared to."

"It's worth a try," Anne said. "Is it a local call? I don't understand American phone numbers."

Josh squinted at the scribbled note. "What's this first number?"

"I don't think that line at the beginning is meant to be a number," she said. "I think it's meant to be the letter *L*."

Josh looked again. "You could be right," he said. "In which case it's a local call. Here goes."

This time the phone was answered promptly. "Boulder Health Connection. How may I help you?"

"Sorry," Josh said. "Wrong number." He hung up.

Boulder Health Connection? Anne hesitated for a moment, then decided to share her idea. "Dom seems to have been a bit worried about his health. The phone directory was open at a listing of doctors. Now he has the number for some health clinic written down."

"The Health Connection isn't a clinic," Josh said after a tiny pause. "It's a club, the sort of place you go to swim and lift weights and take aerobic dance lessons."

"Oh, well, that explains why he has the number." Anne felt relieved. "Dom's a pilot. I daresay he needs somewhere to go and work out the kinks after a long flight."

"Could be that simple. Except the Boulder Health Connection is where the twins are working this summer."

And Laurel's name begins with an L, Anne finished silently. What's more, Dom, according to his friend Trent, had recently acquired a new girlfriend, with a cute body and short brown hair. A girl who looked young enough to be in high school. The description fit either one of the twins perfectly. "How old are the twins?" she asked.

"They'll be nineteen next month. They graduated from high school this June."

Anne debated for a moment before putting her suspicion into words. "Is it possible that Dom and Laurel are involved in some sort of a relationship?" she asked.

"It seems more than possible," Josh said, not sounding too happy at the idea. "Hindsight sure sharpens the picture, and looking back, I can see several signs that they were attracted." His smile lacked humor. "God knows, they have about the same mental age."

"Would everyone in the family be very upset if they're attracted to each other?"

"Nobody would be thrilled. Dom is too old and too irresponsible for a kid like Laurel. But Bree is a pretty indulgent mother, and the twins are scheduled to go away to the University of Illinois in the fall. Nobody's going to zoom off into orbit over something that isn't likely to be more than a summer romance. If Dom and Laurel are dating each other,

I don't know why they feel the need to keep their feelings such a big secret."

"The mind of most eighteen-year-olds is unfathomable to adults," Anne said. "But I know from working with them that teenagers like to dramatize everything. The students in my school are always imagining themselves in the throes of the world's greatest love affair. And for some reason, at that age they always fall in love with the person least likely to make them happy. I sometimes think teenagers only enjoy themselves when they're feeling miserable. If there isn't a real problem in their lives, they rush off and invent one."

"But the twins might be suffering from a few real problems at the moment," Josh said, crumpling the sticky note and tossing it into the trash. "We've all been so busy sympathizing with Bree over her rat of a husband that we've forgotten the rat is also the twins' father."

The phone rang before Anne had time to reply. Josh picked up the receiver. "Hello."

Anne recognized the immediate blizzard of sound. She also recognized the expression of resigned patience that crossed Joshua's face.

Josh finally managed to speak. "No, Aunt Shirley, I'm afraid Carlo isn't here, or Dom, either. But if Dom had been involved in an accident, I'm sure we'd have heard by now. And Carlo left here about ten minutes ago with the address book. He'll be back with you soon."

Another lengthy pause, then, "No, I'm sorry, we can't come over now. Anne and I are just about to leave for...for..." He obviously grabbed the first excuse that flew into his mind. "We're going to Boulder, to the health club. The twins are joining us for lunch." Not pausing to draw breath—no doubt for fear Shirley would launch into another of her marathan orations—he added, "Is Sebastian there? Put him on for a moment, could you?"

Josh visibly relaxed as Shirley departed and Sebastian took over the phone call. "We need to make the arrangements for your dinner tonight, with Anne," Josh said into the phone. He listened for a moment. "Seven sounds fine.

I'll drop her off on my way out to dinner. Can you drive her back to my place?''

The answer from Sebastian was obviously yes. ''That's all settled, then,'' Josh said to Anne as he hung up the phone. ''Sebastian acted as Bertram's accountant, so he's in a much better position than I am to fill you in on the financial and legal technicalities of your grandfather's estate.''

Anne didn't want to think about Bertram's money. It was still an uncomfortable topic for her. ''Are we really going to Boulder?'' she asked, changing the subject. ''Or was that just an excuse to ward off Aunt Shirley?''

''If you don't mind, I'd like to go. It might be helpful to have a chat with the twins, and I know they work the mid-day shift on weekends.''

They walked back out to the car, which was hot after its spell of baking in the sun. With the windows open, the dry mountain air soon blew in, cooling the interior to a pleasant warmth. ''I've no idea what I'm going to say to the twins,'' Josh remarked as they filtered into the flow of highway traffic. ''You're the one with expertise in this field, Anne. How should I approach them?''

''Do you really want my professional opinion?'' she asked. ''Sometimes friends have said they want my advice, and then they've discovered too late that they aren't at all happy to have an outsider poking into the dark corners of their family business.''

''I'm sure. I have hardly any experience with kids this age. I need help.''

''For a start,'' Anne said, ''you would be wise to stop referring to Laurel and Heather as *the twins*. They're not an entity, you know. They're two separate human beings who happen to look alike.''

''Very alike,'' Josh said wryly. ''Identical, in fact. But you're right. We all got into the habit of lumping them together when they were little—you know, *Where are the twins? What are the twins having for dinner?*—and we've never grown out of it.'' He turned to her and smiled. ''Point taken. What other words of wisdom do you have for me, counselor?''

"Well, you don't actually need to speak to *the twins* about Dom, do you? You need to talk to *Laurel*. Maybe you could invite Laurel for a milk shake, and I could do the same with her sister, but sit at separate tables. For their sake, even more than for yours, you need to start showing them that their lives are likely to take very different paths from here on out. This summer would be a good time to start emphasizing their individuality, the uniqueness of what they each have to offer the world.''

Josh was silent for a moment. "You know, it's amazing," he said. "When I visualize sitting down with Laurel alone, just the two of us without Heather, it's much easier to think of what I want to say to her about Dom. Thanks, Anne. I appreciate your insight.''

"Don't mention it. And by the way, when you're having your heart-to-heart with Laurel, you might ask her where Dom has gone this weekend. I'm sure she knows.''

"He'd better not be anywhere too close," Josh muttered. "When I catch up with him, he's in danger of being strangled.''

THE TWINS HAD JUST finished leading an aerobic dance class when Anne and Josh arrived at the health club. With their faces drenched in sweat and their hair clinging damply to their heads in identical wet curls, they looked even more alike than usual. Josh, however, had no difficulty in telling them apart. "Hi, Heather," he said as a twin wearing a purple body suit and sleek black tights walked across the gym to greet them. Her sister followed, wearing the same sort of tights, but her body covered by a huge cotton sweatshirt, artistically tattered in a style made fashionable by the heroine of the movie, *Flashdance.*

"Hi, Laurel," Josh greeted her. "We hoped we'd catch you both in time for lunch.''

"Uncle Josh! What are you doing here?" Anne's sensitive ear detected a definite note of anxiety in Laurel's question.

"Hoping you'll agree to join me for lunch."

Laurel pulled a face. "I'm sorry, Uncle Josh. I can't. I'm not eating lunch today. I'm on a diet."

"Me, too," Heather said, running a hand over her perfectly flat stomach. "I gained a whole pound last week."

"Come and have a carrot juice, then. Or a diet soda. I'd really appreciate a few moments to talk with you, Laurel."

"Well, we're kind of busy," Heather said. "We need to shower and change, and then we have a bunch of paperwork to finish up before our other class."

Josh glanced at Anne, his smile rueful. "Actually," he said, "I don't need to speak with both of you. I was hoping to have a few words alone with Laurel."

Laurel and Heather looked astonished. Anne wondered if she had imagined the flicker of panic in Laurel's eyes before her expression settled into mere surprise.

"I noticed a terrific swimming pool as we drove up," Anne said. "Surely you two can allow yourselves a five-minute lunch break. Why don't we go outside by the pool, and Heather can tell me about her plans for next fall while Josh has a quick chat with Laurel. A tall glass of ice-cold lemonade would be wonderful outside in the sunshine." She used the brisk, authoritative tone of voice that worked so well with her students, and was relieved to discover she hadn't lost her touch. Heather and Laurel exchanged glances, then agreed reluctantly to break for a lemonade.

Having agreed to come outside, Heather had no intention of making any further concessions. She accepted her frosty glass with a mumbled word of thanks, then hunched her shoulders away from Anne, staring angrily across the pool to where Josh and her sister were sitting.

"Why does Uncle Josh need to talk to her and not to me?" Heather demanded angrily. "Laurel and I tell each other everything. She'll tell me what he said as soon as he leaves."

"That's her choice, isn't it?" Anne said. "Just as Josh is entitled to have a few private words with her if he wants to."

"I hope he isn't nagging her."

"Josh doesn't strike me as the nagging kind," Anne said mildly.

Heather's head jerked up. "Are you falling in love with him? Women do, you know. All the time. He won't get married again. Merrilee burned him but good."

The brash question jolted Anne more than she liked to admit. She had avoided examining her feelings for Josh; now Heather—of all people!—had sensed something in Anne's voice that she herself hadn't known was there. However, Anne wasn't a trained counselor for nothing. She was adept at wresting conversations away from dangerous topics.

"I hardly know your uncle," she said, making sure her smile was friendly and open. "But I've certainly enjoyed his company these past few days."

There was nothing like damning a person with faint praise to allay suspicion, and Heather wasn't experienced enough to penetrate Anne's polite facade. While Heather stirred melting ice in her glass, Anne quickly recovered the initiative. "Does Laurel feel as protective toward you as you do toward her?"

"I'm older," Heather said with perfect seriousness. "I was born fifteen minutes before her, so I've always kind of looked after her. She's shy, you know, and that makes it tough for her."

"I do know, because I'm shy, too. But sometimes the best medicine for shy people is to make them stand on their own two feet."

"We like being together. I like helping her out."

"It wouldn't mean that you and Laurel loved each other less just because you developed a few independent interests," Anne suggested gently. "Perhaps when you start university next autumn, you and your sister could take different courses, and make one or two different friends.

Sometimes twins need to make a special effort to reach out to other people.''

''We're both going to be business majors,'' Heather said flatly. ''We want to open our own health club when we graduate.''

So much for her efforts at a five-minute pop cure for eighteen years of conditioning, Anne thought wryly. ''Are you looking forward to starting college?'' she asked.

Heather shrugged. ''It'll be okay, I guess. It's my mother who wants us to go. I guess she doesn't want us to end up like her. A forty-year-old has-been, with no husband and no job prospects.''

There was a wealth of pain beneath the bitter words, and Anne responded instinctively. ''Don't underestimate your mother, Heather. She's going through a difficult time right now, but forty is young these days. Lots of women in her situation discover they have talents they never dreamed of.''

''Like what?'' Heather sneered. ''Crying on Uncle Josh's shoulder? Clucking over me and Laurel? Doesn't she realize we're *grown up?* We're nearly nineteen, for heaven's sake!''

The perennial cry, Anne thought sadly. From the three-year-old protesting he could tie his own shoes, all the way up to near-adults like Heather, only the young ever felt confident they were grown-up enough to handle life's challenges.

''Wait five years,'' she advised Heather. ''By then your mother may have accomplished some things that will surprise you.''

''She never even graduated from college,'' Heather said, her shoulders still hunched, her gaze still fixed on her sister at the other side of the pool. ''She only married Daddy because—'' She stopped abruptly. ''Thanks for the lemonade. May I go now? I need to change into a fresh leotard before class.''

Heather had said more than she intended; that much was clear. It was equally clear that she planned to say nothing more. Anne glanced across at Josh and Laurel. Their chat also seemed to be ending. As she watched, they stood up and began walking around the pool toward the main club building. From the shuttered expression on Laurel's face, she gathered their talk hadn't been a success.

The twins were perfectly polite as they said goodbye to Anne and Joshua, but they didn't attempt to hide their eagerness to escape to the locker room, away from the probing eyes of their intrusive elders.

"Heather basically told me she and Laurel are both fine, and would I please mind my own business," Anne said as Josh started the car. "How about you? Did you manage to get Laurel to open up a little?"

"On the contrary. She told me that I was crazy to think she had any special feelings for Dom. She and Heather had left boyfriends behind in Chicago, and they were planning to meet up with these young men at college in the fall. Plus she wouldn't dream of going out with anyone as old as Dom. She pointed out that Dom is only a couple of years younger than I am, and she made thirty-five sound like six months away from senility."

"We could be mistaken," Anne said. "I suppose we were building an awful lot on one scrap of notepaper and my feeling that the pair of them were play-acting yesterday when they heard about Dom's disappearance."

"I don't think we're mistaken," Josh said. He eased the car into the highway traffic and leaned back, mouth grim. "I think Laurel was lying through her teeth. What's more, I think she was scared." He drummed his fingers on the steering wheel, his body stiff and awkward with tension.

"It's the damnedest thing," he said. "Until we came up here and spoke to the twins, I never for one second thought anything was wrong with Dom. Now that I've talked to Laurel, my mind's suddenly a sinkhole of suspicions. Where the hell is he? What's going on with Laurel?"

"And what does Dom know about my kidnapping?" Anne added mildly.

Josh looked at her, then drew in a deep breath. "Yes," he said, finally admitting that Dom's behavior the night Bertram died wasn't entirely beyond question. "We need to ask him that, too. Hell, when Dom does condescend to put in an appearance, he's going to need some powerful earplugs. When Aunt Shirley gets through blasting him, I'm going to start."

Anne felt a drop of water splatter on her arm. She glanced out of the car window and saw that it had started to rain. "Is this another one of Colorado's ten-minute afternoon showers?" she asked Joshua.

"There's no rain in the forecast," he said. "It's sure to be a quickie. You might want to close your window, though, or you'll get wet."

Anne had not yet mastered the electronic wizardry of Josh's Toyota. She pressed a button in the armrest control panel, but it was the wrong one. Instead of closing the window, the back of her seat collapsed in a whoosh, stretching her out almost prone behind her seat belt.

Josh yelled, a loud frightened yell that seemed entirely out of proportion for the minor nature of her mishap.

"Sorry if I distracted you." Anne scrambled upright, and bent over the armrest control panel, making another search for the correct button. The wind was blowing the rain into the car, making it decidedly uncomfortable. The sooner she closed the window the better.

"I've—been—shot."

The car swerved in a violent loop across the highway, banging Anne's head against the door. Blinking, half-blinded by the pain, she swung around and tried to focus her smarting eyes on Josh.

Blood. Dark red blood was splattered all across his chest in an obscene pattern. Dear God! *Did he really say he was shot?* The car swerved again, and she saw Josh's eyes close.

"No!" she shouted. "You mustn't faint! Josh, take your foot off the accelerator."

She saw the huge effort with which he forced himself to absorb the meaning of her instructions. His foot slid off the accelerator and plopped onto the floor. The car slowed a fraction.

"Thank you, Josh!" she breathed. "You're a wonderful man!" Unlatching her seat belt, she leaned across and grabbed the steering wheel. The instant she took control, Josh's hands flopped into his lap and his head lolled forward, as if he'd exhausted every scrap of his energy. No way she could reach the brake pedal without moving Josh, Anne realized. No way she could move Josh while the car careered along the highway at fifty-five miles per hour. A hill, she prayed fervently. Please God, just one little hill. No hills appeared, but Josh groaned, and her panic level lowered a millimeter. People who groaned couldn't be dead.

Gradually she realized that the wailing noise she could hear over the yammering of her pulses was getting louder. A police siren! Wonderful, wonderful noise. Police cruisers had radios, and could call medical help. The road ahead inclined very slightly upward. Not exactly a *hill,* but something. Thank you, God. The speedometer now read a mere forty-three miles per hour. But soon after roads incline up, they have a tendency to incline down. Panic returned, full-blown and choking. On a steep downward slope, the car could reach sixty miles per hour in no time, perhaps even more. She had to stop the car! What would happen to a Toyota traveling at forty-three miles per hour that was deliberately crashed into the median barrier? Anne felt sweat bead on her forehead. But it wasn't sweat making her T-shirt wet. It was blood. Joshua's blood. *I have to stop the car.*

A sign flashed past. Something-or-other exit ahead.

An exit. Maybe one with an upward-climbing exit ramp? Anne would have crossed her fingers, except that they were clamped to the steering wheel in a death grip. Hah! Death grip. Very funny, Anne. Josh is bleeding to death, and you're a comedienne. . . .

Louisville Exit. And the exit ramp climbed steeply upward! Anne drove the car off the highway, onto the ramp. The engine sputtered, then chugged groggily along, soon losing speed. At the Stop sign that marked her final emergence from the ramp onto a local road, she swung the car right and rolled to a gentle stop in a grassy drainage ditch.

When she realized that by some miracle they had avoided causing a multicar pileup on a busy highway, she didn't know whether to laugh, cry, shout or faint. In the end, her teeth were chattering so hard she couldn't manage anything more than a squeaky gasp. *Louisville Exit, I love you.*

Josh was still bleeding. His blood oozed away in a warm, life-threatening trickle. Anne unbuttoned his shirt and gently eased it away from his skin. She pulled off her own T-shirt and held it against the wound, temporarily staunching the bleeding. Where were those damn policemen? They'd be tooling up fast enough if she didn't need them.

As if summoned by her irritated wish, a young police officer appeared at the side of the Toyota.

"Out of the car, miss. Are you aware it's an offense— Oh, my God!"

Anne said the first thing that came into her head. "I've never driven before in America. You all drive on the wrong side of the road." And to her absolute fury, she burst into tears.

Chapter Eight

The bullet wound in Josh's chest was, according to the paramedics, superficial. The emergency room surgeon agreed with that diagnosis. Josh had seemed to lose so much blood because the bullet had skimmed along the surface of his flesh, gouging out a bloody groove about four inches long and a quarter-inch deep. However, his dramatic loss of consciousness had occurred not because of this wound, but because he'd banged the side of his head when the car swerved.

"Looks as if you've knocked your head about more than once in the past few days," the doctor said, peering at Josh's scalp. "There's an older contusion here."

"A ... rock fell on me up in the mountains."

"You want to watch where you're climbing," the doctor said cheerfully. In his view, accustomed as he was to treating all the more hideous forms of bodily damage that mankind inflicted on itself, Josh was not a worrying case.

"You're going to feel uncomfortable for a few days," he said, applying a final stitch, then stepping back to admire his handiwork. "But I'd say you're a very lucky man."

Josh managed a wan smile. "This much good luck I don't need."

"We'd like to keep you in for observation overnight." The doctor scribbled on his chart. "That way we can make sure there's no concussion. And you'll feel stronger if we replace the lost blood and give you a glucose drip overnight.

Plus the antibiotics you need are more effective when we administer them intravenously."

Josh would have protested, but at that moment his mother and Shirley Rossi arrived in the emergency room, in response to a police call alerting them to the accident. After listening to five minutes of his mother's anxious questions and Shirley's protestations that she would nurse him with more care than Florence Nightingale, Josh wisely decided that he would spend the night in the tranquil isolation of a hospital room.

Ellen seemed satisfied with this decision, but Shirley was not so easily pacified. Deprived of her preferred prey, Shirley immediately turned her attention to Anne. "But my dearest child, you are covered with blood! Have you, too, suffered some monstrous wound?"

"No, I'm fine, thank you. Don't worry, Aunt Shirley. I just haven't had time to shower and change my clothes. This is Josh's blood you can see on my shirt."

She'd made a bad mistake, Anne realized, almost as soon as the words left her mouth. Shirley erupted in a fresh spasm of anxiety, and only calmed down when the doctor threatened to have her booted out of the hospital if she didn't stop making so much noise.

"How the hell can I put this dressing on with you screeching in my ear like a banshee?" he demanded.

"Really, these technicians," Shirley said, thoroughly miffed. "They do not understand the nervous soul of a great *artiste.*"

Anne silently thanked her lucky stars that Carlo had stayed home in Denver.

As soon as the doctor left the cubicle, Ellen started questioning Josh again. Anne could see that she tried to stop herself, but anxiety had eroded her self-control, and the unanswerable questions kept pouring forth. *Who shot you? What do the police say? Why would anyone want to shoot you? Was it an accident? A hunter? Have they put detectives on the case?*

Josh could say nothing except that Detective Goodine had been notified and the police were investigating. He soon began to look gray with fatigue. His mother's fear was wearing enough, but Shirley in full histrionic flood would exhaust anyone, let alone a man missing an four-inch strip of chest.

"You know, I'm feeling really shaken up," Anne said, not entirely without truth, but chiefly because she could see Josh needed rescue. "Aunt Shirley, do you think you could come with me to the coffee shop? Perhaps we could have some tea before I call for a cab to take me home."

Josh gave her a look replete with gratitude, and even his mother managed a smile of appreciation. "Don't go without saying a proper goodbye," Josh murmured.

"As if I would." Anne took Ellen's place at his bedside and reached out to touch his shoulder, one of the few spots on his upper body not swathed in bandages. The muscles bunched and rippled beneath her touch, and she felt confused by the wave of emotion that swept over her. She covered the confusion by speaking in her usual brisk schoolteacher voice. "I'm glad the bullet didn't touch anything vital, Josh."

"Yeah, who needs skin, anyway?" His smile faded and he reached for her hand. "Thank you, Annie," he said quietly. "You saved both our lives."

She hated to be called Annie, so she had no idea why her body reacted to his use of the nickname with a flush of pleasure. Her schoolteacher voice was called into service again. "Try to get a good night's sleep, Josh."

"I'll be as good as new in the morning. Especially if you give me a kiss to help me feel better." The intensity of his gaze was at odds with the teasing lightness of his words.

"Kisses only work with little children," she said, afraid that she sounded as breathless as she felt. Where was her stiff British upper lip when she needed it?

"You're wrong, you know. They work even better with grown-ups. Let me show you."

She felt the space between them charge with energy, becoming taut and sensual, but she didn't move away.

"Annie?" He reached up and curved his hand lightly around the nape of her neck, exerting the merest hint of downward pressure.

How could she refuse him? Anne asked herself. The man was wounded, after all, and might get a fever if he was thwarted. In fact, he was probably feverish already. Why else would he behave so outrageously? But with his mother and aunt looking on, he wasn't likely to make a simple kiss into a big production. Strictly for the sake of his health, Anne lowered her head.

The second their lips met, she knew she'd been wrong about the big production. This kiss was going to be pure Hollywood, with full violins, pounding pulses and a rapturous heroine.

"Close your eyes," Josh whispered.

She obeyed, and in the sudden darkness her other senses seemed both heightened and distorted. Josh's kiss felt richer, headier, warmer than anything she'd experienced before. His mouth caressed hers, and she felt drunk from the swift, intense rush of sexual desire. The hospital noises faded into a steady hum that pulsed in rhythm with her heart.

When the kiss finally ended, she was dizzy and disoriented. She stood up, blinking in the reality of fluorescent light and hospital clatter. She wondered if she looked as bemused as she felt.

Josh raised her hand and held it briefly against his cheek without speaking.

"Sleep well," Anne muttered. "I have to go now."

Ellen Kennedy's expression was thoughtful as she watched Anne walk out of her son's cubicle. Thoughtful, and not too happy.

ANNE SOON DISCOVERED that when Shirley wasn't playing tragedy queen, she was not only a pleasant companion, but she was also surprisingly efficient. Shirley found a washroom, insisted on getting real soap and a cloth towel from a passing orderly and waited without a sign of impatience while Anne cleaned up the most-visible effects of the accident.

By the time Anne was ready to search out the cafeteria and order tea, Shirley had already called Sebastian and asked him to drive Anne home. To Anne's protests that she was being a nuisance, Shirley merely replied, "My dear, you can't possibly take a cab, not in those clothes," and then entertained Anne, and the people at nearby tables, with funny stories about her years as a world-famous diva.

Sebastian arrived, looking more frazzled than Anne had previously seen him. "This is dreadful," he said as soon as he was within speaking distance. "I've just seen Josh—" He paled, and tried again. "If that bullet had gone even a fraction of an inch deeper, we'd have lost him."

"But the bullet didn't go deeper," Shirley said with amazing practicality. "And Josh is going to be out of here by tomorrow morning. Will you drive Anne home right away, Sebastian dear? I really need to go upstairs and hold Ellen's hand. First Bertram, and now this. It's really more disaster than the poor woman can be expected to cope with in the space of two weeks."

"Of course I'll drive Anne, it'll be my pleasure." Sebastian turned to Anne with a smile. "Especially if you'll agree to spend the night with me. I'm sure you don't remember, but we were supposed to be having dinner together tonight and I have a meal already prepared for us."

Anne appreciated Sebastian's offer, although in many ways she would have preferred to go back to Josh's empty town house and curl up in front of the television. Some mindless game show, she thought, where the people look as if they've never heard of death or attempted murder.

"You don't want to be alone tonight," Shirley said firmly. She seemed to have abandoned her role as the family's resident hysteric for a new role as manager-in-chief. "Besides, you can't get into Josh's house, you haven't got the keys."

"Actually a policeman gave me Josh's keys. But you're right, both of you. This probably isn't a good night to spend alone." She smiled at Sebastian. "Thanks for the offer to put me up."

"Not at all. Let's go now," he said. "You're going to need a few hours to unwind before bedtime."

"Wait!" Shirley rummaged in her purse and finally pulled out a little gold pillbox. She flipped up the lid. "Sleeping pills. Nothing too strong. The doctor prescribes them for me when I cross time zones. I hate to have insomnia." She pressed the box into Anne's reluctant fingers. "Take them, my dear. And keep the box. It's a pretty thing. I believe it belonged to one of the Borgia's. It's been in my husband's family for years."

"Think about what the Borgias probably kept in there," Sebastian said with a dry laugh. "Poison, love potions—"

"Well, all I have in there are sleeping pills," Shirley said. She gave Anne a resounding kiss. "Good night, my dear. You're a sweet thing, even if you do wear the strangest clothes. I'm glad Josh is attracted to you. He needs a woman like you after eight years of living with Merrilee. I'll walk you both to the main exit."

She left them with effusive hugs, bestowed as liberally on Anne as on her own son. Sebastian gazed after his mother, his expression of mingled exasperation and affection one Anne had seen several times on Josh's face when he dealt with Shirley.

"My dear mother can be so clever at times," he said. "And on other occasions, I wonder if she's moving in the same reality zone as the rest of us."

"I'm sure she's not," Anne said, smiling. "But her world is probably much more interesting than ours, don't you agree?"

"If you like your whole life to play like grand opera, I guess so. Personally I prefer my day-to-day living to be a bit more humdrum." He laughed ruefully. "But then I'm an accountant, and we're not people known for riotous living. High drama for me is adding two columns of figures and discovering that they don't balance. Sometimes I wonder if I'm a changeling. Dom and Carlo are so much like my mother, and I don't even look like her.''

''Perhaps you take after your father,'' Anne suggested.

''Perhaps.'' Sebastian didn't seem thrilled by that idea. He stopped next to a blue car, big by the standards of most English models. The logo read Buick LeSabre. ''Here we are, this is mine,'' he said, unlocking the door on the passenger side and waiting politely for Anne to get in. ''We're only a half-hour drive from my condo. Hop in, you must be exhausted.''

''I am tired,'' Anne admitted, fastening the seat belt and leaning back with a small sigh.

''Too tired to tell me exactly what happened this afternoon?'' Sebastian asked.

Anne wasn't enthusiastic about repeating her story yet again. She'd told it to two sets of police officers, as well as Detective Goodine, and then repeated a shorter version three times at the hospital. But Sebastian had been kind to come to pick her up, and he deserved to hear the details of the attack on Josh firsthand. He listened intently while Anne explained what had happened, then was silent for a few seconds.

''Do the police think it was a serious attempt to murder you?'' he asked finally. ''Or are they trying to pass it off as an accident? Have they given you any advice about what you should do? Would going back to England take you out of the danger zone, so to speak?''

Anne swiveled around in her seat and stared openmouthed at Sebastian. ''But it was Josh who got shot, not me!''

Sebastian glanced at her, then stared quickly back at the road. ''I'm sorry. If that's what you... I mean, I must have misunderstood something the nurse said to me when I visited with Josh. I only saw her for a minute, so I probably got it all wrong.''

He sounded totally unconvincing. Sebastian, Anne realized, was not a good liar. "What did the nurse tell you, Sebastian?"

He cleared his throat uncomfortably. "It never occurred to me that you didn't realize. Of course, it might have been an accident, a stray shot not aimed at anyone...."

She kept hold of her irritation with extreme difficulty. "Sebastian, what are you trying to say?"

He drew in a deep breath. "The nurse said that the bullet hit Josh from the right and emerged on the left. That means the shot came from the right-hand side of the car. Your side. The police think the shot came from a car passing Josh's Toyota on the inside lane. From that position, the logical intended victim is you, not Josh."

Anne didn't say anything for a long time. She wasn't sure she could speak. Dear God, but she was a fool! Of course the bullet had come through the open window on *her* side of the car. The only reason she hadn't been killed was that she didn't understand the buttons on the control panel of Josh's Toyota. She'd avoided death because her seat back had collapsed when she'd pressed a button intended to close the car window.

"Anne, are you okay?" Sebastian sounded worried. "I'm sorry. I didn't mean to scare you."

"You didn't scare me," She said. Strangely enough, that was the truth. Anne felt a combination of anger at her unknown assailants and frustration at her inability to pin down why she was their target. But for some reason, she no longer felt fear. Perhaps, during those dreadful days of isolation in the cabin, she'd plumbed the limits of her capacity for terror and now simply accepted that she was a target.

"I was thinking," she explained. "Going back over the few seconds before the accident occurred and wondering if I had even a subliminal memory of the gunman or his car."

"And do you?"

"I'm afraid not. I was thinking about the rain, looking up at the sky... There's absolutely nothing buried for me to dredge up. And the fact is, even if I'd seen the car clearly, I doubt if I could identify it. American cars all look rather similar to me. Big and sleek."

"Now I've worried you to no purpose. Believe me, I'd never have brought this up except that I assumed you realized..." Sebastian's voice tailed into remorseful silence.

"Don't feel that way. I'm grateful to you for pointing out the reality of the situation. The police probably explained some of this to me, but I was pretty shaken up right after the accident, and I don't seem to have absorbed what they were saying."

"Sounds to me as if those doctors in the emergency room should have taken a few minutes to check you over and give you a tranquilizer."

"Did you see the waiting area? They were rushed off their feet."

"Well, I'll have to take extra care of you tonight. From now on, we're going to ban all conversation about this crazy incident. And about your kidnapping, too. During dinner, you can tell me about life in London, and I'll regale you with anecdotes about Uncle Bertram."

Sebastian was true to his word. As soon as they arrived at his condo, he showed Anne to the shower—another American extravaganza of gleaming tile and oversize bath towels—and provided her with a padded Chinese silk robe in brilliant peacock blue. "Have fun wearing it," he said. "My mother brought it home from Beijing years ago, before the Chinese government discovered how much money foolish Western tourists were willing to waste on hand-embroidered goodies. One of the few times in her life my mother has ever condescended to buy something inexpensive."

Her T-shirt he tossed into the trash, saying he had dozens he could lend her, and the rest of her clothes went into the washing machine, churning themselves to cleanliness while Anne sipped a glass of Chardonnay and watched Sebastian make salad dressing. Life in the United States, she decided, was long on practicality and comfort. Always provided you could manage to avoid getting murdered.

Sebastian's pampering of her continued. Over a delicious meal of grilled sole, tossed salad and crusty bread, he entertained Anne with wonderful stories about her grandfather, emphasizing the exciting days when Bertram's small agricultural products company had first started to grow into a major corporation.

"It was in the midsixties, I guess, right after your father left to go to Cambridge. Uncle Bertram was always so proud of Paul's brilliant mind. I've often thought what a shame it was that Paul never managed to swallow his pride and write the old man before he took off for Vietnam. Paul's death left a hollow in Bertram's life that was never filled."

In many ways Anne agreed, although she couldn't help thinking that a man as generous as her father must have had good reason for his stubborn refusal to be reconciled with Bertram Kennedy. Or was it just the familiar story of two good people unable to cope with the special intensity of the father-son relationship?

"What triggered the initial burst of growth in my grandfather's company?" she asked, not wanting to spoil the pleasant mood by hashing over past family bitterness.

"In some ways it was luck," Sebastian said. "If anything about the Vietnam War can be considered lucky. Bertram made a good, steady living manufacturing various agricultural chemicals needed by the U.S. military. He had a successful small manufacturing company, but nothing that was going to make him a multimillionaire. Then he accidently discovered one day when he was messing about in the lab that a small change in the formulation of one of his weed killers produced a very useful mutation."

Anne was too much her father's daughter to let that comment go unchallenged. "I hate to think what sort of chemical the U.S. army would consider useful."

"It was nothing toxic to humans, I know that much, but the actual details are still shrouded in secrecy. The U.S. government bought up the rights to his formula for a generous price, then licensed the actual production of the chemical back to Bertram. When the Vietnam War ended and demand for his secret product ended, Bertram took the money from the sale of his formula and used it to build up his company's research facilities. He was always a brilliant manager, and with a well-funded research department to back him up, his company developed some of the most effective agricultural chemicals of the early seventies.''

Anne's scalp prickled with the awareness of an important connection that cried out to be made. Her mind whirled and tumbled, trying to grasp the random facts that needed to click into place to form a coherent picture. Here, surely, was the answer to one of the puzzles about the estrangement in her family. Her father had volunteered for lifesaving service in Vietnam. Her grandfather had supplied chemicals that the U.S. military used to defeat the Vietnamese. Her father would have hated to think of Bertram making a fortune out of military production, and Anne now understood part of the breach between the two of them. However, it didn't explain the fact that Bertram and Paul had been at odds several years before her father had volunteered for service in Vietnam.

"When you think about it," Anne mused aloud, "my dad and my grandfather were following quite similar paths in their research. Only their end purpose was different."

"Do you think that was what they quarreled about?" Sebastian asked, clearing their dinner plates from the table. "No, don't get up. There's almost nothing to do."

He returned with a small bowl of chocolate-dipped strawberries and a pot of fragrant coffee, and his question was forgotten. Anne bit into one of the fat red berries, her opinion of American cuisine rising by the moment. "This has been a delicious meal," she said. "Thank you, Sebastian."

"My pleasure."

Anne finished her strawberry and sipped the excellent coffee. Her mind drifted lazily around the subject of her father and his work papers. The prickle she had felt earlier returned. Then a more immediate memory destroyed the fuzzy connection.

"Richard Durbin!" she exclaimed, returning her coffee cup to the saucer with a distinct rattle. "Oh, that poor man! I just remembered Josh was supposed to meet him for dinner tonight. He must be fuming at being stood up."

Sebastian helped her find Richard's phone number in the directory. She explained Josh's accident to a sympathetic Richard, who expressed his dismay and willingness to help out if he could.

"By the way," he concluded. "It probably doesn't seem all that important right now, but I've finished reading those papers you two wanted me to look at."

"Did you manage to make head or tail of them?" Anne asked.

"As far as I can see, pages are missing completely at random. But enough material is lost making it difficult to reconstruct any coherent account of what your father was doing."

"Difficult or impossible?" Anne asked.

"Difficult. I could work on it some more if it's really important."

"I'm not sure how important it might be," Anne said. "Have you reached any conclusions at all?"

"Your father was obviously a brilliant chemist, way out of my league in the leaps of creative imagination he was able to take. And the missing pages don't help me to follow his train of thought. But it's clear he was way before his time in awareness of the damage chemicals do to the environment. He was trying to develop a cure for the fungi that destroy rice crops. He'd formulated a spray that killed the fungi, but if it was applied during the germination process, the spray destroyed the entire rice crop. Your father wasn't prepared to let such a potentially harmful product out on the market. His greatest contribution was that he planned to make sure his fungicide didn't poison plants, animals or humans along with the fungi. Not many people were concerned about that twenty years ago."

A prickle of warning flashed tantalizingly across Anne's mind, then disappeared back into darkness. Were these old work papers of her father's really important, or was she just imagining that they somehow lay at the root of his dispute with Bertram Kennedy? Maybe the missing pages had been lost quite by accident. After all, her luggage had been searched, and the sheets of paper were twenty years old. Easy enough for them to come loose from the ring binder and get scattered...somewhere. The kidnappers might have lost the pages. That didn't mean they'd deliberately set out to mutilate the record of her father's research.

Anne sighed. Too many questions were chasing too few answers. "Thanks for your efforts, Richard. I really appreciate the help."

"Don't mention it. Tell Josh I expect that dinner as soon as he can enjoy a hearty meal. What would you like me to do with these papers?"

"Hang on to them, would you? I'll pick them up as soon as I can."

She hung up the phone and explained to Sebastian what her conversation had been about. He had no suggestion about her father's missing work papers, other than the fact that the pages could surely have been lost at any time during the past twenty years. But he was delighted, for Anne's sake, that her luggage had been returned.

"Strange that the kidnappers returned everything," he said. "What did the police make of that?"

"Who knows?" Anne said resignedly. "I think Detective Goodine half suspects I put them on his doorstep myself."

"And we're breaking my own rules," Sebastian said. "We're not supposed to be talking about your kidnapping tonight. Come and sit in the living room. I have some fun stuff to show you."

Sebastian was an opera buff, and he had kept many mementos of his mother's famous performances: a chest of dazzling fake jewels from the Vienna Opera House production of *Faust* spilled in gaudy brilliance over a corner table. Fans and head combs from *The Marriage of Figaro* were grouped in a decorative semicircle over the fireplace, and steel-bladed swords from *Rigoletto* guarded the archway into the small dining alcove.

"I assumed stage performers always used plastic swords nowadays," Anne said, feeling the edge of one of the blades. It wasn't supersharp, but sharp enough to cause substantial harm if a singer didn't move correctly during a fight scene. "Aren't these rather dangerous, not to mention heavy?"

"They have special retractable blades on the swords they use in actual fight scenes," Sebastian explained. "And you can be sure every sword battle is choreographed to the last half step. But plastic never manages to catch the light like metal, or clang like steel. So the director nearly always decides to go ahead and stage the fight with real weapons. With the points blunted, of course. These were made at a factory in Toledo, Spain." He pulled down one of the swords from its clip mounting. "See the decorative gold-work on the handles? I'm very fond of this pair. They're actually fine pieces of craftsmanship."

"Come to think of it, I've never heard of a single actor or singer getting accidently injured during a stage duel. That's interesting, isn't it? Actors must be quicker on their feet than most people credit."

Sebastian gave an embarrassed little cough. "Actually I've always been fascinated by the amount of danger actors and singers willingly expose themselves to. In fact, I've written a script for a movie that deals with the problem. In my script, a famous tenor is murdered on stage during the last act of *Aida*. Someone substitutes a real knife for a fake dagger."

"What a wonderful idea for a movie!" Anne exclaimed, thinking that she would have to stop being so swift in her judgments. Who would have thought that Sebastian had the soul of a scriptwriter lurking behind his sober accountant's exterior? "And you have so much inside information to make the script sound authentic."

"The idea of on-stage murder isn't new," Sebastian said. "But I've tried to give the old story a new twist. The motive for the murder is all tied up with Eastern Europe and international politics. I guess the theme of the script is that old-school politicians can still protect corrupt fiefdoms even if they aren't called communists anymore. All in all, I think it's a damn good script, even though I say so myself."

"It sounds exciting," Anne said. "Have you had any luck in making a sale? I expect that's very difficult to do, isn't it?"

Sebastian actually blushed. "I've been lucky," he said. "My script's been optioned already. By Gene Holstein. I don't know if you've heard of him."

Even Anne knew the name of one of Hollywood's most successful directors. "Why, that's marvelous," she said, genuinely impressed. "When will the movie be released, Sebastian?"

He laughed wryly. "Don't buy your tickets for opening night just yet," he said. "There's a lot of negotiating to do before a movie script progresses from the option stage into production."

At Sebastian's suggestion, they sat in the kitchen while he prepared them both a hot toddy. "Much better-tasting than Mamma's sleeping pills, and probably just as effective," he commented. Anne sipped the sweet, pungently spiced drink and listened to Sebastian talk about his movie. He had flown out to Hollywood two or three times to meet with Gene Holstein, and had several fascinating anecdotes to recount about the legendary director. By the time they'd finished the toddy, Anne felt herself drooping.

"It's been a long day," she said. "I think I'm going to bed now, if you don't mind."

"You know where your room is," Sebastian said, smiling. The ring of the phone interrupted him before he could say anything more, and Anne left him to answer his call in private. She was already in bed and half-asleep when Sebastian tapped on her door.

"Come in!" she said.

He poked his head around the door. "Sorry to disturb you, but that call was from Dom. My little brother is back in town, and seems astonished that any of us had been worrying about him." Sebastian sighed. "Honestly I sometimes wonder if Dom is ever going to grow up and behave responsibly."

"I'm glad he's safe," Anne said sleepily. The traumatic events of the day seemed to be catching up with her, and Sebastian's toddy was making her feel as woozy as if she'd actually taken one of Shirley's pills. She forced herself to smile at Sebastian. "Great to have Dom back. I'll look forward to meeting him."

And that was an understatement, she thought groggily as her head drooped onto the pillow and she fell instantly asleep.

BABE WAS SO EXCITED she didn't know how she managed to stay quietly in bed. Her lover was back in contact with her again! She'd finally spoken to him on the phone, and tomorrow they were going to meet. Being young was such a bore! Imagine living in the same town as the man you loved and not being able to date him freely just because of the old bats in your family. She could hardly wait for the morning.

A shadow fell briefly over the glow of Babe's happiness. Tomorrow she would have to explain why she'd returned Anne Clarence's suitcases. Her lover had insisted that she was to hide them until he gave her further instructions. But when she explained her reasoning, he would understand that Anne needed to be gotten out of the way and sent home to England. Anne Clarence was an interfering busybody, a typical nitpicking schoolteacher who saw far too much with those big blue eyes of hers.

Her lover wouldn't be angry with Babe for returning the suitcases. He'd be pleased. Wouldn't he?

Chapter Nine

Anne slept deeply and without nightmares, either thanks to Sebastian's toddy or because of her own state of exhaustion. She woke at eight the next morning, feeling more refreshed and energetic than at any time since her arrival in Colorado. She and Sebastian just had time to share a cup of coffee and a toasted English muffin—which bore no resemblance, of course, to any muffin Anne had ever tasted in England—before he left for his office.

Sebastian refused to listen to her thanks for his hospitality. "Don't mention it. Now you'd better hurry up and get dressed. Ellen's going to be here at nine-thirty to take you to the hospital," he explained. "Josh is being released at ten. It's all arranged. And by the way, I've left a selection of T-shirts on my bed. Choose whichever one you'd like and please don't bother to return it. I have literally dozens."

Anne wasn't sure that she relished the prospect of a half-hour drive to the hospital with Joshua's mother, who tended to look at Anne as if she were something unpleasant that the cat had left half-eaten on the doorstep. In the event, however, Ellen was cool but gracious. Her chief preoccupation, other than the state of Josh's health, was a photograph album Bertram had prepared to give to Anne when she arrived in Denver, and which Ellen only now realized had disappeared.

"He spent hours selecting pictures of Katrina and your father," she said. "He was so much looking forward to sharing the family history with you. He took it with him when he went to your hotel room. When he died, there was so much confusion, no one gave it another thought. And now the album has disappeared." Surprisingly Ellen didn't sound as if Anne were her prime suspect in the mystery of its disappearance.

"I expect Dom knows where it is. We can ask him."

"That's true. Now that he's finally back in town. He called his mother at midnight last night, full of apologies for forgetting their dinner date. Really, it's time that young man took a hard look at himself and started behaving like a responsible adult."

For once, Anne found herself in total agreement with Josh's mother. "He called Sebastian, too. It must be a relief for Aunt Shirley to know he's safe."

Ellen obviously decided that intimacy had gone quite far enough. She steered the conversation back into neutral waters, and demonstrated for the remainder of the drive how it was possible to keep conversing while saying absolutely nothing intimate, friendly or even of much consequence.

The sight of Josh, fully dressed and sitting impatiently at the end of his bed, should have relieved Ellen's mind of at least one worry. Josh clearly wasn't suffering any serious aftereffects from his encounter with a speeding bullet. Anne was alarmed at the fierceness of her desire to go to him and hold him close. When he smiled at her and said, "Hi, Annie," her repressed, schoolteacher heart lurched with ridiculous pleasure. She compensated for her foolishness by scowling fiercely and letting his mother do all the talking.

Despite Josh's protests, Ellen insisted on doing the driving back to Josh's town house. Anne sat quietly in the back of the car and listened to the two of them chat. Either Ellen felt inhibited by Anne's presence, or she wasn't a woman who enjoyed intimacy, even with her son. Her conversation with Josh was friendly, but it wasn't much more personal or revealing than her earlier conversation with Anne.

How odd that Grandfather Bertram should have chosen to marry such a reserved and proper woman, Anne thought.

From all the anecdotes and stories she'd heard about her grandfather, she'd built up a picture of a man who radiated energy, determination and a certain devil-may-care attitude. Ellen didn't seem at all the sort of woman to make Bertram Kennedy happy. And yet by all accounts, she had. Marriage, Anne reflected, was the chanciest of lotteries.

Josh gave a pleased exclamation when he saw his Toyota parked in the driveway outside his town house.

"There was no damage to the car," Anne explained. "Once the police saw that the bullet hadn't lodged anywhere in the bodywork, they had no interest in it. So they asked me what you wanted done with the car, and I asked them to arrange a tow. I hope that was all right."

"It was perfect," Josh said. "Do you know what happened to the keys?"

"I have them," Anne said.

"Then I suppose you won't be needing this spare set of house keys that I brought," Ellen said, sounding somewhat offended, as if Anne had overstepped the boundaries of polite behavior by deciding what should happen to Josh's car without consulting anyone in his family. Ellen dropped her bunch of keys back into her purse with a decided snap, and got out of the car.

"Are you ready to let us in, Josh? I have a League of Women Voters luncheon at noon, and I'd like to see you settled before I have to leave for that." She stalked toward the front door of the town house.

Josh took his own set of keys from Anne, draping his arm casually around her shoulders, indifferent to his mother's rigidly disapproving back. "I'm wounded," he said to Anne. "I need your support." Lowering his voice, he murmured, "I need more kisses."

His mother glared at Anne as if she were the one demanding to be kissed, then—with the air of a martyr—moved aside to allow Josh room to unlock his front door.

He gave his mother a teasing smile. "Stop trying to look like a dragon, Mommy dearest. You'll get wrinkles." He turned the key, swung the door open and stepped into the

living room. Before Anne or his mother could follow him
inside, he quickly swung around and came out again,
latching the door behind him.

"Don't go in," he said flatly.

His mother stared at him. "What in the world is going on,
Josh? Why can't we go inside?"

Apart from his bandages, Josh had looked perfectly fit at
the hospital. Now he looked pale, and a line of sweat stood
out in beads across his forehead. If he'd asked for Anne's
support right at that moment, she would have believed he
genuinely needed it.

"Mom," he said. "I don't want you to go into my house.
There's been—there's been an accident."

"What sort of accident? Did the toilet overflow? I've seen
wet carpets before. And a lot worse, too." Without doing
anything as unseemly as pushing, Ellen Kennedy sidestepped her son and walked into the house. A split second
later, Anne heard her scream.

"Hell!" Josh muttered, dashing inside.

Anne hurried after them into the little entrance alcove,
then stopped. The body of a man—with a steel-handled
knife sticking out of his back—lay crumpled on the carpet
not six feet from the door, a trail of blood marking the
pathway the murder victim had followed in his pathetic dying effort to reach either the door, or perhaps the phone that
stood on a special stand in the arched entrance to the living
room.

Josh gathered his mother into his arms, turning her head
away from the terrible sight. He propelled her into the living room, sitting her in a chair that faced away from the
front entrance.

Anne knelt beside the body, numb with the horror of
witnessing violent death at such close quarters. She was
thirty years old, and this was the first time she'd ever seen a
dead person. Television movies made murder seem ordinary, as if a bleeding body was something to be treated with
no more than perfunctory regret. The reality was something infinitely sadder and more powerful.

Hand shaking, she reached out to find a pulse. There was no need for more than a quick touch. The body was already cold with the frigid inhumanity of death. Gently, averting her gaze, she lowered the man's eyelids. Even that wasn't as easy to do as it looked on television.

She rocked back on her heels, trying to calm herself. Then she dashed to the bathroom and washed her face and hands over and over, first in hot water and then in cold. At long last, she felt able to walk back into the living room and face whatever needed to be faced.

Josh was on the phone, calling the police. Anne circled the body, keeping her gaze averted, and went to sit near Ellen in the living room. Ellen looked up at her with eyes that didn't quite focus.

"It's Dom," she said. "Can you believe it? That body on the floor over there is my nephew. Dear God, whatever am I going to say to Shirley? I was so irritated with her when she kept on spouting that nonsense about her mother's heart sensing Dom was in trouble. But she was right all the time. How will she bear it? She loves him so much."

"That's Dom? Oh, my God!" Anne couldn't help the exclamation. She jumped up and ran back to the hallway. Swallowing hard, she knelt once again alongside the body and forced herself to look more closely at the dead man's face. So this was Dominick Rossi. Even in death, Anne recognized that he had once been a handsome man. Even in death, she could see the faint similarity to his brother Carlo. When she looked closely, she recognized that she had seen him before.

Dominick Rossi was the bellman who had come to her hotel room the night she arrived in Colorado. Dominick Rossi had been one of her kidnappers. Anne couldn't help feeling frustrated that she was never going to be able to ask him why.

UNTIL YOU HAD BEEN through the dreary routines of a murder investigation, Anne thought, you had no idea how grim the consequences of violent death actually were. It seemed an eternity before the police technicians had finished their grisly tasks and the remains of the young man who had been Dominick Rossi were removed to the morgue for a postmortem.

Bad as it was to deal with the rituals of a murder investigation, Anne knew she was escaping lightly. She could only be thankful that she wouldn't have to face the truly dreadful task of informing Shirley that one of her sons was dead.

That task fell to Ellen, who showed remarkable strength of character in the swiftness with which she regained outward composure. They couldn't risk calling Carlo, in case it was Shirley who answered the phone. So Ellen placed the call to Sebastian, telling him that his brother was dead, and when he arrived—gray cheeked and hollow eyed—she was enough in command of herself to be able to offer him some comfort as they set off to convey the awful news to Shirley and Carlo. Anne's opinion of Joshua's mother rose several notches in the wake of this heroic effort.

Anne had thought nothing could be worse than the phone call to the funeral director, the tramp of police officers in and out of the house, the endless questions from Detective Goodine, the harrassment from reporters crowding around the front door. But when the last police technician gathered up his jars of fingerprint powder, and the last reporter dashed off to file his story in time for the early-evening news broadcast, Anne realized that the silent aftermath of death was far worse than the earlier intrusions. The bloodstains stared up at her from the carpet in mute, macabre reproach. Josh, of course, was suffering far more than she was. He had answered the detective's questions clearly and concisely, without showing very much stress. Now he stared out of the window, as if even the power of speech had been drained out of him.

"Shall I make us some tea?" Anne asked, desperate for something to do. She felt embarrassed at the inadequacy of her offer in relation to the stark misery etched into Josh's face, but was helpless to think of anything that might help more.

"Thanks. Sounds like a good idea." Josh tried to smile, but he didn't move, and in the end, Anne got up and led the way into the kitchen, carefully avoiding the red splotches on the carpet that were already turning an ugly rust brown.

Once in the kitchen, Josh sat down at the tiny breakfast counter, gazing at the brightly patterned curtains without seeing them. When she put a cup of steaming tea in front of him, he looked down as if he wasn't quite sure what it was or what he was supposed to do with it.

"Drink some while it's still hot," Anne suggested quietly. "I put the sugar in already."

He sipped obediently until the tea was gone, then crashed the cup into the saucer, reaching out blindly to pull Anne into his arms. She went willingly, resting her cheek on his shoulder and reaching up to stroke his hair until the spasm of grief passed.

"Why would anyone want to kill Dom?" Josh asked, his voice harsh with pain. "I've known him since he was a baby, and he didn't have an ounce of harm in him. He was irresponsible, but he was charming and friendly...."

His voice faded away, and for a moment Anne didn't respond. Was this the moment to tell Josh that Dom wasn't quite the harmless charmer he had seemed? In the end, Anne decided that she needed to speak up. Detective Goodine had asked her if she'd ever met Dominick Rossi, and she'd lied by saying no. But someone in the Kennedy family had to face up to the truth. Josh, unfortunately, was the person most capable of bearing that burden.

"Josh," she said, hesitating even as she began to speak. She began again. "Josh, you're not going to like hearing this, but I'd seen Dom before...before we found him today."

Grief and shock had not made Josh slow-witted. His body snapped to attention. "Where?" he asked curtly. "When?"

"In the hotel, the night I arrived in Colorado. He was the bellman who came to my hotel room and kidnapped me."

"How can you be sure? Didn't you say the bellman wore thick, horn-rimmed glasses—"

"I'm sorry, Josh. I'm absolutely positive. The bellman and Dom are one and the same person."

Josh paced the kitchen, his body radiating tension. "Damn it, why would Dom do such a crazy thing? For God's sake, why?"

"The same reason any other kidnapper would have done it, Josh. For money. It must have been for money. He planned to hold my grandfather up to ransom."

"I can't believe he'd do something so *wrong*." Josh sat with his head in his hands, his body sagging with grief. It was a long time before he lifted his head.

"I don't understand," he murmured. "How did Dom organize something so complicated? He couldn't even plan a family picnic without screwing up." Josh snapped his fingers in irritation. "The how doesn't even matter. *Why* would he resort to something outright criminal? Damn it, Bertram loved Dom. If Dom needed money, he could have asked Bertram. Or me, for that matter. He didn't need to steal the damn stuff. The money was his for the asking."

"Perhaps not," Anne said. "What if he needed money for something you and Bertram would both have disapproved of?"

"Such as?"

"Drugs," she suggested. "Drugs are the obvious answer."

Josh shook his head. "No way. That's impossible. Quite apart from the fact that he never gave the smallest sign of having a drug problem, he was a pilot. Alliance Air routinely test its pilots for drug and alcohol abuse. He could never have gotten away with a serious drug habit. And I'm willing to swear that he didn't have an alcohol problem. Dom liked a couple of beers now and again, but if he was addicted to anything, it was women, not booze or cocaine."

"Then perhaps one of his women may know why he needed money," Anne said. "His latest girlfriend, for example." She let the suggestion hang in the air, without attempting to identify any specific woman.

Josh turned to her. "Laurel?" he asked slowly. "You think Laurel might know something to explain all this?"

Anne chose her words with care. "I said all along that I thought the other kidnapper that night was a woman."

"But Laurel isn't a woman," Josh protested. "She's just a young girl—"

"That's precisely what makes me think she was there," Anne said quietly. "Remember I told you that something about the way the kidnappers talked reminded me of my school in England?"

"Laurel doesn't have an English accent. In fact, she has quite a strong midwestern twang—"

"It wasn't her accent," Anne said. "It was her tone of voice, her attitude when she spoke to Dom. It reminded me of the students I hear in my counseling sessions. The woman in my room that night was young, Josh. Very young, and totally infatuated with the man giving the orders. That's what my subconscious picked up on when I listened to her. I hear that tone of voice all the time, you see, in my work."

Josh carried his cup over to the sink. "Sounds like we'd better talk to Laurel right away," he said. He closed his eyes and pinched the bridge of his nose in a gesture replete with weariness. "If Laurel really was involved with Dom to the extent you're suggesting, she's going to be devastated by his death."

"I'm afraid you're right," Anne said. "But I don't think you should talk to Laurel over the phone, Josh. She's going to need some strong family support to get through this. Even more important, if she and Dom really did try to kidnap me, someone has to make her understand that she committed a serious criminal offense. We're not talking about a young woman joyriding in the neighbor's car without asking permission. We're talking about a crime that carries a heavy jail sentence. At least, in England it carries a heavy sentence."

"Here, too. It's a federal offense." Josh drew in a deep breath. "Are you going to ask the police to prosecute?"

"My grandfather's dead, and I'm unharmed. I can't see that prosecution would bring any benefit to Laurel or to me at this point. But if it turns out that I'm right, and she was involved in the kidnapping, somebody has to see that she gets professional help."

"You mean counseling?"

"A *lot* of counseling from somebody experienced in handling rebellious young adults. If it's any consolation, young girls who fall in love with older men often show appalling lack of judgment and behave very badly for a while. Then they turn into respectable, contributing members of society once their hormones stop controlling their common sense."

Catching Anne's own sense of urgency, Josh strode out of the kitchen. "Throw a few clothes in an overnight bag," he said. "Let's get out of here and find Laurel. The twins never work the evening shift, so they should be home."

By tacit mutual consent, they avoided the ill-fated Toyota and drove to Josh's mountain house in the Jeep. The evening air was at once balmy and crisp, the darkness pierced by the glow of silver starlight. The mountains loomed alongside the roadway, distant shadows of sharp-edged purple velvet. On such a night, in such a setting, Anne thought sadly, death deserved no place.

It was obvious as soon as Bree opened the door leading from the garage into the kitchen that news of Dom's death had preceeded them into the mountains. "Sebastian called. What's going on, Josh?" Bree asked, her face drawn taut with worry. "Why are all these—accidents—happening?"

"I don't know," Josh said, giving his sister a hug. "But right off the bat, we have to stop fooling ourselves about what happened. Dom's death wasn't an *accident*—it was murder."

Bree whirled around to confront Anne. "It's your fault," she said hoarsely. "Everything was fine until you came over here. Your father hated Bertram, and now all the old hatreds are starting up again. If you'd stayed in England, none of these tragedies would have happened."

Josh's expression hardened. "Bree, you may be distraught, but that's no excuse for such crazy accusations."

Bree's face crumpled and she burst into tears. "I'm sorry, Anne," she mumbled, reaching for a paper towel to blow her nose. "I should never have said that. I know these deaths aren't your fault. I just can't bear to think that someone—" She choked off the end of her sentence, unable to complete the treachery of her thoughts out loud.

Josh handed his sister another paper towel. She gave her eyes a final, fierce wipe, then sniffed and squared her shoulders. "Would you like a cup of coffee, Josh? Anne, how about you?"

"Thanks, but later maybe." Josh kept his voice casual. "I don't see the twins. Where are they?"

"Up in their room," Bree said. "They've taken the news very badly. Heather's been crying ever since Sebastian phoned us, but they won't let me into their room. I decided maybe it was better to let them comfort each other."

"We need to talk to them," Josh said. "It's important."

Anne could see Bree prickle at the word *we,* but the woman didn't say anything overtly hostile. "You know where their room is, Josh. If you can get them to come out and eat dinner, I'd be grateful. Crying themselves sick isn't going to bring Dom back. But I guess they're too young to realize that when life is a mess, sometimes you have no choice except to keep plodding forward as best you can. Heck, I forget it myself far too often." Bree turned to Anne. "I really am sorry for the way I've behaved since you arrived in Colorado. I'm not always this much of a witch, you know. I'd like to blame my rotten behavior on my husband for being such a louse over our divorce, but the truth is I've always felt insecure around fragile, beautiful blondes like you."

Americans, Anne was discovering, were a great deal more frank about their emotions than their English counterparts. A few days ago, Bree hadn't bothered to conceal her dislike; now she was equally sincere in her apology. Almost against her will, Anne found herself responding. At this rate, she thought wryly, Bree and I will be bosom buddies by the time I go home.

Upstairs, Josh tapped on the twins' bedroom door. "Heather, Laurel, it's me. Could we talk?"

A voice, breathless with tears, responded. "We don't have anything to say. Please go away."

"It's important for us to talk," Josh said.

"We want to be left alone right now. We're nearly nineteen, and I think we're entitled to some privacy."

The same twin had done all the talking, but Anne had no idea which twin that was. "Is that Laurel answering you?" she asked Josh.

"No, it's Heather."

Anne frowned. "It's not a good sign that Laurel's allowing her sister to do all the talking. If Laurel really was involved with Dom to the extent we suspect, I think it's important for us to see her without delay. Do you mind if I try something more forceful than a polite request to chat?"

"Go right ahead. I agree with you. We need to get them out of hibernation."

"Laurel, this is Anne Clarence. I need to talk to you about the night I was kidnapped."

"She doesn't know anything."

"Lost your tongue, Laurel? Or are you just too scared to open this door and tell me face-to-face why you and Dom locked me in a deserted cabin for five days?"

This time there was a moment of silence before Heather replied. "You're crazy. My sister didn't kidnap you. Go away."

"Why did Dom need the ransom money, Laurel?" Anne paused for effect. "You can tell me yourself, or I'm going downstairs to call the police and ask them to investigate."

The door flew open to reveal a twin with tousled hair, her red-rimmed eyes sparking with fury. "*I've told you already*. Laurel has no idea what you're talking about. You've no right to make such crazy accusations. It's libel. We'll sue!"

"Slander," Anne corrected calmly. "Libel is written, slander is spoken. And truth is accepted as a defense in both instances."

She looked past Heather and saw Laurel huddled in a chair by the window, her arms wrapped around her knees, her face stark white and frighteningly void of expression. Recognizing all the symptoms of shock, Anne walked into the bedroom without waiting for Heather's permission. She squatted down so that she was at Laurel's eye level.

"I think we have lots to talk about," she said, keeping her voice soft and nonthreatening. "Would you like to come out onto the porch and tell me about you and Dom?"

Laurel blinked; otherwise her face remained rigidly without expression. After an endless moment of silence, she finally managed to speak. "Dom's dead," she whispered.

Heather stormed over to confront Anne. "Can't you see she's upset, for heaven's sake? Why do you have to keep on nagging at her?"

"I don't want to nag, but I'm pretty sure she'll feel less sad if she shares the pain she's feeling. She needs to talk about Dom with somebody."

"She talks to me," Heather said. "We talk all the time."

"Perhaps tonight she needs to talk to someone who isn't so close to her. Sometimes, when we're feeling stressed, strangers make better listeners than the people we love."

"Maybe some strangers, but you're way too strange for anyone to talk to," Heather said with a sneer.

"Heather!" Josh interjected sharply. "You may be upset, but that's not an excuse for rudeness."

Heather blushed, but that was the extent of her apology. "Laurel and Dom were just good friends," she said defiantly. "They went to a few parties, a few bars, that's all. Nothing to make a big deal out of. Jeez, how many times do I have to say it? We should be allowed to date anyone we want. We're nearly nineteen."

"Right, and in another nineteen years you may have some sense," Josh snapped. "Not to mention some better manners."

"Heather, perhaps you don't know that Dom is the man who kidnapped me," Anne said quietly. "And he had a woman with him, helping him. I think that woman was Laurel. The night I was kidnapped my grandfather died in my hotel room, which means that my kidnappers are facing manslaughter charges, as well as kidnapping ones." She had no idea if that was true, but she doubted if the twins would know, either, and she needed to scare them into honesty.

"You and your sister had better think hard about who you want to talk to, Heather. Right now, your choices are me, or Detective Goodine of the Denver police, or a special agent from the FBI. From your sister's point of view, I'd say I'm definitely the best of the bunch."

"Anne and I will wait outside on the porch," Josh suggested. "If neither of you is downstairs in ten minutes, we'll place a call to Detective Goodine."

"That's up to you," Heather said, rallying her defenses. "You'll sure look silly if you do."

"It's okay, Heather, I want to talk to Anne." Laurel spoke so softly that her voice was barely audible. The moment she'd finished speaking, she turned to look out of the window, refusing to meet anyone's eye.

"Laurie, you don't have to tell her anything." Heather rushed to her sister's side and hugged her, whispering some impassioned, inaudible plea into Laurel's ear.

Laurel stared stonily ahead. "I want to talk to Anne," she said, her voice firmer this time.

Josh came and took Heather's hand. "Come on, honey, let's give them some space. I think your mother could use some help in planning dinner."

Heather hesitated on the brink of refusal, then with an impatient shrug, allowed herself to be led out of the room.

As soon as the two of them were alone, Laurel swiveled around in her chair and confronted Anne. Her brown eyes were dark with despair.

"You know, don't you?" she said.

"About you and Dom being the kidnappers?"

"No. About... the other."

"Yes, I suppose I do." Anne's voice softened with compassion. "Would you like to talk about that first?"

Laurel raised her shoulders in a gesture of defeat. "I have to tell someone. It may as well be you."

"Then let's start at the beginning. How many weeks pregnant are you, Laurel?"

Chapter Ten

Laurel didn't answer the question directly. "How did you know? About the baby, I mean."

"I work as a guidance counselor, remember? When a girl in my school starts to look worried, and she isn't doing drugs, an unplanned pregnancy is one of the things I'm trained to consider."

"Is that all it was? Your training? Mom doesn't suspect a thing."

"It wasn't only my training," Anne said. "There were some other clues. Josh and I went to Dom's apartment yesterday, and we noticed he'd left the phone directory open to a listing of doctors. Not just any doctors, but obstetricians, and I couldn't think why Dom would be needing those. Then, when I saw you at the health club in that great big sweatshirt, I wondered why you'd chosen to lead an aerobic dance class in something so cumbersome. The only reason I could think of was that you were trying to hide the changes in your body. Spandex bodysuits like the one your sister was wearing highlight every tiny blimp, don't they?"

Laurel stared at the spruce tree outside the bedroom window. "I'm seventeen weeks pregnant," she said. "I diet all the time, but the baby's not a tiny blimp anymore. He's already a bulge."

"Seventeen weeks!" Anne exclaimed in surprise. "But you haven't been dating Dom that long, have you?"

"Dom and I fell in love last Christmas," Laurel said. "He had some vacation time in April and he came to visit me in Chicago. That's when...that's when it happened." She poked her finger into a hole in the knee of her jeans and tugged nervously at the frayed threads. "Dad and Mom were fighting all the time about their divorce settlement. Mom cried every day, and Dad kept yelling that he'd supported her for all these years, and now it was time for her to get off his back. He said he'd never wanted to marry her in the first place. That he'd only married her because... because..."

"Because she was pregnant with you and Heather?" Anne prompted softly.

"Yes. How do you know all this stuff before I tell you?"

"Secrets of the trade," she replied lightly, not wanting to tell Laurel how many times she'd heard similar stories. To Laurel, her situation seemed unusual, if not unique. To Anne, it was part of a sad litany she'd heard far too often.

"When I was with Dom, I didn't have to deal with my parents' hassle, you know? He was such good fun, and he made me feel terrific." She cradled her arms around her abdomen, rocking back and forth in pleading rhythm. "He did love me, really love me, not like his other girlfriends. He wanted us to be a proper family." She looked up, still young enough to take a childish pleasure in watching the effect of her final bombshell. "Dom and I were married, you know. We got married in Reno over the July 4 holiday."

With a supreme effort at self-control, Anne suppressed her shock at Laurel's revelation. Her professional instinct warned her that Laurel didn't want to be bombarded at this moment with questions. What she needed to hear was reassurance that she'd been loved.

"I'm sure Dom loved you and wanted the baby," Anne said, wondering if her words might even be true. Dom could certainly have found more convenient women to entertain himself with than Laurel, and the bonds of matrimony had always seemed way down on his list of priorities. "But I don't understand why the two of you decided to keep your marriage such a big secret."

"Heather knew we were married," Laurel replied evasively. "I have our wedding certificate in my drawer. Want to see it?" Without waiting for Anne's reply, Laurel jumped up and pulled out a drawer in the tallboy, revealing a typical teenager mess of odd socks, T-shirts and crumpled papers. She located a pink form and waved it triumphantly under Anne's nose.

"See? He must have loved me if he was willing to marry me. He asked me, you know, as soon as I told him about the baby. I didn't try to persuade him or anything."

"I'm sure Dom felt something very special for you, Laurel."

The girl sat down again, her eyes forlorn, clutching the certificate like a talisman. Looking at her, Anne felt torn between pity and anger. Pity because Laurel lacked the maturity she so desperately needed to cope with the consequences of Dom's death, and anger because she had waded so thoughtlessly into waters far out of her emotional depth.

It was a familiar situation for Anne. After six years of working in a high school in one of London's poorest neighborhoods, she wasn't surprised by Laurel's self-centered reaction to Dom's murder. Her lack of interest in such obvious questions as who had caused Dom's death was typical of an adolescent suffering from emotional overload. And emotionally Anne had no doubt Laurel was still an adolescent, unable to think and feel beyond her own immediate problems. Anne sighed. The poor girl would have to do a lot of growing up in the next five months if she wanted to become an adequate mother.

Tentatively Anne reached out her hand and laid it over Laurel's. "I have some questions I need to ask you, Laurel. Tough questions. Are you willing to answer me?"

"Maybe." Laurel shrank into a defensive ball. "Maybe not."

"Well, let's start with an easy one first. Can you help me to understand why you and Dom were so secretive about the fact that you were in love? Your family might not have approved, but other than the age difference, what objections could they have had? You and Dom aren't blood relatives. And once your mother knew you were pregnant, I can't imagine she'd have prevented you marrying. Anyway, how could she? You're eighteen, a legal adult.''

For a moment it seemed that Laurel would refuse to answer, then she sighed. "What's the difference now that Dom's dead? You may as well know." She drew in a deep breath. "We didn't care about the family knowing, not really. It was—other people we were afraid of. Dom said we must keep our marriage secret to protect me.''

A chill ran down Anne's spine. "Protect you?" she asked. "What from? Why would you be in danger if people knew you were married?''

Laurel didn't answer, and Anne pressed her question. "Tell me, did you and Dom know that he might be in danger?''

"Yes, but I didn't think he was going to die," Laurel said in an anguished whisper. Tears gathered in the corner of her eyes, then began to roll down her cheeks, faster and faster. The tears turned to great gulping sobs, and she didn't resist when Anne took her into her arms and stroked her back in a silent offer of comfort.

When the racking sobs finally tapered off, Anne got up to find some tissues. She handed Laurel the box. "I think it's time we talked about the night you and Dom kidnapped me," she said. "Is that connected with the danger you and Dom were in?''

Laurel shredded the tissue. "I didn't want to kidnap you, Anne, but Dom needed the money real bad. We never meant to hurt you.''

Anger surfaced before she could control it. "Right. You thought five days in an empty cabin with almost no food, no light and no hot water would be a relaxing holiday for me.''

"We never meant for you to be there so long!" Laurel protested. "But Uncle Bertram died, and everything started to go wrong. Dom had to go out of town right after the funeral so Jimbo's men wouldn't get him, and Mom took Heather and me to stay with Aunt Ellen—''

"Hold on a minute there! Back up, please. Let's start at the beginning. Who is Jimbo?''

"He's a...man. He and Dom were kind of involved in a business deal.''

"An illegal business deal?''

"Not exactly.''

"I need the truth, Laurel. Was Dom running drugs?''

"No!'' Laurel sounded horrified at the suggestion. "Why in the world do you think he'd do something awful like that?''

"I can't imagine,'' Anne said. "Unless it's because he's been murdered. Or because he flew all over the Rocky Mountain region in private planes, and because little things like kidnapping didn't phase him.''

"Dom would never have dealt drugs,'' Laurel repeated. "He'd never even smoked pot except for maybe a couple of joints in high school. He hated drugs and what they do to your body. We're both into physical fitness,'' she added seriously. "Keeping fit is very good for your health.''

"Then if it wasn't drugs, what the dickens was he involved in that was so threatening?'' Anne demanded.

Laurel shredded another tissue. "He...owed Jimbo a lot of money,'' she admitted reluctantly.

"What for?''

"I guess there's no way to hide it anymore. He... gambled. Dom used to gamble a lot.''

Gambling. All those weekend pleasure trips to Las Vegas with his girlfriends, Anne thought, the picture suddenly coming clear. Perhaps the trips had started innocently enough with taking in the shows and enjoying the nightlife. Eventually Dom must have found himself addicted to the tables.

"How much money did he owe?'' Anne asked.

"I don't know exactly. Maybe...maybe a quarter of a million dollars. The interest just kept piling up.''

A quarter of a million! Anne's mind reeled under the size of the number. "How in the world did he manage to get that much credit to throw away?" she asked. "Surely no bank would advance that sort of a loan to a pilot?"

"Getting credit was easy. Not from a regular bank, you know, but from loan sharks. Everyone knew Dom would inherit millions of dollars as soon as Uncle Bertram died."

"Then I don't understand the problem," Anne said. "The loan sharks extended credit with Bertram Kennedy's estate as security. The estate didn't vanish, so why was Dom suddenly in trouble?"

"Jimbo decided Dom's credit wasn't good anymore."

"Laurel, please help me to understand why. My grandfather didn't lose his money. Dom was still one of his major heirs. The loan sharks wouldn't care that Dom obviously had an addiction that needed treatment, so what was their problem?"

"Uncle Bertram threatened to cut Dom out of his will," Laurel admitted wearily. "Lord knows how, but Uncle Bertram heard that Dom had a gambling problem, and he told Dom to get treatment and shape up or he wasn't going to inherit a penny. As soon as word got out that Dom was disinherited, the sharks started circling."

"So instead of getting treatment for his addiction, your husband then came up with the brilliant scheme of kidnapping me and holding my grandfather up to ransom."

"We didn't mean to hurt anyone!" Laurel cried. "We just wanted the money Uncle Bertram had promised to give Dom. He owed it to us. Why did we have to wait until Uncle Bertram died?"

"Is that what Dom told you? That Bertram *owed* you the money to bail Dom out of trouble?"

Laurel's pale cheeks washed with color. "Dom had stopped gambling," she said. "Since he fell in love with me, he hasn't bet a single dime. He just needed to get out from under his debts. He only borrowed a hundred thousand. All the rest of the money he owed was interest. If you look at it logically, the quicker he paid it off, the less money he would waste. Uncle Bertram was throwing money away by not giving us our fair share of our inheritance."

Dom might have been as much fun as a barrel of monkeys, Anne reflected, but neither he nor Laurel seemed to have possessed even a smidgen of old-fashioned moral fiber. "We'll forget the morality of your schemes for the moment," she said. "How did you and Dom plan to extract money from my grandfather without him finding out that you were the people who'd kidnapped me?"

"Dom worked everything out." Laurel sounded rather proud of her husband's achievement. "I made the phone call to Uncle Bertram, pretending to be you. I asked Uncle Bertram to go to your hotel room right away. Then I drove you to the cabin, while Dom took care of getting his uncle to the hotel. We never meant to hurt you," she insisted. "I put some food into the cabin, even though we expected to free you almost at once. The plumbing worked, so you could use the bathroom. It's summer. It's not as if you were cold or anything. You were totally safe there."

"How about the drug you put in the milk powder, Laurel? What's your explanation for that?"

"It was only a tranquilizer," she said, her voice sullen. "Dom mixed it in with the milk powder to help you. We didn't want you to worry."

It seemed far more likely that Dom didn't want Anne to be thinking clearly enough to plan her escape or to remember too many inconvenient details of her kidnapping, but there was no point in confronting Laurel with that fact. The girl appeared entirely oblivious not only to the torment they had inflicted on their victim, but also to the multitude of risks she and Dom had been taking. Had they really both been naive enough to believe that Bertram Kennedy would fork over a quarter of a million dollars without making any attempt to discover who was behind the kidnapping? Laurel obviously didn't realize that Bertram's death was probably the single factor that had prevented their kidnapping scheme from unraveling almost as soon as it began. With jail sentences waiting at the end of the unraveling for the two chief plotters.

"How did you plan to make your ransom demands?" Anne asked. "Why was it so important for Bertram to go to my hotel room?"

"We knew nobody would suspect Dom of being involved if he was the person who discovered you missing." Once again, Laurel sounded naively proud of her skill in deception. "We left the ransom note on the bed in your hotel room. We wrote it with letters cut out from newspaper headlines so no one could trace it back to us."

A good old Nancy Drew standby, Anne thought wryly. In fact, Dom and Laurel sounded as if most of their planning had been lifted straight out of a children's mystery novel. "So my grandfather read the ransom note, and that's when he had his stroke?" she asked.

"Oh, no! Nothing like that." Laurel leaned forward, suddenly earnest. "It wasn't our fault Uncle Bertram died, truly it wasn't. Nothing happened the way we'd planned it. When Dom got to your room, the ransom note was missing! He couldn't think what to do, so he wandered around, pretending to look for you. Then the phone rang. Dom grabbed the phone, thinking it might be me. But it wasn't. It was some man—Dom didn't recognize the voice, but all of Jimbo's henchmen sound sort of the same. Mean, you know. And vicious. The man ordered Dom down to the lobby."

"And Dom went? Just like that? Leaving my grandfather alone in the hotel room?"

"Well, he didn't know Uncle Bertram was going to have a stroke," Laurel protested. "And anyway, Dom had no choice. The caller threatened to tell Uncle Bertram who'd kidnapped you if Dom didn't go downstairs."

"Didn't it occur to your husband that he was putting my grandfather at terrible risk by leaving him alone?"

Laurel looked blank. "Why? Jimbo doesn't—didn't—have any quarrel with Uncle Bertram. Dom would have been in trouble if he didn't go down to the lobby, but Uncle Bertram was perfectly safe.''

Anne gave up the attempt to bring Laurel to a realization of the harm she'd caused. She tried another tack. ''Wasn't Dom surprised to hear from Jimbo right at that moment?''

''Not really. His people have been following Dom around for weeks. They probably saw us taking you out of the hotel and wanted to muscle in on the deal.''

Anne had no personal experience with loan sharks, but she supposed Laurel's theory made sense. Loan sharks were greedy people. Extortion would be all in a good night's work for them. They had probably summoned Dom to the lobby to see how much extra money they could shake loose from the Bertram Kennedy money tree. Although the missing ransom note remained a minor mystery. Why would Jimbo's men have removed that?

''So what happened when Dom got down to the lobby?'' Anne asked. ''I suppose Dom met up with one of Jimbo's henchmen, explained about his kidnapping scheme, and Jimbo's man let him go upstairs again.''

''No,'' Laurel said, sounding puzzled. ''It was weird, actually. Dom couldn't spot any of Jimbo's people in the lobby. He hung around for ten minutes or so. Eventually he went upstairs again. When he got to your room . . . when he got up there, Uncle Bertram was already dead.'' Eyes sparkling with tears, she looked pleadingly at Anne. ''We didn't kill him, Anne. His death was just bad luck. We never even told him you'd been kidnapped, let alone made the ransom demand. It wasn't the shock or the strain of what we did that killed him. It was natural causes. It must have been natural causes.''

''That may well be true,'' Anne said, relieved to see that Laurel was capable of feeling some guilt over Bertram's death. ''But I don't understand how I ended up being the villain of the piece in all this.''

''Well, naturally we couldn't tell anyone what had really happened,'' Laurel said, sniffing miserably. ''Dom couldn't say that he'd left Uncle Bertram alone in your hotel room without telling everyone about Jimbo. So he said the first thing that came into his head. He said that you'd been in the room when he arrived, that you had asked him to go down to the lobby, and so he'd left you alone with Uncle Bertram. Then Dom pretended that when he returned to your room, Bertram was dead and you'd run away. Everybody believed him, of course."

"Of course," Anne said, anger churning sickly in her stomach. "Very neat. You and Dom are completely off the hook, and the unwanted visitor from England gets blamed for everything. For once, Dom certainly managed to think fast on his feet.'

"We didn't mean any harm," Laurel repeated, burying her face in her hands. "All we wanted was to pay off Dom's debts so that we could make a home for our baby."

"No," Anne said, refusing to feel sympathy for Laurel. "All you wanted was to pay off Dom's debts without any pain to yourselves, not even the pain of admitting that Dom had a gambling addiction and that he'd made a total mess of his finances. If Dom had been courageous enough to admit to the truth a couple of months ago, my grandfather and your husband might both be alive tonight."

White-lipped, Laurel rose to her feet. "Do you think I don't know that?" she asked, her voice rasping with pain. "We were cowards, both of us, and now Dom is dead." She wrapped her arms around her waist. "The police will never be able to pin Dom's murder on Jimbo, will they? So he has the last laugh, after all."

"Except he hasn't been paid," Anne pointed out. Which, when she thought about it, was reason enough to wonder why Dom had been killed. A little niggle of doubt began to stir. Bertram was dead. Dom stood to inherit more than a million dollars. Why would Jimbo choose this moment to murder him? Laurel spoke before Anne could explore her doubts.

"I guess Jimbo got tired of waiting for Dom to pay up," she said with weary resignation. "They'll come after me, you know. Killing Dom was their way of sending me a message. They want to get paid right now."

"But I thought that was the whole point of keeping your marriage secret! Jimbo wasn't supposed to know you were Dom's wife."

Laurel shrugged. "He found out a couple of weeks ago. That's why Dom flew down to Vegas to see Jimbo this weekend. He hoped to work out a deal. As soon as Uncle Bertram's will had been probated, Jimbo would get paid. I guess Dom couldn't get them to agree to the delay."

Anne was appalled at the bleak acceptance in Laurel's voice. "For heaven's sake, Laurel, promise me that if anyone from Jimbo's organization threatens you, you'll tell me or Josh right away. Promise?"

"What good will that do?"

"If need be, we'll arrange to pay them off," Anne said. Much as she loathed the thought of rewarding Dom's murderers, Laurel's safety was more important. "Loan-sharking is a business. A brutal business sometimes, but a business nevertheless. If you pay off Dom's debt, Jimbo can't afford to keep harrassing you. He has to think of his reputation with his other customers. People won't hustle to pay their debts if Jimbo kills off his clients anyway."

For the first time, a faint spark of hope lighted Laurel's eyes. "You mean Jimbo won't be on my back forever?" she said.

"We'll either get him arrested for murder, or we'll pay him off," Anne promised, hoping to God she could get Dom's murderers behind bars before she had to pay them off with Bertram Kennedy's hard-earned money.

Laurel had just started to say something when a knock came at the door. "Are you people okay in there?" Josh asked. "You've been talking for almost an hour."

"We're fine," Anne said. "Hang on a minute. I think we're going to come downstairs." She looked questioningly at Laurel. "Shall we go down?" she asked. "I think you have a lot to talk over with your mother."

Laurel suddenly looked both young and vulnerable. "Stay with me while I tell her," she said. She pulled another thread from the hole in her jeans. "The stuff about the baby is going to upset Mom. She wanted me and Heather to finish college before we... She didn't want us to get married too young, like her, you know."

Bree was on the point of serving dinner when Josh, Anne and Laurel finally trooped downstairs. Anne suggested that the meatloaf should go back in the oven until Laurel had talked to her mother. As she knew from too many previous experiences, food and high emotion didn't mix well.

Josh looked astonished, and Heather looked acutely uncomfortable during Laurel's revelations, but Bree greeted the news of her daughter's marriage and pregnancy in stony, white-faced silence. The additional news that Laurel and Dom had plotted Anne's kidnapping as a way to shake money out of Bertram Kennedy seemed at first too much for Bree to absorb. When she finally understood the enormity of what her daughter had done, she exploded with an anger made all the more bitter by the inevitable tinge of guilt.

Forcing herself to think professionally rather than personally, Anne managed in the end to get the conversation between Bree and her daughters onto a constructive basis. When the shouting and recriminations finally stopped long enough for everyone to start making tentative plans for the future, she slipped out of the kitchen onto the porch. Dom and Laurel had behaved in a way that was both cowardly and selfish, not to mention criminal. Because of their actions, Anne had been deprived of the chance to meet her grandfather. She needed time and space to work through her feelings of anger and frustration, or she wouldn't be able to behave decently toward Laurel. And although Laurel didn't deserve too much sympathy, the girl was probably going through enough at this point without having Anne snap at her every time she opened her mouth.

The night air nipped at Anne's arms with high-country chill, but she tucked her hands under her sweatshirt and curled up in the corner of the love seat, listening to the peaceful tumble of water over the rocky creek bed. The scent of pine permeated the air, and this far from the city there were no ground lights to diminish the star-spangled splendor of the sky. Her grandfather's family hadn't turned out to be the warm, welcoming group of people she'd fantasized about, although Josh was becoming more important to her than she wanted to admit. At least the natural glories of Colorado were exceeding every one of her expectations. No wonder her father had always spoken so wistfully of the spectacular mountains and sunny climate of his native state.

Josh WENT OUT onto the porch more because he wanted to be with Anne than because Bree and the twins needed time alone. Over the past few days, his feelings for Anne had shifted from reluctant physical attraction to a growing recognition of the fact that when he was with her his chaotic world seemed suddenly to have a calm center.

When he'd first met Anne at Stapleton airport, he'd assumed the worst, for no reason except that she was petite, blond and the possessor of a stunning pair of baby blue eyes—just like Merrilee. He'd believed Dom's story that Anne had panicked and run away when Bertram Kennedy suffered a stroke because he'd *wanted* to believe it. If Anne had left Bertram Kennedy to die, then Josh could convince himself she was just like his ex-wife inside as well as out, a shallow soul packaged inside an enticing body. That way he could ignore the tightening in his gut every time he looked at her. That way he could tell himself he was too damn old to be suckered in by a pair of wide eyes and a set of fluttering lashes. That way he could remind himself that fantasies about making love to a beautiful woman were usually a damn sight better than the reality. Merrilee, he had discovered, was not the only woman whose body promised a warmth and passion her heart was incapable of delivering.

Over the past three days, Josh had realized that where Anne Clarence was concerned, he had been mistaken on almost every count. Physically Anne looked more beautiful every day, as her pale skin took on a golden glow from the

Colorado sun and her body threw off the effects of being imprisoned. Mentally her strength and compassion became more apparent by the moment. Right now, Anne didn't have a reason in the world to think well of Bertram Kennedy's assorted relatives, and even less reason to think well of Josh. Unfortunately for him, his physical attraction was already changing into something much more important. He hadn't yet given a name to what he felt, but he knew that he cared very much what Anne thought of him.

"Mind if I join you?" he asked.

She glanced up, her delicate features silvered by the moonlight. Her smile was sweet, warm, inviting, and his damn-fool heart gave a lurch of happiness. At least she wasn't rejecting him out of hand.

"Please do," she said, patting the love seat. "You can sit close and lend me some body heat."

Josh was all too willing to oblige. His wound was most sore on the right side of his chest, and he managed to put his left arm around her without wincing. She rested her head on his shoulder, taking care to avoid the pad of his bandages. She sighed pleasurably. "This is comfortable," she said softly. Her fingers stroked with butterfly lightness across his chest. "Does it hurt very much? Should I move?"

"No, don't move." The words came out more fiercely than he intended, and so he added quietly, "I like having you in my arms."

The breeze blew strands of her hair against his chin, and he smoothed them back into place. The strands wound themselves into a loose curl around his fingers, and Josh found himself suppressing the urge to bend down and bury his face in the silky softness of her hair.

"It's odd," Anne said, her voice husky. "Lying here in your arms feels so familiar, as if we'd done it dozens of times before. And yet, two weeks ago we'd never even met."

Josh had quite a lot of experience dealing with women, most of it successful except for the grand disaster of his marriage to Merrilee. He knew better than to push his relationship with Anne too far, too fast. He opened his mouth to say something innocuous like *time is relative,* or *friend-ship can't be measured in hours.* Instead, he heard himself say, "I want like hell to kiss you."

She looked up at him, her expression serious. "Why don't you, then?"

It took a moment for the meaning of her words to regis-ter. When it did, he felt a jolt in his gut not unlike the mo-ment when the bullet had first hit his chest. A jarring sensation, but no pain. The pain, he thought with a touch of his usual cynicism, would probably come later.

Her eyes were shadowy pools of invitation, deep enough for a man to drown in. Josh felt himself sinking fast. He was about to go under for the third time, and he didn't even care. Right at this moment, drowning seemed like a won-derful fate, provided Anne drowned with him.

He crooked his finger under her chin and slowly bent his head toward her. Their lips touched, and he felt the electric shock of the contact right through his body. His tongue pressed against the firm outline of her mouth, the warmth of her breath mingling with his. With indescribable gentle-ness, she rested her hand against his chest, holding the weight of her body away from the wound gouged by the bullet's trajectory.

Weaving his fingers into the silkiness of her hair, he in-haled the scent of her softness, and tasted the promise of passion in her lips. All the warmth he had dreamed of find-ing was there. When Anne's mouth opened beneath the ex-ploration of his tongue, desire flared between them, hot, powerful and urgent. For endless minutes, Josh's world contained nothing more than the exquisite reality of Anne's body in his arms and the hard pressure of his own sexual need.

When they finally broke apart, Anne's mouth was swol-len with the imprint of his kiss, and her eyes were clouded with the haze of unfulfilled desire. Gazing down at her, Josh found her unspeakably beautiful.

"I want to make love to you," he said when he could summon enough breath to speak.

"I want that, too," she whispered. "But I'm scared it's too soon for us."

He leaned down and kissed the end of her nose. "I'm not hustling for a night of quick sex. I want to make love to you, Anne. It's not too soon for me to know that the feelings I have for you are special."

She reached out and touched his cheek with fingers that shook slightly. A fresh wave of desire, swift and unexpectedly fierce, crashed over Josh. His hold on Anne tightened, and he pulled her close, deliberately allowing her to feel the extent of his arousal.

"Come upstairs with me," he said. "I want to be alone with you."

She pushed her hair behind her ear and looked up at him, the brilliant blue of her eyes made smoky by desire. Josh laid his hand flat across her stomach, and felt the sharp contraction of her muscles. It gave him a schoolboy feeling of satisfaction to know that she wanted him, at least a little.

His mouth almost touching hers, he said, "If you want me to stop, tell me."

"I... don't want you to stop." Her hands, feather light, sought out the thud of his heartbeat, then moved slowly downward. "I want you to love me. Please."

Josh had never been so willing to oblige a lady.

BABE SCOWLED into the darkness, vividly recreating a mental picture of the passionate kisses she'd seen Josh share with Anne Clarence. English people were such hypocrites, and Anne was one of the worst, preaching sexual responsibility one minute and then running off at the first opportunity to make out with Josh on the back porch. But there was no reason for Babe to feel disappointed just because Anne turned out to be no different from everyone else. Hypocrisy made the world go around. Babe was smart enough to have figured that out years ago. *Do what I say, not what I do.* Except Babe wasn't willing to play that game.

Her teeth started to chatter, and she pulled the covers higher. Why was she so cold? It must be because of what had happened to Dom. Dear God, why had Dom needed to die? In the anonymous darkness, Babe faced the truth. She was more scared now than ever before.

But she must look on the bright side, Babe told herself. She was probably worrying for no reason. The police were going to be told about Dom's debts and about Jimbo, but the whole kidnapping episode was going to be glossed over. That was another way Anne Clarence was like every other woman when you got right down to basics. It was so damn easy to pull the wool over her eyes. She smoothed her hand over her stomach, nibbling her lip thoughtfully.

Babe wasn't like other women, thank goodness. She was too smart to be suckered into believing the obvious. Anne Clarence believed Jimbo had killed Dom, and that was good. Babe didn't believe anything so convenient. Although perhaps, just this once, it would be nice to believe the obvious. Then—maybe—she wouldn't feel so damn scared.

Babe shivered. The bedroom seemed freezing. Or maybe she was lonely without her lover.

She wished she knew who had killed Dom.

Or maybe she was glad she didn't.

Chapter Eleven

After so many days of high drama, Anne found it anticlimactic to get up the next morning and realize that she had nothing special to do. She had finished dressing and showering and was contemplating this extraordinary situation, when Josh, dressed in a business suit with crisp white shirt and silk tie, came back into the bedroom.

"I thought I heard you moving about," he said, perching on the end of the king-size bed they'd shared and tugging her down for a kiss. When they finally broke apart, his shirt was no longer so crisp and his tie was decidedly rumpled.

"Why am I going to the office?" he muttered. "Why aren't we in bed, with the door firmly locked?"

Anne smiled. "You said something about your sales director being in hysterics, the production manager threatening to strike and your secretary claiming that the pile of urgent mail now takes up your entire desk and two shelves of the stationery closet."

"Trivial details," he said, loosening his tie.

"I'll be here tonight, waiting," Anne said, tightening it again.

Josh sighed. "Okay, you win. I'll be virtuous. What are your plans for the day?"

"I promised Bree I'd cook dinner. That's about it. I don't know what to do with myself now that I no longer have to run around town trying to find my kidnappers."

"I recommend the back porch as a mighty peaceful snoozing spot in the afternoon."

"Sounds tempting," Anne admitted, "although you're the one who should be snoozing. How does your wound feel this morning?"

Josh wriggled his shoulders dismissively. "A bit stiff, that's all. The forecast is for ninety degrees and sunny, and there's fresh-brewed iced tea in the fridge. Have I persuaded you to take a lazy day?"

"You talked me into it, although I can't imagine drinking something as weird as iced tea."

"But tea's the staple English drink," Josh protested.

"Hot tea, with milk. Not cold, with ice."

He grinned. "Try it, and you'll see how many good things we colonials can introduce you to. Apart from great sex." He leaned over and kissed her goodbye. "That felt very husbandlike," he murmured. Not disguising his surprise at what he'd said, he added, "It also felt good." He touched her briefly on the cheek. "Take care, Annie, love. I'll be home around six."

Josh had volunteered to drop Heather off at the health club, and Bree was driving Laurel into Denver for meetings with Detective Goodine, an obstetrician and Shirley Rossi, in that order, so Anne had the house to herself. The sunny porch proved every bit as relaxing as Josh had promised, but instead of dozing, Anne found her mind whirling with unresolved questions.

Last night with Laurel, it had been all too easy to consider the mystery of her kidnapping entirely explained. In the bright light of day, Anne began to remember all the minor mysteries that remained unsolved. How many strange incidents could be attributed to coincidence? she wondered. What had happened to the kidnapping note, for example? Dom and Laurel had left the door to Anne's hotel room closed, but not locked, so anyone could have walked in and taken the note. But suppose a maid had found the note, wouldn't she have alerted the hotel management? And if Jimbo's men had found it, why hadn't they left it there?

Then there was the terrifying fact of the shot fired at Josh's Toyota. Because the bullet hadn't lodged anywhere in the car, there was no way of telling what sort of a gun it had been fired from. Was it a random bullet from a hunter's rifle? Or had somebody fired with malice aforethought from a car passing the Toyota on the right-hand side? In which case, according to Sebastian, the intended victim hadn't been Josh, but Anne.

Even Dom's murder didn't seem entirely straightforward. The police surgeon had estimated Dom was killed around three in the morning. What had Dom been doing in Josh's apartment at that strange hour? And why had Jimbo's men chosen to kill him now, when his debt was more likely to get paid off than ever before?

Of course, there were lots of possible answers to all these questions. Dom and Josh were friends, and everybody in the extended Kennedy family seemed to have keys to everyone else's home. And since Dom had been out of town, he wouldn't have known Josh was in the hospital. Perhaps it wasn't surprising that he had chosen to visit Josh late at night and let himself in with a spare key when he found the town house empty. Anne could concoct a dozen reasonable explanations as to why Dom had been where he was, and why Jimbo had been following him. But however long and hard she thought, she couldn't come up with a single reason why a loan shark would want to kill off a client just at the moment he finally seemed likely to pay off his debt.

Lastly—and this was so trivial she couldn't understand why it bothered her so much—there was the strange disappearance of her father's work sheets. Richard Durbin, Josh's scientist friend, had concluded from his examination of the remaining papers that her father had been working on a fungicide to protect rice crops. That wasn't exactly startling news. Anne herself had been able to deduce as much. So why did she feel this niggle of unease every time she thought about her father's research? Why did she feel that the loss of his research papers was somehow deeply significant?

With an annoyed shrug, Anne poured herself another glass of tea, pleased to find that it tasted a little less extraordinary the second time around. She stretched out on a cushioned lounger, and tried to make her mind a blank. She counted sheep and visualized peaceful English hillsides. It worked for about twenty seconds.

Bertram Kennedy's company had originally marketed a variety of agricultural chemicals used by the military. Then, just as the Vietnam War began its devastating buildup, Bertram had sold the U.S. government the formula for a secret substance that was used by the army in Vietnam. Nothing illegal about that, of course, nor even anything immoral from the viewpoint of most people at that time. Her father had been opposed, but his aversion to pouring chemical poisons into the environment had been exceptional twenty years ago. And she had no proof that her father had joined the Red Cross in Vietnam to atone for Bertram Kennedy's sale of this product to the U.S. government. The letters between her father and grandfather dealt with—

My God, the letters! *The letters written by Paul and Grandfather are missing, every darn one of them.* Anne jerked into a sitting position, spilling iced tea all over her hand and shorts.

"Damn!" she muttered, looking around for something to mop up the spill.

"Have a handkerchief," offered a familiar voice. "I'm afraid I don't see any napkins."

"Sebastian! I didn't hear you drive up." She took the hanky with a smile, concealing her disappointment that he wasn't Josh. "You look hot." And sad, she added silently. Dom's death wasn't sitting easily on Sebastian's shoulders. "Let me get you something cool to drink."

"A diet soda would be great."

"There must be a can in the fridge. Come inside."

He followed her into the kitchen. "Looks like I arrived in the nick of time. Whatever you were thinking about didn't seem to be making you very happy."

"It wasn't. I'm probably worrying about nothing," she said, reaching into the fridge for a Diet Coke. "But it's the most peculiar thing. Did I mention to you that several of my father's work sheets were missing when my suitcases finally got returned to me?"

"Mmm, I believe so."

"Well, now I've remembered something else that's missing. My father's letters to my grandfather. Every one of them was gone."

"I'm sorry. They must have a lot of sentimental value for you."

"Not as much as you might think, because the letters weren't exactly personal. Since my dad and my grandfather didn't get on too well, I suppose they found it easier to talk about their research rather than about themselves and their families. But still, I wish I knew what had happened to those letters. The fact that they're missing bothers me for some reason."

Sebastian popped the top on his can of Diet Coke. "Well, it doesn't need to bother you for long, does it?"

"What do you mean?"

"Laurel will be here tonight. Ask her. Either she or Dom must have returned your cases to the police station, although heaven knows what was going through their minds when they did that. And if the letters are missing, Laurel must know why."

Anne stared at Sebastian in silence for a few seconds, then burst out laughing. "Good lord, I'm only using half a brain recently. Do you know, I never even thought about asking Laurel!"

Sebastian grinned, adding ice cubes to his soda. "Glad to have been of service. Any other problems that you'd like me to solve in the next few seconds?"

"Unless you can tell me who was shooting at me and Josh the other day, I don't think so."

He frowned. "I'm afraid I can't help with that. God knows, I wish I could. What's the latest police theory?"

"Who knows? A teenager high on drugs. A hunter. The police don't think it was a serious attempt to kill Josh or me. Speeding cars passing on a highway. Only a crack shot could hope to kill someone that way."

"Jimbo probably has a few of those in his organization."

"I suppose so. But Jimbo has no reason to kill either of us. We'd never heard of Jimbo until..."

"Until my brother died."

"Yes." Anne sat down at the kitchen table, regretting her thoughtlessness in raising a subject that had reminded Sebastian of his brother's death. "What brings you up here?" she asked quietly. "I hope everything is all right with your mother."

He sighed. "She's taking Dom's death very hard, which isn't surprising, I guess. I never thought I'd see the day when I was praying for her to have one of her tantrums. It doesn't seem right for her to be so quiet. Carlo is even worse. He's sitting at the piano, with his hands resting on the keys, staring into space. I don't think he's moved since he heard the news."

For a moment, Sebastian seemed totally sunk in melancholy, then he made a visible effort to pull himself together. "But to answer your other question, I came up here specially to see you. The probate court has issued some documents that need your signature." He reached into his briefcase and pulled out a thin sheaf of legal-sized documents. "Please read them carefully before you sign," he said. "And if you don't understand any of the language, ask me."

The language was opaque, but not impenetrable. The court recognized Anne as a petitioner in the disposition of Bertram Kennedy's estate. In the meantime, pending full settlement, Anne Kennedy Clarence authorized Joshua Donaldson and Sebastian Rossi to continue acting as executors and to make necessary disbursements as they saw fit.

"Do you have a pen?" Anne said when she'd finally finished reading. "This amounts to four pages to say that you and Josh have my permission to continue administering Bertram's estate. Lawyers always like to make simple things complex, don't they?''

Sebastian smiled without mirth. "I couldn't agree with you more. Bertram's will is sixty-six pages long, jam-packed with legal flimflam. And you know what really annoys me? In the end, for all the gibberish his expensive lawyers insisted on, his real wishes probably won't get carried out.''

''Managing such a huge estate must be taking up an enormous amount of your time,'' Anne said.

''You're so right. And with Dom . . .'' He swallowed and turned away. When he spoke again, his voice was husky. ''With what happened to Dom, I have all his affairs to handle, as well. I was in his apartment at six o'clock this morning going through his papers. The state of his file cabinet gives new meaning to the word *chaos.*''

''Have you decided to pay off the money Dom owed to Jimbo? I only ask because Laurel seemed so worried that Jimbo might come after her now that Dom is dead.''

''In a way, the decision's out of my hands. I've no idea how to get in touch with the guy, even if I wanted to pay him off tomorrow. I'm hoping that the police will track him down. And once Jimbo is arrested, Laurel can feel safe again.''

''Do you really believe he killed your brother?''

Sebastian frowned. ''To be honest, I don't know what to believe. People do the strangest things for money.''

''But Jimbo must have known he didn't have to kill Dom to get paid. He would have been paid anyway.''

''The police are asking all those same questions.'' Sebastian hesitated, looking at Anne, then looking away before he finally spoke. ''I don't want my mother to know this, Anne, so please don't say anything to anybody, not even to Josh. But I'm not sure Laurel knew the truth of Dom's business dealings with Jimbo.''

''What do you mean?''

"The fact is, I'm not sure Dom owed Jimbo money. I think..." He drew in a deep breath. "I think they may have been more—partners."

Anne cradled her glass of iced tea with chilly fingers. "Partners in what?" she asked.

"Nothing very bad, I'm sure," Sebastian said at once, obviously trying to reassure himself as much as Anne. "Look, let's wait and see what the police come up with, shall we? There's no point in tormenting ourselves with speculation until we have a few facts to go on."

Anne realized with regret that she had no difficulty in believing that Dom had been involved in some sort of nefarious business deal with Jimbo. Everything made a great deal more sense if they were partners who had fallen out, rather than loan shark and victim. Poor Aunt Shirley, she thought. And poor Carlo, and Sebastian. One bad apple in the family barrel, and everyone became tainted. Sebastian looked so sad she wanted to say something comforting. All she could think of was, "I'm so sorry, Sebastian."

"Well, I guess we'll all survive one way or another." He carried his glass over to the sink, then picked up his briefcase, his face drawn and weary. "I'll see you tomorrow, I expect, at Dom's funeral. God, what a tragic waste!"

THE NEXT DAY, Anne was able to see for herself how devastated Shirley was by the fact of her son's death. Anne had heard of people who appeared weighted down by grief. In Shirley she saw a living example of a woman shrunken beneath the pain of her loss. The flamboyant opera singer had turned overnight into a tired old woman.

A tall, distinguished-looking man stood at Shirley's side throughout the funeral service. As they waited to express their condolences, Josh explained that this was Shirley's husband, Giorgio Rossi e Neroni, the conte de Montania.

"Aunt Shirley doesn't use the title of countess?" Anne asked as they waited in the receiving line after the burial.

"Sometimes, when she's in Italy. But professionally she's always been Shirley Rossi. She married her first husband when she went to study in Milano, but she divorced him before she made a name for herself."

"I didn't realize she'd been married twice."

"Yes. Sebastian is actually a half brother to Dom and Carlo. Sebastian uses the count's family name, but his father was actually a young singer Shirley worked with."

"That explains why Sebastian doesn't look in the least like his brothers."

The few minutes Anne spent with Shirley Rossi and the count were even more harrowing than she'd anticipated, and the encounter with Carlo almost frightening. Carlo's face was pale, and his cheeks slightly sunken, giving a diabolical cast to the perfection of his features. Looking at him, Anne thought she knew exactly how Lucifer must have appeared at the moment of the Fall.

"I'm sorry, Carlo," she murmured, hating the inadequacy of the words. "I'm so very sorry."

He looked at her, eyes hollow. "He wasn't supposed to die," he whispered. "Not Dom."

The words, as much as Carlo's distraught appearance, made Anne acutely uncomfortable. "He was very young," she agreed.

Carlo looked through her. Anne had no idea if he knew to whom he was speaking. "It's my fault," he said. "It should never have happened."

Anne looked around, wishing Josh were with her, but he was deep in talk with Sebastian. "You mean you could have loaned Dom the money he needed?" she asked.

Carlo stared at his mother, his expression agonized. "I wish I knew what to do," he muttered, and walked away without giving Anne another glance.

It was not a conversation to treat lightly, and Anne was grateful for the distraction when Ellen Kennedy sent her into the kitchen in pursuit of the caterers. She passed on the message about the need for more fruit punch, and was gathering up her resources for a return to the living room when Laurel came into the kitchen.

Both twins had worn pale blue dresses to the funeral, but unlike Heather, Laurel had topped hers with a hip-length, loose linen jacket that effectively concealed her pregnancy. In contrast to Laurel's concealing jacket, Anne had noticed at the church that Heather had drawn the belt of her dress so tight that it seemed almost as if she wanted to emphasize the narrowness of her waist and the firm, muscled flatness of her abdomen. Hard as it was for Laurel to be widowed and pregnant, Anne reflected, Heather might be suffering from problems of her own. After years of closeness, it couldn't be easy for Heather to watch her twin undergoing changes that were entirely outside the range of her own experience.

Laurel came closer to Anne, but avoided meeting her eyes. Obviously embarrassed, she addressed her remarks to the floor. "Sebastian was talking to me just now," she said. "He told me about your father's letters. They're missing."

"Yes, I wanted to ask you about them, as well as the research papers in my father's work files. Some of them are missing, too."

"It was Dom who took your cases," Laurel said, as quick as ever to deny responsibility. "He took them back to his apartment because we needed to hide them. But he took great care of them, Anne. He knew it was important not to destroy your passport and visa and things. That's why he returned your cases to the police station. So that you'd have your passport back in case you wanted to go home to England."

"But I can tell from the way my clothes were refolded that Dom searched through my cases," Anne said. "Do you know what he was looking for?"

Laurel shook her head. "No, he didn't search your cases, Anne, honestly he didn't. There was no reason for him to search them. One of them fell open when we were loading them into Dom's Bronco, that's all."

"You mean my father's letters just happened to fall out of my case and you didn't notice they were missing? Surely you must have seen them scattered all over the ground?"

"We were in the hotel parking garage," Laurel explained. "And we heard someone coming. We had to pick up all your stuff really quickly and shove it into the back of the truck. We thought we'd picked everything up, truly, but I guess the papers must have gotten stuck under the body of the Jeep or something. It was dark down in the garage, and we were kind of scared." She twisted the button on her jacket, which was hanging almost off, probably from too much similar twisting. "I'm sorry, Anne. We didn't know those papers were missing. And for sure we didn't know they were important."

"They probably weren't," Anne said, sighing. Laurel's explanation of what had happened was entirely credible and yet—and yet, Anne couldn't rid herself of the uncomfortable feeling that her father's missing papers held some sort of significance. But there was absolutely no reason for Laurel to lie, nothing in her expression or manner to suggest she wasn't telling the truth. Anne gave herself a mental shake. She was becoming obsessive about a trivial detail, allowing the bee of irritation to buzz too long and too loudly within the confines of her bonnet.

"I have to get back to Aunt Shirley," Laurel said. "See you later, Anne." She darted out of the kitchen, looking almost furtive, which didn't entirely surprise Anne. News of Laurel's marriage and pregnancy was undoubtedly circulating among the funeral attendees, causing a lot of comment, and teenagers often found it difficult to be the focus of that sort of gossipy attention.

The last of the guests didn't leave until the middle of the afternoon, at which point Shirley and her husband retired to their bedroom, pleading exhaustion. Carlo had disappeared, a fact for which Anne was somewhat grateful. Bree and the twins left for the mountains and Ellen Kennedy sank into a chair by the empty fireplace, her face drawn into heavy lines of sadness.

"If my mother is going to rest, I'll take the chance to grab a few hours at the office," Sebastian said. "Do you think you can cope, Ellen?"

"With Giorgio here, there's nothing for me to do," Ellen said. "He's helped save Shirley's sanity, I'm sure of it."

"He's always known how to handle my mother," Sebastian said. "If he only had a grain of financial sense—" He pulled himself up in midsentence. "I guess this isn't the time or the place to criticize my stepfather's financial habits," he said. "Anne, can I give you a ride anywhere? Or are you spending the night with Josh again?"

His voice couldn't have been more bland, so Anne didn't understand why she found herself blushing. Anyway, in this day and age, the implication that she and Josh were lovers wouldn't raise an eyebrow. For whatever reason, she felt oddly flustered and said the first thing that came into her head.

"What I'd really like to do is look through my grandfather's old files," she said. "When he sold out, do you know what happened to his original company records?"

Ellen Kennedy straightened in her chair, looking not at all pleased. "Naturally most of his papers went into Agricon's archives after the takeover," she said. "And I must say, even if Bertram's files were all right here, I can't imagine why you'd want to poke around in a bunch of musty old papers."

"I want to know exactly what products my grandfather was producing when he first set up his own company," Anne said. Until she spoke, she hadn't known that was what she wanted to do. As soon as the words left her mouth, the suspicion that had hovered for so many days at the edges of her subconscious crystallized into solid form. "And I also want to find out as much as I can about the secret formula he sold to the U.S. government."

"Well, you'll have to take a trip to Nebraska to find out that," Ellen snapped. "Agricon has all those technical records. Besides, why on earth does it matter what the precise formula was? There was nothing harmful about it, if that's what worries you. If you've heard about the lawsuit brought by that serviceman in South Carolina, then you should know that his case was thrown out of court. Yes, he has cancer of the liver, but the man tried to commit suicide by *drinking* some of Bertram's product. Good God, that's like claiming bleach shouldn't be sold as a laundry aid because babies can die if they swallow it.''

"I'd never heard about the lawsuit," Anne said. "That isn't why I want access to his papers.''

"Then what in the world are you looking for?'' Ellen demanded.

"I don't know exactly," Anne prevaricated, unable to tell the truth to the woman who had loved Bertram Kennedy for so many years. She tried to give a believable excuse, one that Ellen would accept. "Bertram Kennedy was my grandfather, and I was denied the chance to meet him in person, although that was something we both wanted very much. Don't I have the right to try to get to know him through his work?''

"Of course you do," said Josh. "Mother, even if you don't have any company files here, you must have other family mementos. Those early records from Bertram's first marriage belong to Anne more than to anyone else. Katrina was Anne's grandmother, after all.''

With extreme reluctance, Ellen rose to her feet. "The key to Bertram's desk is in my bedroom," she said. "If you want to come with me, Anne, I'll get it for you.'' She walked out of the room without a backward glance.

Sebastian pulled a face. "Aunt Ellen on her high horse positively terrifies me," he said. "I'm going to make my escape while I can. Good luck, Anne! See you later, people.''

Anne was already doubting the wisdom of what she had set in motion. After all, at this late date, did it really matter where Bertram's breakthrough formula had come from? Did she really want to cut open these festering family wounds? "Josh, I'm sorry. I didn't mean to offend your mother. Perhaps I shouldn't insist on seeing these papers.''

"Don't worry about it." Josh sounded distracted. "It's obviously important to you. And what I told my mother is no more than the truth. You're Bertram Kennedy's only direct descendant. You have a right to examine his papers."

Ellen was waiting for them at the head of the stairs. "These are Bertram's keys," she said. "And when you're ferreting around in the past, I wish you would remember that the Vietnam War finished a long time ago."

Josh's frown lifted. "Is that what's worrying you?" he demanded. "Mother, are you afraid we're going to discover something in the records that might link Bertram's military products to health problems in the people who used them?"

"There is no link to discover," Ellen said fiercely. "But who knows how the media might distort the facts. God knows, they've tried to do it often enough in the past. Pesticides, fungicides, herbicides. If that's what your company produces, half the reporters in this country consider you little better than licensed murderers. Bertram was a good man, a patriot, even if his son despised him. He deserves better than to have his granddaughter come over here and stir up all the old propaganda just to vindicate Paul's antiwar views."

"But that's not what I plan to do!" Anne said, appalled. "You've completely misunderstood my motives."

"Then why do you want to search through twenty-year-old files?" Ellen demanded. "What in the world do you think you'll find hidden in Bertram's papers?"

"I believe I can guess," Josh said, his voice very dry. "You don't think Bertram was a murderer, do you, Anne?"

"No," she said flatly. She drew in a deep breath. "But I'm nearly sure he was a thief."

Chapter Twelve

"You're insane!" Ellen exclaimed. "Bertram was the most honorable man I've ever met—"

"He was also a passionate anticommunist," Josh interjected quietly. "And a strong supporter of United States involvement in Vietnam."

"What in the world has that got to do with him being a thief?" Ellen asked, her voice cracking with bewilderment. White-faced, she glared at Anne. "How can you accuse your own grandfather of being a thief?"

"I don't mean he went out robbing banks," Anne said. "But I do think my father invented the formula for the infamous secret chemical Bertram sold to the U.S. government. Which means that Bertram sold something that didn't belong to him."

"Everyone knows your father was working on ways to increase crop production," Ellen protested. "How could he have invented a product that was useful to the U.S. military in Vietnam?"

"By accident," Anne said. "As the result of a failed series of experiments. I suspect that the product Bertram sold to the U.S. military was a fungicide that only affected rice. The American government sprayed it on Vietcong rice crops to cut off their food supply."

"You have no way of proving that Paul discovered any such formula."

"But I think if we get experts to examine his work papers closely, we'll discover that he did. My father was trying to find a fungicide to protect rice seedlings and increase crop yields in Third World countries. Instead, he developed a product that killed the seedlings off before they could germinate. My dad must have been horrified when he realized that my grandfather was going to make a huge profit from something he considered an abysmal failure."

Stricken, Ellen looked around for a chair, and finding none, sank down onto the top step. "You can't be right," she said. "Bertram would never have stolen a dime from anyone, least of all from his own son."

"Perhaps his own son is the *only* person he'd have stolen from," Anne suggested quietly. "With hindsight, I understand the letters they exchanged much better. Of course, I've only seen a small part of their correspondence, just the few letters that happened to end up in my dad's files at the university, and even those are now missing. But I think in one of those letters my grandfather explains that he's made my father a major shareholder in his company. From my grandfather's point of view, selling my father's formula to the U.S. military was the logical exploitation of research that my father considered worthless."

Josh knelt next to his mother, putting his arm around her shoulders. "There were plenty of families back in the late sixties where fathers and sons were talking to each other from such different political perspectives that it was like trying to communicate across the void of outer space," he pointed out. "Bertram supported the war effort. Paul was totally opposed. Bertram thought chemical fertilizers and insecticides were the most efficient way to expand the world's food production. Paul disagreed. Throw in three thousand miles of Atlantic and a history of stormy relations from the time Paul was in high school, and you have a recipe for just the sort of disastrous misunderstanding that may have occurred."

"Anne's right about one thing," Ellen admitted with evident reluctance. "I know that Bertram gave Paul half the shares in his original company. They were assigned in such a way that they reverted automatically to Bertram on Paul's death." Honesty compelled her to add, "I can't quite see why Bertram would have done that unless he felt he owed Paul a debt."

"I think over the years Bertram gradually realized that he'd done a terrible thing," Josh said. "Remember how excited and nervous he was when he first heard from Anne?"

"That was because she was his granddaughter, Paul's child. Good lord, he'd never seen her! No wonder he was excited."

"It wasn't only that," Josh said. "He told us all one night over dinner that God was being good to him and providing him with the chance to right old wrongs."

"We all assumed he simply wanted to heal the breach with Paul's family," Ellen said, meeting Anne's eyes with obvious difficulty. "I hope you'll believe that we none of us dreamed for a moment that there was any more-serious wrong to be corrected." She struggled to regain some of her normal composure. "Although we are rather leaping to conclusions here. We have no proof that Bertram did anything..." She stopped, her sense of honor compelling her to avoid euphemisms, compelling her to say the words that were so painful. "We have no proof that my husband stole the formula for his successful defoliant from Paul."

"That's true," Anne said, taking pity on Ellen. "There's no conclusive proof of anything I've said."

"But now that we know what we're looking for, it shouldn't be all that difficult to find proof one way or the other," Josh pointed out. "Cambridge University probably has copies of reports Paul submitted concerning his work. Agricon certainly has records in Nebraska of the precise formula for the product Bertram sold to the U.S. government."

"At this late stage, I don't really see why any of this matters," Anne said, surprised to find herself feeling sorry for Ellen. "I'm pleased that we've managed to work out what it was that Grandfather Bertram and my father quarreled about. And naturally I'm glad that my grandfather grew to realize that he'd behaved badly and wanted to make amends. But at this point, who cares which of them discovered the darn formula? The Vietnam War is over, the fungicide was used, my father died. What was done, was done."

Ellen and Josh both stared at her in silent astonishment. It was Ellen who broke the silence. "I'm afraid it matters rather a lot," she said dryly. "Not only philosophically, but practically, as well. If Bertram appropriated your father's research, the profits that he made from selling the resulting formula to the government belong to your father. I'm sure a smart lawyer could make a good case for saying that all the successes of Bertram's company grew out of that initial profitable sale. In which case, all the profits from Bertram's company really belong to your father."

"So what? My grandfather is dead. My father is dead."

"Precisely," Josh said. "And that means Bertram's sixty-five million dollar estate really belongs to you."

By DINNERTIME, ANNE WAS heartily sick of talking about Bertram's money, and even more weary of repeating that she had no intention of spearheading an investigation into the precise origins of her grandfather's fortune.

"Why would I want to inherit sixty-five million dollars?" she asked with what seemed to her, unassailable logic. "All of you are accustomed to being rich, so having millions of dollars seems normal to you. I never even considered the possibility, and I'm not trained to take on the responsibility of such a huge sum of money."

"You're deciding too hastily," Josh cautioned. "You haven't taken the time to consider what you're throwing away."

"I've considered very carefully," she said. "I'm throwing away a great deal of trouble. How many diamond rings can a person wear at one time? How many houses can I sleep in? How many dinners could I eat?"

"At least one different house for each season of the year. And at least one fancy dinner a night," Josh said. "And you could always buy a yacht."

"Sailing makes me seasick. And if I ate fancy dinners every night, I'd need to spend half the year in health spas getting rid of the extra pounds I gained. Which would mean that I had no time to live in my houses. Josh, face facts. You're not going to persuade me that I need this money."

"Take her to dinner at Giovanni's," Ellen suggested with an unexpected touch of humor. "His lobster with buttered angel-hair pasta would convince anyone that being rich is fun."

Two hours lingering over Giovanni's exquisite—and ruinously expensive—cooking didn't persuade Anne that she wanted to be a multimillionaire, but it convinced her that Josh was the most intelligent and entertaining companion she'd ever known. Far from regretting their impulsive lovemaking, she realized that the more time she spent with Josh, the more she liked him and the more she wanted to repeat the intense pleasure of a night spent in his arms. She was obviously a slow learner, she thought with a touch of amusement. It had taken her thirty years to discover the joy of sex, but now she was eager to make up for lost time. By the time they arrived back at Josh's town house, Anne was wondering if nine-thirty would be too early to suggest going to bed.

Her erotic, champagne-hazed mood was jarred slightly when she saw the bloodstained carpet in the hallway, a grisly reminder that Dom had paid an exorbitant price for his addiction to gambling. Josh winced as he walked around the rusty brown splotches. "I'll have to arrange for the carpet cleaners to come in," he muttered. "I've decided to put this place on the market. At this point, the fact that it's five minutes from my office doesn't seem all that important."

Once in the living room, he put on a tape of classical music, and the clear, high notes of a flute concerto floated soothingly into the room. Sinking into a chair, he drew in a deep breath. "Damn, but these last couple of weeks have been hell. Thank God, it's all over."

Anne went to him, intending to offer nothing more than comfort, but as soon as he put his arms around her, passion flared, and they kissed with mounting hunger. When the doorbell rang, Josh muttered a curse. "Ignore it," he said, pulling her back into his lap. "They'll give up soon enough."

But the buzzer continued to ring, a shrill, insistent counterpoint to the rippling notes of the flute. Reluctantly Anne stood up. "I think you'd better see who it is. They sound determined."

Josh strode across the room, glanced into the peephole, then yanked open the door. "Yes, what is it?"

"Are you Mr. Joshua Donaldson?"

"Yes."

"I'm Officer Wolnik," Anne heard a masculine voice say. "I have bad news, I'm afraid, Mr. Donaldson."

Stomach clenching, Anne joined Josh at the door. Dear God, what had happened now? Please God, not something to hurt Laurel. A young police officer stood on the step. His squad car, with radio squawking and blue light flashing, waited at the curb.

"What's happened?" Josh asked, his body so rigidly erect Anne knew he was holding himself together by sheer force of will.

"A party of hikers climbed over Smoke Top Ridge this afternoon. They reported that a cabin up there had been vandalized. Paint on the walls, windows smashed in, the whole works. We investigated and discovered that the cabin belongs to your deceased stepfather, Bertram Kennedy."

That was all! Anne's pounding pulses gradually resumed their regular beat. In comparison to the horrors she had feared, the vandalizing of an empty cabin seemed almost unimportant. From the slump of Josh's shoulders, she knew he was feeling the same sort of bone-deep relief. It was a sad commentary on the violence recently unleashed in both their lives that the trashing of Bertram's hunting cabin seemed such a minor mishap.

"Thanks for letting us know," Josh said. "Fortunately the cabin was empty. Not even any furniture. I don't know how much damage the vandals could do."

The police officer referred to his notebook. "I'm afraid among other things, the hikers discovered a dead deer in the middle of the living room. Not at all a pleasant sight from what the police officer up in Estes Park tells me. Seems like a real lot of yahoos got in there, if you know what I mean."

Anne shuddered and Josh reached out to take her hand. "Has the deer been removed?" he asked, sounding so ineffably weary that Anne's bones ached in sympathy.

"We've taken care of it. Notified animal control, I believe."

"I appreciate that." Josh rubbed his hand against the back of his neck. "We'll arrange to get the place cleaned and repaired as soon as possible. Is that what you needed to know?"

"We believe we have the perpetrators in custody, Mr. Donaldson. We'd appreciate it if you'd come with me to sign a complaint and see if you can make an ID against the perpetrators."

"I'll sign the complaint willingly, but surely there's not much hope that I'll make an ID. Do the vandals claim to know me? Was this something personal?"

The police officer took another look at his notes. "It doesn't say anything about the perpetrators' motives, Mr. Donaldson. Sorry."

"Do you know how the vandals were caught?"

"I guess the hikers must have seen them in the act. I don't know how else we could have 'em in custody so fast. But you can ask the officer in charge, sir. I was just assigned to call and pick you up." He glanced at his watch. "It's getting near the end of my shift, so if you could hurry..."

Josh turned to Anne. "Do you mind if I go now? I may as well get this over with."

The police officer glanced at Anne. "The young lady can come with us if you'd like, sir. Maybe it's better if she isn't left alone until we find out why these goons were vandalizing your property." He smiled cheerfully. "If their motives were personal, you never know when they might take it into their heads to start on this house, do you?"

"I think I'll come," Anne said. "If you don't mind, Josh?"

His smile warmed her heart. "You know how much I would like your company."

She had never ridden in a police squad car before, and soon discovered that the combination of protective grill-work and driver-controlled, nonopening doors was distinctly claustrophobic. Officer Wolnik didn't say much to them, being fully occupied with listening to his crackling radio.

Now that the first shock of hearing from the policeman had passed, Anne found herself full of questions. "Josh, doesn't it strike you that our lives are becoming too full of bizarre coincidences?" she asked. "Why did vandals suddenly choose Bertram's cabin to vandalize after years of leaving it safely alone?"

"Of course it seems odd. But what's the alternative to coincidence? Every other explanation I can dream up sounds even more incredible."

"Like what?"

He shrugged. "That Jimbo has a sick mind and flew up from Vegas to Denver to put a dead deer in Bertram's living room. That sort of explanation makes coincidence sound good."

Anne's brow furrowed in concentration. "What if Dom and Jimbo have nothing to do with this vandalism? Suppose somebody has a personal grudge against you, and the only coincidence is that they happen to be working off their hatred right after Jimbo decided to get angry with Dom?"

"Unless we're dealing with a total lunatic, I can't imagine who would have a grudge against me. I haven't won any business contracts against stiff competition. My ex-wife is happily remarried and living in New York, two thousand miles from here. I don't have gambling debts, or any other debts to speak of, apart from the usual mortgages and business loans."

Anne smiled. "Well, have you run into any total lunatics recently?"

"Not that I know of." He stared out of the window, lost in thought, then suddenly straightened and leaned forward to talk to the policeman.

"Officer, where are we going?"

"To the Estes Park police station," the man replied, raising his voice to be heard over the crackle of his radio. "Sorry, sir. I thought you realized that's where they're holding the alleged perpetrators."

"I should have driven my own car," Josh said. "You'll never end your shift on time if you have to take us back to Denver."

"Don't worry about it, Mr. Donaldson. The overtime'll come in useful. My wife's pregnant, so we need the money."

"Congratulations," Josh said.

Officer Wolnik looked pleased with himself. "It's our first baby. The doctor says it's going to be a girl."

Several miles passed in discussion of the upcoming birth and Officer Wolnik's intention to be present in the delivery room. He and his wife were attending prenatal classes and practicing breathing relaxation exercises. Once started on the fascinating subject of his impending fatherhood, Officer Wolnik was a one-man conversationalist.

Anne found his mixture of pride and pleasure rather touching. She wondered what it would feel like to be pregnant with Josh's baby, and was astonished by the wave of intense longing that swept over her. Motherhood had never figured in her plans as more than a remote possibility for some time in the distant future. Suddenly her womb ached and her breasts tingled with the desire to feel Josh's child growing inside her. She tried to put her feelings into perspective. Making love to Josh the other night had been a revelation to her, transporting her to a whole new world of

pleasure and sensuality. Maybe the great sex they'd shared
had triggered a flood of maternal hormones. Wanting to
bear a man's child didn't necessarily mean that she was crazy
enough to have fallen in love with a man she'd cordially
disliked two weeks earlier.

She turned to look at Josh, her mind so full of unexpected questions that she scarcely registered what he was
saying. But something in the taut line of his body penetrated her cloud of daydreams. She blinked as he leaned
forward again, grabbing the mesh that separated the driver
from the rear of the car.

"What the hell is going on here?" Josh demanded. "This
is the road to my house and Bertram's cabin!"

"Didn't I explain, sir?" Officer Wolnik's voice was mild.
"We have to go to the scene of the crime first."

"What for?"

"Well, sir, I guess because I say so."

The driveway leading to Josh's house sailed by on the
right-hand side of the squad car. "Please let us out here,"
Josh said.

The car continued its upward climb at a brisk forty miles
per hour.

"Damn it, Officer, I asked you to stop the car. What the
hell is going on here?"

"I'm taking you to Mr. Bertram Kennedy's cabin, sir."

"I never agreed to come up here."

"You don't have much choice, do you, sir?" Officer
Wolnik sounded as polite as ever, but Anne realized her
teeth were clenching tight with fear. Wolnik was entirely
correct. They were confined to the squad car, with no way
to get out until this crazy policeman chose to release the
door locks.

The cabin loomed ahead of them, a darker shadow
against the shadows of the night. The place appeared deserted. Anne searched for signs of broken windows and
smashed doors, but the cabin looked just as it had always
done. Obviously there had been no attack by vandals. Then
why had the policeman brought them here? Fear turned

Anne's mouth dry and her palms wet. She was back in the nightmare again, back in the terrible dream where nothing made sense.

Officer Wolnik slowed the car, then turned around to give them both a friendly smile. He braked, and the car jerked to a stop. He reached down to his holster and casually extracted a gun. There was, however, no casualness in the way he pointed his weapon straight at Josh's chest.

"Out of the car, both of you."

He released the locks on the doors, and they stumbled out. Josh put his arm around Anne. "I'm sorry, love," he said. "I think I've been damn stupid."

"It's my own fault," she said. "I didn't have to come."

"You're wrong, Ms. Clarence. I had special instructions to make sure you came." Officer Wolnik gestured with his gun. "Keep walking, folks."

They had arrived at the entrance to the cabin. Officer Wolnik pushed sharply on the door, and it swung silently inward. A brutal shove from behind sent Anne toppling forward. She stumbled into the cabin. Immediately the door slammed shut behind her. Blackness descended. Total. Absolute.

"Josh!" She screamed his name in a crescendo of terror. Silence echoed and reverberated through the suffocating room. She couldn't even hear the sound of scuffling feet outside the cabin. What was happening to Josh? She buried her face deep in her hands, shutting out the dreadful darkness. Her body curled itself into a helpless little ball. Everything will be all right, a silent voice crooned. If you lie there, still and quiet, the darkness will take care of you.

No! She wouldn't be tamed that easily. She ripped her hands away from her face and crawled to the door. As she pressed her cheek against the cold wood, the breeze carried a chuckle of laughter to her ears. Officer Wolnik? Josh? She couldn't tell. After a split second of quiet, she heard the hum of a car engine starting up. She beat her fists against the door.

"Josh, don't go! Please God, don't let them leave me here again!"

The only answer she received was the sound of the car driving down the mountain. Gradually the phut-phut of the motor faded into silence. The quiet and the darkness grew together, expanding into a thick, suffocating cloud that smothered her tears and choked off her sobs. Dry-eyed, hugging her body, she rocked back and forth, accepting her fate. Josh was a prisoner, and she would be locked in the cabin until she died.

There was no logical reason why she shouldn't stand, but her body felt too heavy to pull upright. Anne crept toward the center of the cabin's living area on her hands and knees. When she realized what she was doing, she jumped to her feet and shook her fist into the darkness.

"I'm not going to die here!" she yelled. "Do you hear me? I'm going to escape again! You can't keep me locked up. I'll find a way out somehow."

Did you ever escape in the first place?

The mocking question echoed in her mind, stark, uncompromising and totally terrifying. Was it possible that she'd never really escaped? What if she'd imagined the unlocked door and the midnight scramble down the mountainside to Josh's house? Certainly the events of the past few days were crazy enough to be part of a dream. Maybe she'd only imagined the horror of finding Dom dead and the joy of making love to Josh.

The fingers of madness began to stroke beguilingly at the boundaries of her mind. *Dear God, that was the explanation for everything.* She'd never left the cabin, which meant that the events of the past few days were nothing more than the fevered nightmares of her captivity. Her food supply had been almost exhausted several days ago. If she hadn't eaten for three or four days... If she'd been drifting in and out of consciousness... If she'd been dreaming wild, hopeless dreams...

If there was no hope of rescue, Anne thought with sudden cold clarity, then perhaps it would be wiser to allow her mind to seep away into the comforting void of insanity. Why fight the inevitable?

With an effort that was physically painful, she banged her fist into her palm, jolting herself out of the slippery downward spiral.

"No, damn it, I won't give up! I escaped before, I know I did, so I can do it again!" Gasping for breath, her chest heaving as if she'd run a marathon, she patted her hands over her body in frantic exploration. She'd originally been kidnapped wearing beige linen pants and a silk blouse. Now she was wearing a dark cotton dress, hose, high-heeled sandals, a silky underslip and a bra that she'd bought in Denver with Josh—

Her thoughts skittered to a triumphant halt. Her bra! *Bought in America.* If there were only light in the cabin, she would be able to see the label and check that the bra was new. Which would mean that she had truly been shopping in Denver, and that she wasn't imagining her escape from the cabin.

Hope made the darkness seem less absolute. Where before she had seen only impenetrable blackness, now she could see the glow of moonlight filtering through the kitchen window. She ran toward the light, unbuttoning her dress as she ran. By the time she reached the kitchen window, the bodice of her dress hung to her waist, and she had pulled off her bra. With fingers that shook, she held the label up in the moonlight. Squinting, she could just make out the purple letters. Size 34B. Made In The U.S.A.

She gave a yell of laughter that almost wavered into tears, then put her bra back on, buttoning up her dress any old which way. She splashed cold water on her face, washing away the last tendrils of panic. She would get out of this damn cabin by morning, or her name wasn't Anne Clarence.

The intention was great. Turning that intention into reality presented a few problems. After all, she'd spent three days searching the cabin once before and hadn't found any way out. What was different this time around?

Anne refused to be discouraged. Last time, she'd been drugged; this time she wasn't. Last time, she'd been tired and hungry; this time, she'd just stoked up her system with Giovanni's lobster and angel-hair pasta. Better yet, when "Officer Wolnik" had shoved her into the cabin, he'd overlooked the fact that Anne's purse was slung over her shoulder. Like any other woman's, her purse contained a multitude of goodies. Surely one of them would be of some use as an escape weapon? At the very least, she had a pocket manicure set. Between her nail scissors, file and cuticle clippers, she would find some instrument to pick the lock on the front door.

Energized by hope, Anne ran back into the living room, feeling around on the floor until she found her purse. Thank God, it was lying by the door, its flap still closed, its contents safe. In triumph, she carried her prize back to the kitchen and had the purse ready to upend over the counter when she heard the sound of a car returning.

Josh! Her mouth stretched into a huge grin of happiness. Despite his wounded shoulder, he'd overpowered "Officer Wolnik" and returned to rescue her. She should have realized right from the start that Josh would soon be coming back to set her free.

Except, of course, that Josh might not have overpowered Mr. Wolnik. It was equally possible that Josh had been disposed of—she wouldn't allow herself to define precisely what she meant by that vague term—and that "Officer Wolnik" was now returning to take care of Anne.

Her euphoric grin faded, and she sidled back into the living room. Obviously she would be smart to hide until she knew precisely who was coming. But the empty cabin presented few opportunities for concealment. In fact, there was nowhere except the bathroom. Anne hid herself behind the bathroom door, leaving it open a crack so that she could see into the living room. Her angle of vision was quite good, and she had as clear a view of the front door as the darkness permitted.

The car engine was cut. Footsteps crunched over the gravel driveway, approaching the cabin door. Anne only had one possible defensive weapon. She scrabbled around inside her purse until she found the manicure set. She pulled out the little pair of nail scissors. Why isn't real life more like the movies? she thought regretfully. Why wasn't there a brass doorstopper in the middle of the bathroom floor? In the movies, a heroine could always count on finding a convenient weapon to knock out the marauding villains.

Her breath raced as fast and skittery as her thoughts. She heard a key turn in the lock. The cabin door swung open. Her fingers tightened around the nail scissors.

A man came into the cabin. It wasn't Josh. In her heart of hearts, she'd known all along it wouldn't be Josh.

"Anne Clarence?" The man's voice was hoarse, his American accent very thick. "Come out, come out, wherever you are! And meet this fine gent who flew in from afar!"

The man walked purposefully into the center of the living room, his back toward Anne. It took him no more than a couple of seconds to deduce that she must be hiding in the bathroom. So much for concealment, she thought despairingly. The door was jerked open, and she lunged forward.

The man simply skipped backward, easily avoiding her ineffectual thrust with the scissors. "Hey, hey, honey, that wasn't smart. I have this real big .45 Magnum in my hand, and I'd sure hate for my finger to jerk on the trigger."

Anne shrank back against the wall, hiding her scissors in the palm of her hand. The man wasn't lying. In his left hand, he carried a gun that was pointing straight at her belly, his index finger curled neatly around the trigger. A pencil light suspended on a gold chain around his neck shone upward, circling his face in an unearthly halo, highlighting his hooked nose and hideously scarred cheek. Combined with the guttural voice, his appearance seemed almost a caricature of the horror-movie villain.

"I'm glad my associate got you here safely," the man said. With affectionate deliberation, he stroked his right hand along the barrel of his gun. "Although it's always a shame not to use this. It's a real nice gun, you know? Smith & Wesson do a lovely job."

Anne shuddered, not only because of the implicit threat, but also because of the man's puffy, grotesque hands. Obscenely swollen, in the reflected light cast downward by the flashlight, they appeared a horrible, suppurating shade of yellow. She licked lips turned parchment dry from fear.

"What do you want? Wh-who are you?"

"Why, I'm Jimbo Katz, of course, and I've come to talk to you about the money your family owes me." He shook his head. "It's a nasty family you've got, Anne Clarence. People you can't trust, that's what they are. I trusted Dom, and look what happened. He cheated me."

"Dom cheated you?"

"He was a very bad boy. I trusted him to collect on three of my outstanding loans, and he stashed the entire proceeds in an offshore account."

"Wha-what's an offshore account?"

"A hidey-hole in the Bahamas, lady. Or maybe in the Cayman Islands. Someplace accommodating, where the bankers don't feel any need to discuss their business with good old Uncle Sam. It's not the location of the account I object to. It's the fact that I don't know the number, so I can't access the money. I don't appreciate it when my associates rob me of my property. And that's just what Dom did."

Anne's stomach lurched at the realization of her worst fears. Dom hadn't been Jimbo's victim; the two of them had been working in partnership. Unfortunately Dom's murder made much more sense if he'd been killed because of a falling-out among thieves, rather than because he had taken too long to pay off his gambling debts.

"Why are you telling me about this?" she asked. "I never even met Dom."

In the circle of light, Jimbo's teeth flashed into a yellow-tinted smile. "Well, little lady, I thought you might be the best person to do business with, you know? You being an heiress, and all. I'm kinda counting on you to get the money Dom owes me for the property he stole. I'm a poor man, struggling to make ends meet, and Dom walked off with my working capital. I figure we're talking somewheres around one million dollars to make me whole again."

"But I don't have a million dollars!" Anne exclaimed.

Jimbo's smile faded. "Don't screw around with me, lady. Your grandfather died and left you a stinking rich woman. If you want to see Joshua Donaldson alive again, you'd better find it in your heart to shake loose some of that lovely money. Fast. Otherwise..."

Anne swallowed. "Otherwise?"

"You saw what happened to Dom. My boys are real good at their jobs."

As he spoke, Jimbo switched off his flashlight and simultaneously swung his fist upward. With reflexes honed by years of fencing practice, Anne sensed the direction of the blow rather than saw it. Sidestepping on light feet, she swung around and rammed the point of the scissors as hard as she could into Jimbo's hand. They sank into the puffy flesh with a sickening hiss. But Jimbo seemed immune to what must have been intense pain. With a grunt of rage, he lifted his arm and swung it down hard on the side of Anne's head.

A blinding light exploded behind her eyes. Looming over her, she saw Jimbo's face, his scar distorted into a red, peeling, blister.

Pain consumed her. She fell into darkness.

Chapter Thirteen

The phone rang while Bree was measuring water for the coffee brewer. Naturally the toast popped up at precisely the same moment.

"Laurel, Heather! Please will one of you get that," she called. "Darn phone," she muttered to herself, sticking two fresh slices of bread into the toaster and spreading butter on the slices that were ready. "That must be the third call this morning and it isn't even seven-thirty."

The twins arrived together in the kitchen a few minutes later. Laurel kissed her mother's cheek, chugged down a small glass of orange juice and grabbed a piece of toast. "Bye, Mom. Gotta run. I'm working the early shift at the club today."

"I thought we agreed you wouldn't teach any more of those aerobic classes. They're too strenuous in your condition." Bree avoided her daughter's eyes, still looking uncomfortable at the mention of Laurel's pregnancy.

"Don't worry, I'm on desk duty till the end of the summer." Laurel pulled a face. "Hey, I've really gotta go. Coming, Heather?"

"Are you working this shift at the club, too?" Bree asked her other daughter.

"Yes. I'm teaching the advanced, high-intensity aerobic dance classes at nine and at lunchtime." Heather put her hands on her trim waist and flexed her shoulder muscles, then sank into a couple of knee bends. She was only loosening up, but Laurel flinched and looked away, obviously aware that her body had already lost the lithe suppleness of her sister's.

"Quit with the limbering-up routine, okay?" Laurel snapped. "If you want a ride with me, you'd better hurry. Come on, Heather, for goodness' sake."

"All right. No need to get in a snit, I'm coming."

The twins were halfway out of the door when Bree remembered the phone calls. "Who called this morning?" she asked. "I'm expecting to hear from Josh and maybe from Shirley. Are you supposed to have given me any messages?"

"Nah, it wasn't Uncle Josh. It wasn't anybody important. Boring stuff." The front door slammed behind the twins.

BABE'S PULSES RACED, and her heart pounded with anticipation. It was always like this when her lover asked her to help him. Life sometimes got so boring, but when she was doing things for her lover, ordinary, everyday things suddenly seemed exciting. Like the phone call she'd just fielded. It had been fun fooling her mother and sister, pretending the call was nothing important.

It was wonderful to know she was needed by someone so powerful—someone as gifted and clever as her lover. And one day soon, with her help, he'd be rich. Rich enough to support his talent in the way it deserved. Rich enough to sweep her away into the glamorous life she craved.

This was the place! Babe choked back a surge of excitement so intense she could almost feel the adrenaline pumping into her veins. Right around the corner they would come to the place her lover had called to warn her about. They would soon find Uncle Josh.

She hugged her arms around her waist, thrilled to think that she was finally playing a crucial role in her lover's great plans for their future. It was about time. Babe's mouth tightened, and she felt herself scowl. She was tired of playing second fiddle to her twin, tired of always being second-best in everything they did. Even her father loved her twin sister more than he loved Babe.

But now, at last, Babe had found a way to be first. Her lover had shown her the way. She would be first in importance, the wife of a handsome, powerful man, a famous man, an artistic, talented man. It was amazing how people believed what they wanted to believe, saw what they wanted to see. All that stuff about Dom and the kidnapping had been such a clever mixture of lies and truth. Nobody had thought to ask the really important questions.

Babe peered out of the car window, staring intently. Yes! There Joshua was. She could see his feet sticking out from behind the rock at the side of the road just as she'd been warned. She must make sure the car stopped before they got too close.

She didn't want to run over Uncle Josh.

LAUREL PUT her hand to her stomach and pressed slightly. "Yuk, I should never have finished that stupid orange juice. I feel sick. If I stop the car, could you take over the driving?"

Heather turned away from the window and sighed. "Gosh, Laurel, you're such a whiner these days. Always going on about being pregnant. You're not the first woman in the world to get caught with an unwanted baby, you know."

Laurel braked and brought the car to a gentle halt. "You know I didn't get *caught*. Dom and I..." She swallowed hard, using the back of her hand to dash away a tear. "Dom and I wanted this baby. Now that he's—gone—the baby is all I've got left."

Heather flushed. "You're right, I'm sorry I shouted, Laurie. You know me, I'm not a morning person." Heather unbuckled her seat belt and started to scoot toward the driver's seat. "Move it, kid, if you want me to drive. We're gonna be late."

Laurel got out of the car. Her feet had barely touched the graveled roadway before she screamed. Heather jumped out after her sister. "What is it, Laurie? What's wrong— Oh, my God!"

The feet, clad in leather loafers, stuck out from behind a large boulder, protruding a good six inches into the roadway. A car coming in the opposite direction could easily have run over the feet without even noticing they were there. Thank heavens this road was so little traveled. Thank heavens the feet weren't sticking out even farther.

Heather's thoughts twisted and tumbled even as she ran. The loafers, highly polished beneath their layer of dust, gleamed brightly in the morning sun. Laurel, half fainting, leaned against the hood of the Bronco, apparently incapable of moving.

"Is he dead?" she whispered.

"I don't know." *Please don't let him be dead,* Heather found herself praying. Not like Dom. Not like Grandfather Bertram. She knelt beside the body, which was lying on its side, curled around the boulder. Reluctantly she forced herself to peer into the man's face.

"Uncle Josh!" she breathed, her voice rising to a squeak. "My God, Laurel, it's Uncle Josh!"

Laurel's fingers splayed against the side of the Bronco, scrabbling for support. "Is . . . he . . . dead?" she repeated.

Heather pressed her ear to Joshua's chest. "He's not dead," she said, her face lighting up in an enormous smile. "But golly, he smells weird." She sniffed again. "Good grief, I think he's drunk."

"He can't be." Laurel managed to walk over to the side of the road. "Uncle Josh never drinks more than a glass of wine or a couple of beers."

"Smell for yourself."

Gingerly Laurel leaned forward and sniffed, then turned away, gagging. "It could be whiskey," she admitted. "What in the world is going on here?"

"Maybe Ms. Too-Good-To-Be-True Anne Clarence ditched him and he's trying to drown his sorrows."

Laurel looked faintly uncomfortable at the mention of Anne's name. Then she shrugged. "There's a bottle of club soda in the Bronco, shall I get it? Maybe it would revive him."

As if to prove that he was suffering from nothing more than a hangover, Joshua chose that moment to give a huge snore. He rolled over, cushioning his face on his hands, a silly grin plastered onto his mouth.

"You get the soda," Heather agreed. "There's fresh blood on his shirt. I want to see if he's torn the stitches on that bullet wound."

Laurel seemed only too willing to leave her sister to the gruesome task of separating Josh's shirt from the sticky crust of blood that glued the fabric to his skin. She had just found the bottle of club soda in the back of the Bronco when the hum of an engine and a cloud of dust on the horizon signaled the approach of another vehicle.

"Make sure whoever's driving that car stops before he crashes into us," Heather said, taking the soda.

"And how am I supposed to do that?" Laurel demanded, but she stationed herself in the middle of the road, pulled off her jacket and waved it madly. The car slowed at once. "I think it's Sebastian," Laurel said to her sister. "He drives a blue LeSabre, doesn't he?"

"Thank goodness," Heather sighed with relief. "Sebastian will be able to help me lift Uncle Josh into the Bronco. I know you can't, now that you're pregnant."

Laurel kept her gaze fixed rigidly on Josh's bloody chest. "I'm sorry," she said quietly. "I'm really sorry, Heather."

"What for?" Heather's voice sounded more brittle than puzzled, although the reason for Laurel's apology seemed somewhat obscure. Heather jumped to her feet, wiping her hands on the seat of her sweatsuit and giving Sebastian a dazzling smile. "Hey, thank goodness it's you. Look what we found!"

Sebastian didn't return the smile. Grim-faced, he knelt beside Josh's still-inert body, indifferent to the dust and grit clinging to his neat gray slacks and pristine starched white shirt. His mouth pulled down, emphasizing deep lines of worry. "Good grief, how terrible! He must have been attacked again."

Laurel drew circles in the dust with her toe. "Heather says he may have been drinking."

Sebastian sniffed then leaned back on his heels. "He certainly smells of something pretty strong. But how did he get here? Where is his car? Besides, Josh almost never drinks."

"You didn't see his car on your way up here?" Heather asked. "Maybe he left it by the roadside if he felt too drunk to drive."

Sebastian shook his head. "I didn't see anything. But right now, we shouldn't be worrying about how he got here. We need to get him into bed." He put his arm beneath Josh's shoulders and lifted. "Damn, he's absolutely deadweight."

"We have a bottle of club soda," Heather said. "Maybe that would revive him if we could figure out how to open it."

"Give it to me." Sebastian took the bottle and rapped the cap expertly against a jutting ledge of rock. The cap flew off, and soda bubbled out, but the neck of the bottle remained intact. Sebastian splashed the relatively cool liquid over Josh's face, then held the bottle to his mouth. Josh groaned, blinked, sucked thirstily and finally opened his eyes.

"Anne," he groaned. "Got to get her." Josh's eyes closed again, and Sebastian looked at the twins.

"Is Anne Clarence missing?" he asked.

"I don't know," Heather said. "We didn't see her after the funeral, but we assumed she was with Josh, didn't we, Laurel? They were supposed to spend the night at Josh's house in Denver."

At the sound of his name, Josh stirred again, reaching out blindly for the soda and chugging down all that was left in the small bottle.

"Bertram's cabin," he said hoarsely. "The policeman took Anne there. Locked her up. Got to... rescue her."

"The *policeman* took her there?" Heather repeated, astonished.

With an impatient exclamation, Laurel pushed Sebastian aside and knelt beside Josh. "Can you stand?" she asked him. "Uncle Josh, put your arm on my shoulders and I'll help you into Sebastian's car. Then we can drive up to the cabin."

"Laurel's right," Sebastian said. "We need action first, questions second." He positioned himself on Josh's other side. "All right, old buddy? You ready to get up?"

Josh wasn't ready to get up, and he sure as hell knew he wasn't all right. He was totally, one hundred percent, guaranteed lousy. It was a toss-up whether he was more likely to pass out or throw up. In the event, he managed to haul himself to his feet without doing either—a minor miracle. He scrambled, as fast as his shaky legs would carry him, toward Sebastian's car.

"Let's go," he said, and collapsed onto the front seat of the car, consumed with anxiety about Anne. Lord only knew what might have happened to her in that damn cabin. Even if she had been left there entirely alone and physically unharmed, he hated to think how much psychic damage another night of solitary confinement might have inflicted. Sebastian got into the car and buckled his seat belt.

"We must hurry," Josh rasped. His throat felt as though a company of marines had conducted drill practice on his larynx. "Got to get Anne." Although he could think fairly clearly, forming his thoughts into coherent sentences was almost more than his addled brain could cope with.

"Shall we come, too?" Heather asked.

Sebastian was already turning the key in the ignition. "You'd do better to call the police," he said tersely. "Obviously we've all been treating the accidents Josh has suffered far too lightly. Somebody is out to get him, and Josh isn't going to be safe until we have the bastard who's attacking him behind bars."

Laurel turned white. "Someone's trying to kill Josh, you mean? L-like they killed Dom?"

Sebastian squeezed her hand. "No, not like Dom. Don't worry, poppet. If Jimbo wanted Josh dead, he'd have succeeded before now."

With a considerable effort, Josh shook off the lethargy that had wrapped him in a semidaze the moment he was seated in the relative comfort of Sebastian's car. "Take me to Bertram's cabin," he repeated. "We've got to get Anne out of there."

The twins looked at each other, and Laurel seemed about to say something. Sebastian shook his head in silent warning.

"You two go and make that phone call to Detective Goodine, poppets. Let him know Josh and I are on our way to the cabin." Sebastian's voice vibrated with false cheer. He patted Josh's knee. "Anne will be sitting in this car with us before you can say Jimminy Cricket."

Josh didn't bother to reply. The alcohol "Officer Wolnik" had poured down his throat had thickened his tongue and ruined his muscle control, but it hadn't turned him into a total fool. He knew as well as Sebastian and the twins that Anne might not be in the cabin. Or that if she was there, she might be dead. His stomach roiled with the acid of frustrated urgency, and he held his pounding head in his hands. "Let's get out of here," he said for what seemed like the hundredth time.

"Of course, Josh. There's no need to sound so worried. We're on our way." Sebastian put the car into gear and drove swiftly up the mountain.

WHEN ANNE REGAINED consciousness, she was alone, and the living room of the cabin had lightened from impenetrable blackness to murky gray. For about twenty seconds, she felt disoriented, then the events of the previous night returned with total and unwelcome clarity. Officer Wolnik. Jimbo. The fact that Dom had been working in active partnership with a loan shark. And Josh was being held hostage.

That last thought was sufficient to propel her into action. Dragging herself upright, she made her way to the kitchen. She turned on the tap and ducked her head under the swiftly running water. The cold water revived nerve ends that had been peacefully sleeping, and the generalized ache of her head resolved itself into a throbbing pain at the side of her skull. She probed the swelling and felt the stickiness of congealed blood. Jimbo must have hit her with the butt of his gun, she concluded. But she didn't have time to worry about her headache. She needed to escape from the cabin and launch a manhunt to rescue Josh.

Her purse lay in a corner of the bathroom, overlooked or ignored by Jimbo. Her manicure set, minus the scissors, was still safely inside. The nail file and the cuticle shaper would both make excellent substitute screwdrivers, she decided, and sat cross-legged in front of the door, tense with her determination to unscrew the backplate and remove the lock.

Her determination wasn't needed. Jimbo, she discovered, had left the door to the cabin unlocked. He must either have known that his blow would put her out for several hours, or he hadn't cared how soon she escaped from the cabin. A quiver of fear raced down Anne's spine at the latter thought. Jimbo must feel very sure that Josh was untraceable if he didn't care how soon she escaped. Josh, after all, was his hostage for the payment of one million dollars.

Anne pushed open the door. Sunlight streamed into the little cabin, filling the living area with the heady scent of pine and mountain wildflowers. The fresh air was wonderful, but she experienced none of the euphoria that had greeted her previous escape from the cabin. She was tired of being victimized, tired of being attacked, tired of not understanding what was happening to her. She had never before appreciated the pleasures of her humdrum life in England so completely.

The high-heeled sandals she'd worn to Dom's funeral weren't very well suited to clambering down the rutted, rock-strewn road that led to Josh's house. Anne kept her head down, her eyes alert for bumps and crevices. She couldn't afford to twist her ankle, because the longer it took her to reach a phone, the colder the trail leading to "Officer Wolnik" and Jimbo would become.

She was concentrating so hard on not twisting her ankle that she heard the sounds of an approaching car only a few seconds before it came into sight. With lightning speed, she dodged behind a rocky outcropping.

As a hiding place, the collection of rocks left a lot to be desired. No single rock was large enough to conceal her, and a crucial space in the middle of the outcropping was protected only by a scraggy clump of sagebrush. So it was with a sinking feeling of despair, but not too much surprise, that she heard the car slowing, then drawing to a halt. She crouched back, huddling herself into the tiniest possible ball. At this moment, she could think of nobody in the whole of America whom she would totally trust. Except Josh, and he was Jimbo's prisoner. Even Detective Goodine would be suspect after last night's debacle. Maybe Brian had been right all along, she thought with a tinge of hysteria. Perhaps America *is* full of Al Capone gangsters and Wild West outlaws.

Two sets of footsteps crunched over the roadway and halted near the rocks. "Anne, my dear, there's no need to hide. It's just us. Sebastian and Josh."

Josh? How in the world can it be Josh? Her hands were icy cold where they splayed against the rock. Sebastian must be trying to trick me. Somehow he is part of Jimbo's massive conspiracy.

"Anne, sweetheart, are you all right? Thank God you managed to get out of that damn cabin!"

It was Josh's voice, rougher than she'd heard it before, and harsh with unmistakable worry. Happiness washed over her, to be replaced almost at once by suspicion. What was Josh doing here? Why had Jimbo let him go?

Slowy she straightened up from her hiding place, paralyzed by doubt. Her heart pounded with delight at the sight of Josh's outstretched arms, but her feet seemed glued to the ground.

Josh suffered from no such indecision. He covered the few yards separating them in two quick strides, sweeping her into an impassioned embrace and covering her face with kisses. She held herself stiff in his arms for all of ten seconds, then she forgot about doubts and questions and melted into his embrace.

"Thank goodness you're safe," he murmured when he found some breath for speaking. "How long have you been hiding here? How did you get out of the cabin?"

"Jimbo left the door unlocked. How did you escape from the policeman?"

Nobody answered her question. *"Jimbo!"* Josh and Sebastian exclaimed in unison. Their faces registered identical expressions of shock. "Did you say Jimbo?"

"What was that murdering slimebag doing up here?" Sebastian demanded. "I figured he'd keep a thousand miles from Colorado until the pressure of Dom's murder investigation eased up a little."

"Dom stole money from Jimbo," Anne said, too tired and too frazzled to come up with a gentler way to impart the news. "They were working together, and Jimbo wants us to pay him a million dollars in compensation for the money Dom absconded with."

Josh's arm dropped from her shoulders. "I don't believe it," he said flatly. "Jimbo's lying. Dom may have been less ethical than I thought, but he would never have been stupid enough to make off with a million dollars of a loan shark's money. He would never have put Laurel and the rest of his family at so much risk."

"Maybe he didn't understand the risk," Anne said wearily.

Josh's reply was curt. "Dom wasn't that much of a fool."

Anne rubbed her hand across eyes that felt gritty with fatigue. "Well, Jimbo sounded pretty convincing to me. And one thing's for sure, he wants a million dollars from us right away."

"How does he want us to pay him?" Sebastian asked, ever the accountant. "A CD? Securities? Or does he expect us to hand over a suitcase of hundred-dollar bills?"

Anne slumped down onto the rock. "He never said how we were to pay him," she said dazedly. "I haven't the faintest idea how we're supposed to get in touch with him. He didn't say that, either."

Josh swore cogently. "So until Jimbo abducts one of us again, we just sit around afraid even to open the door. That's great."

"I'm sorry I didn't think to ask him for his calling card," Anne snapped. "The gun he had pointed at my stomach didn't help to clarify my thought processes."

"Oh, Anne, I'm sorry." Josh moved to take her into his arms again, but Sebastian interrupted. "This probably isn't the best place to hold a discussion about Jimbo Katz," he said. "I don't want to alarm either of you, but you both look as if you could use the services of a good doctor. Let me drive you to Josh's house. At the very least, you need to report what happened to the police."

"That's for sure," Josh agreed, his voice grim. "I'd like to see that phony Officer Wolnik strung up by his thumbs. With Jimbo hanging right there next to him."

Anne's legs wobbled as she walked toward Sebastian's car. He put a guiding hand under her elbow and helped her into the passenger seat. "You'll see," he said kindly. "Everything will seem better after you've had a shower and a cup of tea. The British think tea cures everything, don't they? I found that out when my mother was singing at Covent Garden Opera House. Don't fret, my dear. We don't need to talk about what happened to you last night until the police get up here."

When they arrived at Josh's house, one of the twins was waiting outside on the front porch. "Thank goodness you're back safely," she said, rushing down to meet them. "Mom is having a fit. She's called Detective Goodine and the local police at least three times."

"Are they here yet?" Sebastian asked, unlocking the car doors. "The police, I mean."

"They're on their way," the twin said, offering her arm to Anne. "Gosh, you have the most terrible bruise on the side of your face. You poor thing! What happened?"

"Questions later, Heather," Sebastian said. "Right now, what Anne needs is a shower and a handful of aspirin."

Anne looked at the twin next to her with a vague feeling of surprise. She couldn't always tell Laurel and Heather apart, but she'd assumed this twin was Laurel. Why had she made that mistake?

"You're wearing Laurel's jacket," she said, not even realizing she'd spoken aloud until Heather replied.

"No. This is mine. Laurel has a jacket in the same style, but hers is a darker blue."

Anne was frowning as she walked into the house, and she listened to Bree's exclamations of genuine horror and concern with only a tiny part of her attention. She didn't want to think about Dom and his relationship with Jimbo, so instead her mind squirmed around, worrying at the totally minor problem of why she had misidentified Heather as Laurel.

Finally, with a definite sense of triumph, Anne realized what had triggered the mistake. At Dom's funeral, when Laurel had sought Anne out to explain about the letters missing from Anne's suitcase, she'd worn a jacket like Heather's. And Anne had specifically noticed that the bottom button was loose, pulled away from the fabric by the twin's nervous habit of twisting it while she spoke. There was an identical loose button on this jacket of Heather's, and—seeing the button—Anne had simply leapt to the conclusion that it was the same jacket and that the twin wearing it must be Laurel.

The resolution of this minor mystery left Anne feeling oddly reassured. It was good to know that at least some problems in her crazy world had logical solutions. She drank her tea, swallowed three aspirin and made her way upstairs to the bathroom.

She emerged from her shower twenty minutes later feeling almost strong enough to face the world. But not strong enough to face Josh. It wasn't fair that he should be sitting on the bed, his face white with pain, his expression determined. He wasn't going to wait, she thought with weary resignation. He was going to fight with her to protest Dom's innocence. He couldn't accept that his childhood companion had been involved with a loan shark.

"I want to know what Jimbo said to you," he demanded without preamble. "This story he told you about Dom is a lie, and I want to find out why he told it."

Anne sighed. This was going to be as tough as she'd feared. "Josh, I know you loved Dom, but you aren't seeing him realistically. Dom was a man who got a young girl pregnant while she was still in high school, a man who kidnapped me and kept me locked in a deserted cabin for five whole days. This was a man who was willing to hold his own uncle up for ransom. We know for a fact that Dom did all those dreadful things to people he should have loved, or at least respected. Is it so difficult to believe that he was capable of stealing money from a loan shark?"

"Yes," Josh said quietly. "Anne, you never met Dom while he was alive, so you had no chance to judge him as a person. Dom was totally spoiled and irresponsible, I'll grant you that. He was immature in his attitude toward money and women. I can imagine him gambling away money he couldn't afford, and then cooking up some crazy scheme like your kidnapping to recoup his losses. But he was incapable of becoming partners with a crook like Jimbo, and even less capable of risking his life by stealing a million dollars. Dom wasn't naive. Damn it, Anne, he would have known that stealing money from Jimbo was the equivalent of writing his own death warrant."

"Then what was the purpose of last night's escapade?" Anne demanded. "Why would Jimbo lie? What reason does he have for locking me up in Bertram's cabin and telling me Dom stole a million dollars if he didn't?"

"I don't have any easy answers," Josh admitted. "But if we accept Jimbo's lies, then we're never going to get to the truth of what's going on. From what he said last night, Jimbo obviously knows that you're about to inherit a lot of money. Maybe he thinks you're an easy mark to frighten out of a quick million."

Anne sat down on the bed, aware that she was fast reaching the end of her rope. She was tired of mysteries, exhausted by the strain of doubting everything and everybody. She rarely cried, but now she knew that she hovered on the verge of tears. She felt the tears welling up in the back of her throat, and she swallowed hard, forcing them down again. She turned away, embarrassed to let Josh see her weakness.

Josh put his hands on her shoulders. "Look at me, Annie," he asked softly.

"No." She gulped. "And I hate it when people call me Annie."

She heard the smile in his voice. "I'm not people," he said. "I'm me. And I think I've fallen in love with you."

She froze on the edge of the bed, trying to absorb the meaning of his words. "Annie," Josh whispered. "Please look at me. A man gets nervous when he tells a woman he loves her and all she does is hunch her shoulders."

She twisted slowly around, and he cupped her face in his hands, brushing his thumbs over her mouth. "You're very beautiful," he said. "Did I ever mention that?"

"You're quite good-looking yourself," she said. Her eyes gleamed with a spark of mischief. "Although not quite as beautiful as Carlo."

He laughed. "No one is as beautiful as Carlo, not even you." He gazed deep into her eyes, and the air between them quivered with anticipation, then his mouth came down hard over hers. Her arms slid around his neck, and she returned the kiss with a hunger that equaled his. When their kiss finally ended, Josh leaned back against the headboard, his smile rueful. "I've got to rest up for a few minutes. In my delicate state of health, your kisses pack more of a punch than I can handle."

Anne curled next to him on the bed, the tumble of questions returning the moment their kisses stopped. "Josh, if Jimbo was lying about Dom, why were we kidnapped?"

"Not because Jimbo is in urgent need of money," Josh said. "Otherwise, he'd surely have set up a better method for collecting payment."

"Then what the dickens did he want? Think how much effort Jimbo must have put into this operation. He presumably paid someone to impersonate the policeman. Then he had to modify some car to look like a squad car. He flew up to Denver from Vegas, putting himself at risk of being arrested by the Denver police for Dom's murder. And to achieve what? By breakfast time this morning, the two of us were both safely home and getting ready to report his activities to the police."

Josh got up and paced the room. "We can say Jimbo's crazy, but that doesn't seem a very likely explanation. In which case, we have to assume he did achieve something last night. Now all we have to ask ourselves is what. Would you recognize him if you saw him again?"

"I sure would." Anne described the man's beaky nose, scarred face and revolting hands. Josh looked more and more thoughtful.

"He's certainly a memorable figure. Did he make any attempt to hide his features?"

"On the contrary. He had one of those pencil flashlights suspended around his neck. His entire face was illuminated the whole time we were speaking."

"In fact," Josh suggested, "about the only thing that really happened last night was that you were frightened, and you met Jimbo—a criminal you could now describe with extreme accuracy."

"Yes." Anne drew in a deep breath. "Are you saying Jimbo deliberately disguised himself so that I'd give a false description of him?"

"Either that. Or perhaps the man you saw wasn't Jimbo."

Anne spent a few minutes trying to work out the implications of that incredible idea. "So somebody went to all the trouble of kidnapping the two of us just so that I could give a false description of Jimbo? Or a false description of a man pretending to be Jimbo? Josh, that sounds like the sort of idiotic red herring Hollywood used to churn out in their B movies."

"Do you have any better suggestions?"

"Maybe what happened to me was a diversion," Anne said. "Perhaps it was you they were really trying to contact."

"In that case, they did a lousy job. Wolnik, or whatever his real name is, locked me into handcuffs in the back of the squad, car, then he drove me to a parking lot in an abandoned building project on the west side of Boulder. We waited in the squad car for maybe twenty minutes, with me trying to break free and Wolnik pouring alcohol down my throat. At that point, another car drew up. Wolnik flashed his lights at the other driver, opened my door, and the next thing I knew, I was lying by the side of the road covered in sand, stinking of whiskey, and Sebastian was dumping club soda over my face."

"So the only thing Jimbo achieved as far as you're concerned was to keep you unconscious for the night."

"And out of the way while you were with him."

"Not much of a return for such a lot of effort," Anne suggested.

Josh's smile was wry. "Isn't that where we came in? We're going around the circular maze again."

A tap on the door intervened before Anne found any reply, and one of the twins stuck her head around the door. Laurel, Anne decided. This was definitely Laurel. And she looked distraught.

"Hey, guys, I've been sent upstairs to fetch you." Laurel cleared her throat nervously. "Detective Goodine is downstairs with another police officer. He says—" Laurel paused, looking young and very frightened. "Oh gosh, this is so awful. He says they went to your house in Denver, Josh. And it's been totally trashed. There isn't a piece of furniture that's left in one piece."

Horrified, Anne glanced across at Josh. He gave a bark of hard, unamused laughter. "Well, what do you know," he murmured. "I guess we've just discovered why Jimbo needed me out of the way last night."

Chapter Fourteen

Detective Goodine was not in a good mood, and it showed.
His attitude conveyed the message that he was tired of the
strange goings-on in the Kennedy family. He admitted—reluctantly—that he had no cause to arrest anyone right at this
moment, but he didn't hesitate to make Anne and Josh feel
that he expected to arrest either or both of them sometime
very soon. The rest of the family didn't fare much better,
with the absent Ellen Kennedy and Shirley Rossi included
along with Sebastian and Bree in the detective's general attitude of condemnation and suspicion.

"Something's going on here, some problem in the family, and I'm darn sure you're not telling me the whole
truth," he said irritably.

"We don't *know* the whole truth," Anne protested.
"Believe me, Detective Goodine, nobody could be more
confused than I am."

"And that goes for the rest of us in spades," Sebastian
said. "My brother was murdered. Josh was shot at and his
house has been vandalized. Last night Anne and Josh were
abducted—and you're acting as if *we* were the criminals. It's
outrageous! We're looking to the police for protection, and
quite frankly, I don't see that we're getting it. Simply a great
deal of unnecessary harrassment."

Detective Goodine's reply to this was a grunt, although he
did finally stop his questioning and agree that everyone except Josh could continue with his or her schedule for the

day. Josh asked Anne to return with him to Denver to inspect the wreckage of his town house, and she willingly agreed.

Detective Goodine offered them a ride into town, but his motives were not exactly friendly. "We have an hour to kill while we're driving," he said, settling into the backseat of the car between the two of them. "I'd like to hear a repeat of your story about the police officer who abducted you in broad daylight, then kept you out of action for the entire night. Amazing how easily he tricked you both."

"He showed us ID," Josh protested. "He came in a squad car! Good grief, how were we supposed to know he was an impostor?"

"He didn't come in a squad car," the detective said. "Every law enforcement agency keeps a strict log on all official vehicles. There's been no unauthorized use reported in the last twenty-four hours. Not within a two-hundred-mile radius."

"Well, it looked like a squad car," Josh said. "The door had a police logo painted on it, and inside there was a grill separating the backseat from the driver's seat in the front. If that wasn't a genuine police car, someone must have spent days turning a regular car into such a convincing fake."

"You're overestimating the difficulty." Detective Goodine rubbed the stubble on his chin and smothered a yawn. "We have word on a stolen 1988 white Chevy, navy blue interior. The airport security people reported finding it out at Stapleton, abandoned in one of the long-term parking lots. They noticed it because at first they thought it was a cop car. They soon realized it wasn't, of course."

"How?" Anne asked.

"The badge on the door was some sort of removable decal. The metal grill separating the front from the rear is sold for people who transport dogs. Plus the original registration was still in the glove compartment. I doubt if it took your fake Officer Wolnik more than thirty minutes to transform the car once he'd stolen it."

"But what about the police intercom we heard?" Jos
frowned. "Wolnik kept it on the whole time, and I think b
even replied to some of the incoming calls."

The detective gave another of his grunts. "I don't know
of course, but I'd guess there never was an intercom. Yo
probably listened to a recording. All the guy needed was
tape deck and a mike he could talk into to make things loo
authentic. The mike didn't need to be functional. He wasn'
really trying to send anyone a message. He could easily cal
culate the timing of his responses."

"I can't believe we were so easily fooled!" Anne mut
tered.

"People see what they expect to see," the detective said
for once sounding marginally sympathetic. "That's wh'
eyewitness accounts of crimes are so unreliable. So we're stil
twenty minutes from Denver. Let's have another go a
making sense of what happened once Officer Wolnik had
you in his clutches."

He listened to the retelling of their story with his usua
stolid expression, only interrupting when Anne finished he
description of Jimbo Katz. "Humph. Scarred cheek
hooked nose, puffy, yellow hands. Sounds like a makeup ki
straight from the Halloween store, if you ask me."

Of course! The moment the detective spoke, Anne won
dered why she hadn't realized the truth hours earlier. She
and Josh had suspected Jimbo of applying a false scar to hi
cheek, but she'd never considered the possibility that hi
grotesque hands had also been fakes. Now she realized
they'd been an artful creation of soft Styrofoam and late
rubber. That was why she hadn't wounded him when she
stabbed him—the tiny nail scissors hadn't been long enough
to penetrate the layer of Styrofoam. And that was why there
had been no blood even though she'd stabbed him with al
the force her strong arms could muster.

Jimbo had set out to deceive her, and, by golly, he'd suc
ceeded. She'd been so fascinated by his horrible hands, and
his all-too-visible scars, that she'd paid no attention to the
man's other physical details. He had been of average buil

and average height, but whether he was five-eight or five-ten she would hesitate to say, and she had no idea of the color of his eyes or the shape of his face. She remembered that his hair had been dark and sleek, brushed back like a forties gangster from the movies. But the hair could easily have been a wig. Probably had been a wig, in view of all the other disguises Jimbo had employed, Anne thought resignedly. She said as much to Detective Goodine.

"Right. Wouldn't surprise me at all." He nodded. "In other words, miss, you and Mr. Donaldson were abducted last night by a man calling himself Officer Wolnik who has now disappeared into thin air. But you're suggesting, Mr. Donaldson, that before this phony cop disappeared, he drove you up to Estes Park, poured alcohol down your throat and deposited you by the roadside, conveniently close to your mountain home, where one of the members of your family was quite likely to find you. Is that correct?"

"More or less, I guess. Minus the sarcastic overtones."

"Minus the sarcastic overtones, Mr. Donaldson, is that a correct interpretation of last night's events as far as you are concerned?"

"Yes."

Detective Goodine permitted himself a thin-lipped smile. "And in the meantime, while Mr. Donaldson was sleeping peacefully as the result of imbibing a pint or so of whiskey, you, Ms. Clarence, were terrorized by a man who apparently had free access to your recently deceased grandfather's cabin."

"Yes, that's right," Anne said.

"This man was of average appearance, except, of course, that he had chosen to wear a false nose, a false scar and a pair of hands borrowed from a kid's Halloween monster makeup set. The obvious conclusion we have to reach is that there is no way in the world you would be able to identify this mysterious Jimbo Katz."

"No, I wouldn't be able to identify him. But I don't see why that's a problem. Surely the police in Las Vegas know him."

"Interesting you should mention that, Ms. Clarence. It so happens that we've already been in touch with our colleagues down in Las Vegas and they tell us that they do indeed know of a Jimbo Katz. Seems he's a relatively innocuous fellow as loan sharks go. Breaks a few knees now and then, but has never actually been known to commit a murder. But the intriguing fact is, his colleagues claim he's on vacation in Hawaii. They say he's been there for the past week."

"Then they're lying."

"Maybe. Except that we contacted the police in Hawaii and they checked around for us. Sure enough, there's a Mr. Jimbo Katz registered in the very hotel on Waikiki that he's supposed to be staying in. Seems the Jimbo Katz in Waikiki is a blond, portly gent, about fifty years old. That's the same description we were given by the police in Vegas." Detective Goodine leaned back in his seat and rested his hands neatly on his stomach. "Now, perhaps you'd like to explain to me, Ms. Clarence, how Mr. Katz could be up here in Colorado terrorizing you, at the same time as he's getting himself a suntan out there on the beach in Waikiki."

"Anne has no reason to lie," Josh said tightly. "Maybe one of his henchmen impersonated Jimbo."

"Seems like a lot of impersonating going on around you two folks, wouldn't you say? Unless you keep something mighty valuable in your town home, Mr. Donaldson, I can't think why it would be worth anyone's while to stage such an elaborate abduction. It's easy enough to see how the trick with Officer Wolnik was worked, but it took a heck of a lot of planning and a lot of setting up. Someone must have been keen to get into your condo to go to so much trouble."

Josh suddenly looked bone weary. "I have nothing valuable in my town house. I have a collection of nineteenth-century woodcarvings that's increased a lot in value recently, but I keep those in my house in the mountains. And I don't store cash in either place."

Detective Goodine leaned forward, his features hardening into anger. "Then can either one of you give me a single reason why I should believe this crazy story you're trying to pass off on me?"

"Because we're both of us far too intelligent to have invented something so unbelievable," Josh said wearily. "How's that for a start?"

"Lousy. That hoary old chestnut won't work, Mr. Donaldson. You've no idea the outright stupid lies I get told in this office by people whose IQs are higher than Einstein's. The more intelligent folks are, the more they enjoy inventing these loony stories."

"Then you tell us what you think happened," Anne suggested. "We'd love to hear your theories. Believe me, I'm getting tired of being kidnapped for no good reason."

"I'm underpaid and overworked," Detective Goodine said. "I don't have time to construct theories. I just like to keep my turf clean and trouble free. So I'm recommending to you, Ms. Clarence, that you take yourself back to England on tomorrow's plane. It might take care of a whole heap of my difficulties. America's a free country, of course, so I can't make you go. But let's just say if I get another call from you saying you've been abducted, I'm going to put you in jail so fast your skin will squeak. Strictly for your own protection, of course. Do I make my meaning clear?"

"Crystal clear," she said stiffly.

"As for you, Mr. Donaldson, I recommend you get yourself a good lawyer some time real soon. My investigations are continuing, and after fifteen years on the force, I've developed a kind of low and simple mind. When a man keeps coming to the attention of the police, I'm so dumb I start thinking he must be doing something illegal."

Having delivered his warnings, Detective Goodine relented sufficiently to escort them into Josh's town house and point out the worst of the damage. Surveying the destruction, Anne wondered how many hours of hard labor it would take just to sweep up the pieces of broken glass, let alone determine what was missing or find out what furniture could be salvaged.

"Do you think he really believes we did this ourselves?" Anne asked Josh as the detective returned to his squad car.

"I doubt it, otherwise he'd have taken us down to the police station. And he'd probably have insisted on questioning us with lawyers present."

Anne walked into the kitchen, crunching over a layer of glass and a nauseating mixture of ketchup, coffee grounds and stale soda. She ran hot water into the sink, which by some miracle seemed clear of debris, and searched around for a mop or broom.

"Leave it," Josh said. "I'm going to call a cleaning service and have them haul the whole mess away. And as soon as they've cleaned up, I'll call a Realtor and put the place on the market. Thank God I have no sentimental attachment to this house."

"Not like your place in the mountains."

"No." He laughed without mirth. "I'm beginning to see silver linings in even the darkest clouds. Instead of being furious that this place is destroyed, all I can think of is how glad I am that the vandals didn't decide to trash my home in the mountains."

Anne pulled the plug and let the water drain out of the sink. "If you're not planning to clean up, there's no point in staying here, is there?"

He put his arm around her waist and led her out of the ruined kitchen. "You're right," he said. "Let's go home."

They didn't speak much during the drive back into the mountains. Anne's body was beginning to remind her of all the indignities it had suffered the previous night, and she ached in a dozen different places. She was almost dozing off when Josh finally turned into his driveway.

"We're home," he said. "There's a lovely bed waiting for you to sleep on once we get inside. Or you can snag a lounge chair on the back porch, if you'd prefer."

Each time she saw the quaint, Victorian exterior of Josh's mountain home, Anne liked it better. Today, after viewing the devastation in his town house, the peaceful, sunwashed yard and perky lace woodwork looked particularly appealing. Even the sound of the kitchen radio, floating around from an open window, seemed homey and welcoming.

Bree opened the front door and ushered them inside. "I made fresh coffee cake," she said. "Do you think it's proof that I'm middle-aged that I've started baking every time there's a crisis?" She pulled out a chair for Anne, and offered Josh a cushion for his shoulders. Her attitude toward Anne seemed to have mellowed considerably.

"The kettle's boiling," she said, puttering around nervously. "Tea will be ready in a couple of minutes. Gosh, you both look terrible, even worse than this morning, and that's saying something." She picked up an oven mitt, then put it down again without taking anything from the oven. "Do you need me to call the doctor? Maybe he ought to take a look at your stitches, Josh. And that bruise on your head, Anne—"

"Bree." Josh reached out and took his sister's hand. "Bree, what's wrong?"

Bree sank into a chair, her face drawn. "How can you ask that? Everything. Nothing."

"That's pretty comprehensive," he said, giving her an encouraging smile. "Think you could narrow down the area in the middle that's causing all the *angst?*"

"You've been shot at. Bertram's dead, Dom's dead. Laurel's not even nineteen years old but she's a widow, and pregnant. Anne's been abducted twice, Aunt Shirley is a walking shadow of her former self, Carlo is loonier than ever and you want to know what's bothering me?" Bree shook her head. "Gee, I can't imagine why I'm so uptight. It must be the hot weather."

Josh grinned wryly. "Okay, I asked a dumb question. But I've known you for thirty-five years, Bree, so you can't fool me very easily. Something else is nagging at you, something more personal. What is it?"

Bree glanced at Anne, then looked down at her hands, obviously debating whether to speak in front of someone she still considered a stranger. Worry overcame discretion. "I guess I don't understand what's happening to our family, Josh. I used to think we were the luckiest people in the world. When Mom married Bertram, he made her so happy, and he was such a great stepfather to the pair of us, and we both married people that all our friends envied. And then what happened? It turned out you'd married the greediest woman in the state of Colorado, with nothing between her ears except dollar signs, and the stinker I married dumped me for his prepubescent nurse so he could indulge his obsession for sex on the hour, every hour.''

Josh covered his sister's anxiously kneading fingers with his hands. ''Bree, look at me.'' He waited for her to obey, then said quietly, ''We married the wrong people, for the wrong reasons. We're both divorced. Maybe we're wise enough now to manage our emotions a little better, maybe not. That's the way life is. Now tell me what's really bothering you.''

Bree drew in a great, shuddering breath. ''It's the twins,'' she said. ''They're fighting with each other.''

In comparison to people getting killed and murdered, and marriages dissolving in a welter of bitterness, Anne thought that a pair of teenagers squabbling didn't sound like a problem to get too worked up about. And yet Bree seemed one of the least likely women to agonize over anything trivial. Anne would have pegged her as a woman who believed all emotional problems could be solved by a cookie, a glass of milk and a teaspoon of sturdy common sense.

But Josh didn't treat his sister's comment lightly. ''What are they fighting about?'' he asked.

''That's just it, I don't know. But something's happened to Laurel, Josh. She's absolutely on the brink. I get the feeling that any moment, if I don't catch her, she's going to topple over into the abyss.'' Bree looked embarrassed at her own rhetoric. She put the teapot on the table and poured out three cups of fragrant, mint-flavored tea with hands that shook.

''Heather doesn't even want to be around her sister anymore, and you know how close they've always been. In eighteen years, they've never fought because they never disagree about anything. Now they're in such fundamental disagreement, they don't even want to be in the same room. I'm not imagining problems that aren't there, Josh.'' Bree put a pan of golden brown cake on the table and looked up, her eyes hazy with tears. ''Laurel's hiding some dreadful secret, I know it.''

Josh put his arm around his sister. ''Honey, there's no secret. You know what the problem is. Laurel's pregnant, and probably ambivalent about whether she wants the baby or not. Her husband is dead and she's eighteen years old. And our encounter last night with Jimbo Katz can't have helped. She must be wondering if he's going to come after her for the money Dom supposedly stole. That's a heavy load for a kid fresh out of high school to carry. And from Heather's point of view, she has to cope with her twin going through important experiences that she isn't sharing. No wonder they're both uptight.''

''That's all true, but I'm telling you, Josh, there's more going on in their lives than we know. Laurel's hiding something. Something so bad she's afraid to tell me.''

''Have you told Laurel's counselor about your worries?'' Anne asked.

''Yes, and she simply says it's the baby, and I'm imagining things.''

Anne hesitated, wondering if she could ethically intervene when another counselor had recently taken professional charge of Laurel. In the end, she decided she had the right to approach Laurel as a family friend. ''Would you like me to talk to her?'' she asked. ''Young people need to work up quite a lot of courage before they can confess their problems to a parent. I'm enough of an outsider that she might find it easier to confide in me.''

For a moment, she thought Bree would refuse. Then she smiled, a smile that showed Anne for the first time some of the buried sweetness of Bree's character. ''Thank you,'' she said. ''You've been very kind to us all, Anne, much kinder than we deserved. I'd appreciate any guidance you could give Laurel. I'm sure she needs the help.''

"Where are the twins?" Josh asked.

"They're at work. Laurel said there was a lot of paper-work to catch up on, and Heather volunteered to take the afternoon aerobic class, since she missed this morning. They'll be back around five. What are you two planning to do?"

"I'm going to put in a couple of hours at the office," Josh said. "Otherwise, pretty darn soon my secretary will fire me. Worse yet, she might quit."

"Josh, you should rest," Anne protested.

He leaned over and kissed her. "Tonight I'll rest," he said. "You can take me to bed early and build up my strength. I want to look like a fine, healthy specimen of American manhood when you take me home to meet your parents."

"Is that what I'm going to do?" Anne asked.

Josh kissed her again, thoroughly. "Count on it," he said.

BABE ALWAYS LOVED the secret hours she spent with her lover. Stealing away to share a glass of wine with him in the afternoon when everyone thought she was at the health club made even the dullest day seem exciting.

This was the first time in ages that she'd been able to sneak away for more than a few minutes. Her sister was be-coming such a bore: always complaining about covering for her; always threatening to tell Mom or Uncle Josh the truth about her lover. What was the truth, anyway? He was a tal-ented man who would be recognized one day very soon as a creative genius. Her lover had no mysterious dark side. Her twin was jealous, that was all.

Today her lover was behaving the way Babe liked best: talking to her as if she were his equal, pacing about the room, radiating power and masculine strength. He looked so unbelievably handsome as he discussed the progess of his new work that she felt little shivers of pleasure creep up and down her spine as she watched him. She was sure he would soon ask her to marry him, and then she would become the wife of one of America's most exciting men. *Her* life wouldn't be humdrum and boring like her mother's. Her life would be spent surrounded by fascinating, talented people. Creative people like her lover.

He stopped pacing and came to sit beside her. He took the glass of wine from her, and set it down on a side table. Then he leaned forward and kissed her gently on the lips.

"Babe, honey," he whispered. "I need you. You know how much I want to be with you, but I can't make everything come right for us without your help."

"You know I'll help you," she breathed, wishing he would kiss her again.

"I have to find some papers of Bertram's that are missing," he said.

"What papers?"

"Actually it's another copy of his will. I really need to find it, Babe."

She sat up straighter on the sofa, the doubts that had been clouding her mind for weeks returning in force to haunt her, even though her lover was kissing her in a way that made her insides feel as if they were melting.

"Wh-what do you mean?" she asked, when he finally stopped kissing her. "The lawyers have dozens of copies of Uncle Bertram's will. What does one more matter?"

"This one's important, Babe."

"Why?" He didn't answer, and she drew in a deep breath. "Did Bertram change his will when he found out about Anne Clarence?"

Her lover chuckled. "Baby-cakes, you ask too many questions."

"Please tell me the truth," she whispered. "Uncle Bertram wrote a new will, didn't he? Did he cut you out of his new will? Is that why you're so worried about money?"

He stroked her face with long, slender fingers. "Babe, Babe, sometimes you come up with the craziest ideas. Why would Bertram cut me out of his will? You know how much he admired my work."

She usually couldn't tell when her lover was lying. This time she had no doubts. She knew, as surely as if he'd told her in plain words, that her grandfather had revised his will before he died, and under this new will, her lover was no longer a beneficiary. Babe's stomach contracted with a sensation she recognized as full-blown fear.

"Did you . . . did you kill Bertram Kennedy?" she asked. Until the moment that she heard herself ask the question, she hadn't realized how strong her doubts had become.

"The old man had a stroke," her lover said, sounding annoyed. "The doctors said so and the autopsy confirmed it."

Babe let the relief wash over her. "I know he had a stroke," she said. The awful, niggling doubt came again. "You didn't cause his stroke somehow, did you?"

"For heaven's sake, Babe, you know better than to keep on chasing the same subject when you can see I don't want to talk about it. Men don't like women who ask too many questions. We hate to be nagged, you know."

Her lover got up from the sofa, his back radiating disapproval, and Babe reached out anxiously to pull him back. "Of course I'll help you," she said. "I didn't mean to upset you. I didn't mean to nag."

He turned around, his face once again wreathed in happy smiles. "Thank you, Babe, I knew you'd support me. You're the only person in the whole world who really understands me." He returned to his former seat on the sofa, tilting her chin up and cupping her face softly in his hands. Then he kissed her, probing with his tongue until Babe felt her nerve endings start to tingle. She gave a little murmur of pleasure, and her lover deepened the kiss.

"Babe," he whispered. "It's great to know I can count on you. You're a wonderful, exciting woman. Together we can really go places, Babe."

"Yes," she whispered, relieved that her powerful, clever lover was pleased with her again. "I want to help you."

"I'm trusting you with an important task. A really important task."

Babe's heart swelled with pride. "Tell me what you need me to do."

ANNE WAS LYING in the backyard, dozing with guilty pleasure, when Bree poked her head around the screened kitchen door.

"Anne, I just had a phone call from Giorgio, Shirley's husband. They're leaving for New York and Milan tomorrow, Carlo, too, and Giorgio says Shirley really wants to speak with me before she goes. Will you be all right if I leave you here alone?"

"I'll be fine. You should go, Bree. I expect Aunt Shirley wants to bombard you with instructions about the care and nurture of her unborn grandchild."

Bree still looked doubtful. "After all that's happened, I'm not sure I should leave you alone. I don't think Josh would approve."

Anne stirred herself from her sun-induced lethargy. "If any fake policeman comes calling, I'll barricade myself in the bedroom," she said. "Don't worry. I promise not to get kidnapped while you're gone."

Bree managed a smile. "Be suspicious of everyone. If any firemen or Boy Scouts, or people wearing nun's habits come calling, lock all the doors and call Josh."

"I promise. And if nobody abducts me, I'll make a salad for dinner," Anne said. "That should keep me safely occupied until Josh and the twins get home. How are you getting into town? Didn't Josh take the car?"

"He has an old rattletrap Jeep up here with no roof. It's bone jarring, but safe. I'll take that." Bree frowned. "Giorgio sounded worried. He says Shirley isn't handling Dom's death at all well. He says she's barely spoken to Carlo since she heard the news, although the two of them have always been very close." Her brow cleared. "Still, it's early yet, and how can we expect a mother to accept the death of her child *easily?* Don't wait dinner for me, Anne. I'm sure I'll eat with Shirley and the rest of them in Denver."

Once Bree had left, the house echoed with emptiness, but Anne found the absence of human noise relaxing. Her days alone in Bertram's cabin had been too filled with fear for her to enjoy the solitude, but here, in Josh's home, she felt at peace. Chopping green pepper and slicing tomatoes in front of the picture window in the kitchen, she savored the mountain quiet. After so many years of living amid the hustle and bustle of London, she had forgotten how the strident clatter of everyday human life cut off awareness of the more-subtle sounds of nature. She couldn't quite hear the grass growing, but she could hear a squirrel chattering and the peaceful splash of water over the stones in the creek. A knot of tension in her stomach—one that she hadn't even realized was there—slowly dissolved. She could easily understand why Josh had decided that the pleasures of living in the mountains year-round would more than compensate for the lengthy commute to his office.

Anne had just finished arranging cucumber slices and chunks of avocado on a bed of shredded lettuce when the phone rang. It was Carlo.

"Anne? Is that you? I didn't expect to be so lucky as to have you answer the phone," he said, sounding worried rather than flirtatious.

"Actually I'm the only person here. Everyone else is at work and I'm feeling a bit guilty about being so lazy."

"But where is Bree?"

"On her way up to your house. Hasn't she arrived yet? Your parents wanted to see her before they leave for Italy tomorrow. She was driving the old Jeep, so I hope it hasn't broken down somewhere between here and Denver."

"She is almost certainly safe. I've been clearing up some papers in Dom's apartment, and so I have been away from Aunt Ellen's house all day. I didn't know Bree planned to visit with my mother."

He fell silent, and Anne could feel tension jangling along the telephone wires. When Carlo failed to break the silence, she could think of nothing more inspired to say than, "How are things going, Carlo?"

He hesitated before replying. "If I am honest, I must admit not well. I'm afraid that I have found something here in Dom's apartment which will bring much sadness to my family."

He's found evidence that Dom stole money from Jimbo Katz, Anne thought. "I'm really sorry," she said. "Is there some way I can help you, Carlo?"

"In fact, I wish very much to talk with you," he said. "Before I decide what steps to take, we need to confer about several things. Perhaps if we share our information, things will become clearer. If you will please remain in Josh's house, I'll drive up right away to speak with you."

"Of course, I'll stay here," Anne said. "How long do you think it will take you to get here?"

"At this time of day, traveling in that direction, it's hard to say. I will be as quick as I can."

"Drive safely," she said. "I'll be waiting."

An hour had already passed when she heard the sound of a car engine chugging up the drive. She glanced out of the window and recognized the twins' Bronco. Two minutes later the car door slammed, and one of the twins entered the kitchen from the garage. "Hello, Heather," Anne said.

The twin gave a little giggle. "You always get us mixed up, Anne. I'm Laurel."

Surprised, Anne took another look. Sure enough, this twin wore one of the baggy sweatshirts and loose-fitting jeans that had become Laurel's trademark. Anne apologized. "I wasn't paying attention, Laurel, I'm sorry. It must be infuriating when people keep confusing the two of you."

"Sometimes it's fun," Laurel said, smiling. "When we were in school, looking just like my sister had its advantages."

Anne returned her smile. "Yes, I'm sure of that. So where is Heather?"

"She volunteered to stay on at work to teach a late class for an instructor who called in sick. I didn't want to hang around until ten o'clock, so one of the assistant managers agreed to drive her home. I get tired early these days."

"That's one of the most common symptoms of pregnancy, so I've heard."

"I guess so." Laurel walked to the fridge and rummaged around for a snack. Reaching for a leftover muffin, she changed her mind and grabbed a celery stick instead, crunching down with almost ravenous hunger. Bree was certainly right, Anne decided, watching Laurel's restless pacing. Beneath the girl's smiles, tension was swirling thicker than a fog in Victorian London.

"I made some iced tea," Anne said. "Would you like to try some? I don't guarantee that I've made it properly."

Laurel accepted the iced tea, but she still didn't sit down. "Where's my mother?" she asked. "And when is Josh coming home?"

"Your mother went to Denver to visit with your Aunt Shirley before she goes back to Italy. And Josh is at the office. I don't know when he'll be home. As a matter of fact, Carlo called, and I'm expecting him to stop by for a visit at any moment."

"That'll be nice." Laurel carried her glass to the sink, rinsed the glass and stacked it into the dishwasher. Despite the simple actions, Anne had the impression that the girl was wound tight with anticipation.

"What are your plans for tonight?" Anne asked.

"Nothing special." Laurel glanced at the clock, and at that moment, the phone rang. She swooped to pick it up.

"Hello." She paused for a moment. "Oh, hello, Carlo. Where are you calling from? Anne's expecting you up here any minute." She listened for a while. "Sure. I could do that. You'll be at Dom's apartment?" Her voice shook slightly. "No, that's okay. I have to face seeing it again some time."

"That was Carlo," she said unnecessarily as she hung up the phone. "I don't know what this is all about, but he says he's spoken with Bree and his mother and they've decided it would be better if we drove into Denver instead of him coming up here. He says it's real important for him to see you."

Anne thought rapidly. The girl was sending off waves of almost manic energy, and the drive into Denver would give Anne the chance to probe tactfully as to what was worrying her.

"We'd better leave a note for Josh," she said. "Or maybe we should call him."

"Oh, just leave a note." Laurel was already scribbling on the telephone message pad. She tore off her effort and stuck it with a magnet in the middle of the fridge door: "Josh and Heather: It's 5 o'clock. Anne and I have gone into Denver to see Carlo. Don't know when we'll be back. Catch you later."

Anne added a p.s. "We'll be at Dom's apartment."

Laurel tossed the Bronco keys from hand to hand. "Are you ready?"

"My purse is upstairs. I won't be a second." Anne hurried out of the kitchen.

BABE GRABBED the note off the fridge and stuffed it into her pocket. Then she picked up the phone and dialed hurriedly. The phone was picked up on the first ring.

"We're on our way," she said, her voice staccato with tension. She listened to the man at the other end, her fingers twisted around the phone cord. "You won't...hurt... her, will you?"

She listened one final time. "I love you, too."

When she hung up the phone, her body was trembling so badly she had to cling to the kitchen counter to control the shakes.

Sometimes being in love wasn't easy.

Chapter Fifteen

"How does Heather like the idea of becoming an aunt next January?" Anne asked as they joined the stream of traffic heading toward Denver. She had decided that the counseling technique of asking Laurel to discuss the feelings of a close family member might produce some valuable insights into the girl's own emotions. Anne had often found this method helpful in the past, but even so, she was startled by the vehemence of Laurel's response.

"What does Heather think? I'll tell you what she thinks. She thinks the whole pregnancy bit stinks. Dom was so immature. He'd have made a rotten father, and now the whole family is acting like he was the most sainted human being ever to walk the earth. It's ridiculous."

Quite apart from the fact that she'd heard nobody singing Dom's praises, Laurel's phrasing struck Anne as very curious. "I don't understand," she said. "Is that what *you* think about Dom, or is it what Heather thinks?"

For a split second, Laurel seemed confused, then she shrugged. "Oh, I was just mouthing off like Heather does at me, all the time. Personally I believe Dom would have made a wonderful father. Of course I do, otherwise I wouldn't have fallen in love with him. I'm nuts about kids. Not like Heather. She doesn't want to be pregnant ever. Pregnancy is gross. At least, that's what she says."

"Are you angry that your sister doesn't share your opinion of Dom and motherhood?" Anne asked.

Laurel definitely looked angry, but all she said was, "I've got other people to love me. Heather's opinion doesn't matter."

"Doesn't it? You two have always been unusually close. Why wouldn't you care what Heather thinks? She's your sister, after all, and your best friend."

"We're not so close anymore," the twin muttered. "Besides, nobody cares what Heather thinks. Laurel has always been everyone's golden girl, doing everything first, winning the prizes and all the applause. Heather's just the second-class twin who tags along for the ride."

A chill of understanding feathered down Anne's spine. "I'm surprised you feel Heather is the second-best twin. I thought Heather was born first."

"She was. She's older, she ought to be more important. If we were princesses or something, Heather is the one who'd be crowned queen."

"Mmm, I suppose so. But being the elder has responsibilities, too. Heather told me that she has to take care of Laurel."

"I don't remember telling— I don't remember Heather telling you that."

"Well, she did. That day Josh and I came to visit you and your sister at the health club. Heather and I spoke to each other out by the pool, remember?"

The twin drew in a deep breath. "I remember now. Yeah, Heather's right, I guess. She's fifteen minutes older so she has the right to be in charge."

Anne spoke softly. "But are you in charge, Heather? Or does it seem to you that recently Laurel has called the tune and you've been doing all the dancing?"

"Wh-what do you mean? Why are you calling me Heather?"

Anne looked at the girl driving the car and said, "You're not Laurel, you're Heather."

The girl smiled. "Are you sure, Ms. Know-It-All Clarence?"

"I'm sure. And this isn't the first time you've lied to me about your identity. You lied at Dom's funeral, too. It was you who came and spoke to me in the kitchen, wasn't it? Why?"

"I have no idea what you're talking about."

"You know exactly what I'm saying, Heather. Why did you pretend to be your sister? You invented a story about losing some important papers written by my father, and prevented me finding out from Laurel what had really happened to them."

Heather stared straight ahead, her expression surly. Then she tossed her head and laughed. "Gee, you're so uptight about everything, Anne! It was just a lark. Laurie couldn't have told you anything about those papers anyway. I was the person who knew where your luggage had been put."

"Why was that? Did you help Dom and Laurel with the kidnapping?"

"I didn't know anything about the stupid kidnapping. But afterward, I found the cases—" She stopped abruptly. "I found them in...in a closet and returned them to the police station. So what, big deal. You make such a fuss about things that don't matter. Laurie and I have been trading places like this ever since we were tiny kids."

"Twins who trade places to trick their first-grade teacher are just having fun. It's a way for them to learn something about their own individual identities. You and Laurel are too old to play that kind of trick."

"You love preaching so much, you should buy yourself a pulpit, Ms. Clarence. Can't you take a joke?"

"I like jokes if they're funny, but I don't think this habit of switching places is amusing."

Heather gave another toss of her curls. "Carlo wants to see you. You want to see Carlo. What difference does it make whether I drive you into town or Laurel does?"

"I have no idea, Heather, you tell me. Why did you lie?"

"No reason," she said. Her voice was casual, yet Anne was sure she was lying. However unwilling Heather might be to reveal her motives, she had had a reason for lying. She gave another toss of her curls. "Give me a break, will you? Stop psychoanalyzing me for five seconds."

"It's a deal if you'll tell me why you're so uptight."

"I'm not uptight."

"Then why have your fingers been strumming on that steering wheel for the last ten minutes?"

Heather's fingers instantly stopped their restless tattoo, and instead curled themselves around the steering wheel. Within seconds, her knuckles had turned white from the force she was exerting.

"You keep picking on things that don't mean anything," she said. "Why shouldn't I be relaxed? I have no worries. I'm not pregnant. I'm not a widow. It's my sister who's loaded with problems, not me."

"Are you scared of getting pregnant, Heather?"

"No, I'm not scared of getting pregnant. Haven't you heard about birth control, Ms. Clarence? There are pills you can take to stop all those messy complications. I told you. I'm relaxed. I'm cool."

And sexually active, Anne noted silently. Aloud, she said, "Except that you're just a little bit jealous that Laurel is going to have a baby, aren't you, Heather? This is one more time when your sister is going to do something important first. And since Dom is dead, Laurel's baby is going to be doubly precious to Shirley's family, as well as to your mother and sister."

"You're crazy, I don't want to be pregnant!" Heather denied, cheeks flushed with anger. "Men hate women when they get pregnant."

"I don't think that's true," Anne said. "A lot of men feel proud and happy when they see their wife pregnant with a child they've helped to create."

"Not glamorous, exciting men. Not successful men."

Understanding dawned in Anne's mind. "Are you in love with an exciting and successful man, Heather?"

Heather hesitated just a second too long for her answer to be convincing. "I'm not in love with anyone."

"You and Laurel always did everything together," Anne pressed. "Why not falling in love?"

"Falling in love isn't like deciding to take ice skating lessons, you know." Heather sounded justifiably scornful. "You can't fall in love to order. Laurel went dancing with Dom one night last Christmas and *kaboom,* it happened for them. It didn't happen for me."

"Who did you go dancing with, the night Laurel and Dom fell in love?"

"One of the pilots Dom hung out with all the time. Some jerk called Trent something-or-other. He was so boring it was sickening, although he was an okay dancer."

Anne began to wonder if she had imagined that fractional hesitation earlier on. Heather sounded convincingly heart-whole. And yet... And yet, Anne had learned to trust her instincts where teenagers were concerned, and her instincts were screaming at her that Heather was involved with a man. Although why Heather felt the need to keep her attachment such a closely guarded secret was yet another mystery to file away along with all the other mysteries of the past couple of weeks. One thing was certain, Anne thought, looking out the window as they stopped for a traffic light, Heather needed counseling every bit as much as her sister.

A shopping plaza that looked vaguely familiar whizzed past on their left. Anne frowned, trying to orient herself. "How far are we from Dom's apartment?" she asked.

"We're almost there," Heather said. Her fingers started strumming again, but she stopped as soon as she realized what she was doing. "This route avoids some of the traffic during rush hour. It's hopeless trying to drive anywhere at this time of night with all the people finishing work."

Anne chuckled. Accustomed as she was to the horrors of eight million people moving themselves around and through central London, the Denver roads struck her as almost empty, regardless of the time of day. She was still smiling when Heather drew the Bronco to a halt outside a vaguely familiar town house complex.

"But this isn't Dom's apartment complex, is it?" Anne asked doubtfully.

"Carlo asked me to bring you to this place," Heather said, putting her hand in the small of Anne's back and urging her up the narrow ornamental path. "Come on, Anne. We've taken ages to get here, they'll be getting impatient."

Heather pressed the buzzer on the front door, but she didn't wait for an answer before depressing the brass latch on the ornate brass handle. The door swung open. "Go in," Heather urged Anne. "You know we're expected." Her voice was husky with strain and some other emotion.

Excitement, Anne thought. She's literally vibrating with excitement.

As soon as Anne stepped into the small foyer, she recognized Sebastian's house and knew she'd made a big mistake. It hadn't been Carlo who'd summoned her to Denver, she realized with a flash of belated insight; it had been Sebastian. *Heather's lover.* When Laurel fell in love with Dom, what better boyfriend could Heather find than Dom's half brother?

Sebastian greeted them with a smile. "Hello, my dears," he said. "Shut the door, Heather, and lock it. We don't want any intruders." He cocked his head to one side and gave a little chuckle. "I'm so glad you accepted my invitation to stop by, Anne, my dear."

"I didn't know the invitation came from you."

"No, I made sure of that. I thought Carlo's name might be more persuasive than mine." Sebastian moved to the left, revealing what his body had previously concealed.

Carlo, his arms and ankles bound and his mouth tightly gagged, sat tied to a chair. His normally tanned complexion had turned a mottled, sickly green, and the muscles of his chest bulged as he strained against the cord binding his arms to his body. He glared at his half brother, his eyes burning with a potent mixture of pain and helpless fury.

One of the benefits of her years of training as an Olympic athlete was that, in a crisis, Anne's body often reacted before her brain had time to think. The moment she saw

Carlo, she stepped back toward the front door, grabbing a porcelain vase from a pedestal that she hadn't even consciously registered stood just to her right. She knew Heather still stood behind her. Without stopping to look, she thrust her left elbow hard into Heather's solar plexus at the same time as she swung around, bringing the vase crashing down on Heather's head. With a startled grunt, the girl crumpled into a heap at Anne's feet.

In normal circumstances, the thump of Heather's body slumping onto the floor would have stopped Anne in her tracks. But now, with the adrenaline flowing, she didn't hesitate. Unfortunately she needed to step over the obstacle of Heather's body to unlock the front door. In the two seconds it took for her to make the leap and reach for the bolt, she heard a great roar of sound, then the plop of a bullet lodging itself in the wall less than four inches away from her head.

"Don't move," Sebastian said. "Next time I'll aim to kill, and I am a crack shot. One of the few useful skills my late, unlamented father imparted to me."

Anne didn't delude herself for an instant that he was bluffing. Her body froze into immobility. Sebastian clucked approvingly.

"Good girl. A wise decision. Why don't you turn around? Slowly, please, so that I don't get nervous and pull the trigger."

Anne turned around. Sebastian watched her, his eyes glittering. Shorn of his glasses, with his usual tailored slacks and baggy knit shirt replaced by black jeans and a sleek black turtleneck, he looked nothing like the pleasant, unremarkable accountant Anne had grown accustomed to meeting. His brown hair was thick and tousled, his body hard with muscle. With an unwelcome sense of shock, she registered the fact that Sebastian looked cruel, powerful and sexually riveting. At this moment, it was all too easy to understand why Heather had fallen under his spell.

"Go and stand next to Carlo," he said. "That way I can keep an eye on both of you at the same time."

He followed her progress across the room, holding the gun in his left hand and stroking the smoking nozzle with his right forefinger, like an animal lover caressing a pet. When she was still a couple of feet away from Carlo's chair, he ordered her to stop. They stared at each other in silence for a while, then his gaze shaded into mockery. He gave his gun one final stroke.

"It's a .45 Magnum," he said. "Smith & Wesson do a lovely job, don't they?"

The words and gesture struck a responsive chord in Anne's memory, just as he'd intended. "Jimbo," she breathed. "That wasn't Jimbo in Bertram's cabin last night, was it? It was you."

The mockery of Sebastian's smile deepened. "At your service," he said, and laughed. "Poor Dom, so deeply in debt to his wicked loan shark. Except that the loan shark was me."

Sebastian's attitude suggested that he wanted Anne to ask questions, and she wished she could frustrate him by remaining stubbornly silent. But she needed to know the answers more than she needed to deny him satisfaction. "Why?" she asked. "Why did you deceive your own brother like that?"

"Half brother," Sebastian corrected coolly, as if the difference were of great significance. "And I did it because I needed him to become desperate for money. Poor Dom was a well-meaning young man in many ways, but he had no brains to speak of. He really believed that the plan to kidnap you was all his own idea. Amazing how we can fool ourselves, isn't it? But then, neither Dom nor Laurel had a grain of common sense to share between the pair of them. They were so boringly easy to bend to my will."

A smothered growl of outrage came from Carlo, and Sebastian smiled as he glanced at his youngest half brother. "Are you enjoying listening to my conversation, little brother? I trust you are finding it educational?"

Carlo didn't indicate by word or gesture that he was aware of Sebastian's existence, much less that he had heard the questions, but Anne saw the veins bulge in his neck, and knew what it cost him in terms of self-control to feign such indifference.

"You're a stiff-necked fool," Sebastian said. "I wonder if you would remain so indifferent if I broke your fingers?"

Carlo is a virtuoso violinist, Anne remembered Josh saying. Dear God, she couldn't let Sebastian destroy Carlo's hands! How could she draw Sebastian's attention back to herself?

"Were you the person who planned my kidnapping?" she asked, pretending a surprise she didn't feel. "Goodness, for a man as clever as you are, the job was bungled pretty badly, wasn't it?"

"Nothing that I planned was bungled," Sebastian snapped. "If Heather hadn't been so damn stupid as to return your luggage before I gave her permission to do so, your curiosity wouldn't have been aroused, and you would have flown back to England as I intended that you should."

"Are you sure?" Anne asked. "Josh might have persuaded me to stay."

But Sebastian wasn't easy to provoke. "I'm quite certain you would have gone," he said. "I read all the letters you sent to Bertram. You were a very shy and self-effacing young woman. You would have left for England on the first plane if I could have carried out my original plan."

A groan from Heather punctuated his comments. Keeping the gun trained dead center of Anne's chest, he walked over to the entrance lobby. He prodded Heather gently with his foot. She stirred, but didn't regain consciousness.

"She's such a mixed-up kid," he said, rubbing his foot absentmindedly over her stomach. "But she's so anxious to please, and so touchingly loyal. She's been quite useful in reporting to me on your activities and helping me to carry out my various plans."

"You're sickening. To use a young girl's infatuation to help carry out your criminal plans..."

The smile that he gave Anne was cruel. "How judgmental you are, Ms. Clarence. I simply gave Heather the loving attention the rest of her family failed to provide. Young people have insatiable appetites for love, you know."

"But you didn't give her love. You have none to give."

"Maybe not. What is love, anyway?" Sebastian asked meditatively. "Do you know the answer to that, Ms. Clever Counselor? I know it's not something I ever received from my parents. My mother was off on her first singing engagement when I was six weeks old, and my father was too busy seducing the nursemaids to notice what was happening to me. Until I was five or six, I thought parents were people you waved goodbye to. How shocked I was when I learned to read and discovered from my storybooks that most children have parents they see every day."

"I'm sorry," Anne said. "You must have been very lonely."

Sebastian smiled. "I learned to survive. I've a brilliant mind and a great creative talent, which helps."

"You're certainly clever," Anne agreed, almost choking on the words. "Too clever for me. I have to admit, Sebastian, I don't have the faintest idea why you arranged my kidnapping."

"Come now, I'm disappointed in you." Sebastian stopped prodding Heather's inert body and returned to lean against the end of the sofa. "The answer is very simple. I needed a cover for the murder I was planning. Bertram Kennedy simply had to go."

"You killed my grandfather?"

"I confess. I am the culprit. The brilliant perpetrator." Sebastian sounded highly pleased with himself. "In the few minutes that Dom left Uncle Bertram alone in the hotel room, summoned downstairs to the lobby by my phone call, I slipped into the hotel room and injected air into dear old Uncle's veins. The symptons of stroke and heart attack naturally followed."

"Oh, my God! You murdered him!"

Sebastian looked pained. "Please don't keep stating the obvious, Anne, my dear." He walked over to one of the bookshelves and pulled out a bound manuscript. His gun, unfortunately, never faltered in its aim. "Do you see this? It's the script for *Sweet Poison*, one of Gene Holstein's earliest movies." He tossed the script onto the coffee table. "It's a predictable little effort, but I got the idea of how I could murder Bertram from here, which just goes to show how educational old movies can be. Of course, I had to do a lot of research in various medical texts before I was confident I knew exactly how the method would work. But everything turned out well in the end. Nobody except Dom suspected anything other than natural causes, and I'm sure that was only because Dom was right there in the hotel."

"Did you..." Anne swallowed. "Did you murder Dom, too?"

"I'm afraid it was necessary. That weekend when he disappeared, he flew to Vegas and discovered that he didn't actually owe Jimbo Katz any money. Jimbo was indiscreet enough to explain that I'd bought out the loan. What with one thing and another, Dom started to become suspicious about my role in Uncle Bertram's death. I must say, I was very sorry to kill Dominick. He was an amusing fellow to spend an evening with."

"I don't understand," Anne said, keeping her hands meekly clasped in front of her, but edging slowly toward the dining alcove. If she could just position herself by the entrance to the alcove, she would have a chance of knocking the gun out of Sebastian's hands.... She looked straight at Sebastian, trying hard to keep her thoughts from showing in her face.

"I don't understand why you needed to murder my grandfather," she said. "What had he done to deserve death?"

"Tut, tut, you're slow today, little Annie. You aren't showing any of that spark of creative intelligence I so much admired in you." Sebastian sounded like a sad parent reproving his favorite child. "I murdered Uncle Bertram for his money, of course. What else? Money means power. Money buys love. Money provides everything that a man could want in this world. Now that you've smelled the intoxicating scent of Bertram's millions, you must surely understand how I crave money. It's what murder is almost always about." Prosaically he added, "And then there was the minor problem that I'd spent a great deal of money trying to get my movie into production. Bertram was about to discover that I had been borrowing heavily from his accounts. Regretfully I decided that he had to go."

"But my grandfather was eighty-two years old, and not in good health! If you'd waited a couple of years—perhaps only a couple of months—you would legally have inherited what you killed to obtain."

Sebastian jerked as if he'd been prodded with an electric pole. "Don't you dare poke fun at me, you scheming witch!" His face contorted into a snarl of rage. Anne had read that phrase a hundred times, but until this moment, she had never actually seen human features twist themselves into the image of a hungry predator, closing in for the kill.

"Don't mock me, damn you! Carlo's already told me that he gave you the photograph album early this afternoon." Breathing hard, Sebastian fought to bring his voice back under control. "I've been searching for that blasted album ever since Dom told me about it. I searched every nook and cranny of Dom's apartment, and yet Carlo had to be the one who found it."

Anne looked at Carlo, frantically seeking guidance. There was almost nothing he could do except squirm and nod his head, but somehow—by some combination of eye contact and body movement—he managed to convey the message that Sebastian had not gone crazy and that the photo album was of supreme importance.

If the album was important, surely the more people who knew about it, the less reason Sebastian would have for killing to keep its secrets? Anne decided to risk acting as though she knew exactly what Sebastian was talking about.

"Carlo and I aren't fools," she said, taking another discreet step toward the alcove. When Sebastian showed no signs of reacting, she let her hands drop to her sides. "We've told everybody Carlo found the album. Josh and Bree know all about it."

Sebastian's features smoothed out of their snarl and took on a look of supreme satisfaction. "Not a clever lie, my dear. Josh is at work, and Bree is with my mother. They know nothing about Carlo's discovery. No, now that Dom is dead, only you and Carlo realize that Bertram placed the copy of his new will in the back of the photo album. Unfortunately my uncle decided to make reparations for the formula he stole from your father, and nothing I said would convince him to change his mind. In the new will, he leaves virtually his entire fortune to you."

She was the heir to sixty-five million dollars! And she would have traded every penny for the chance to meet with her grandfather, Anne thought. Lord but she was tired of hearing about Bertram Kennedy's fortune.

She inched backward. One more step, and she'd be flush against the wall holding the stage swords that had been used in one of Shirley Rossi's productions of *Rigoletto*.

"Sebastian, don't be a fool," she said, more to distract him than because she had any hope of persuading him to change his mind. "You'll never get away with killing Carlo and me. What are you going to do with our bodies?"

"Colorado is full of canyons where bodies can disappear for a dozen years. And long before the pair of you are found, I shall have started a new life in Paraguay. A most convenient country with banks that never ask awkward questions, and a legal system that denies all requests for extradition."

"Paraguay only takes in criminals who have plenty of money."

Sebastian laughed. "I'm not short of funds, thanks to you. You should really pay more attention to the documents you sign, my dear. Those papers you so agreeably penned your signature to yesterday enabled me to cash in sufficient funds from Bertram's estate to keep me in comfort for the rest of my life. I understand the cost of living is remarkably low in Paraguay. Apart from bribes, of course.''

Anne had finally managed to position herself directly in front of the wall-mounted swords. She felt behind her back and curled her fingers around the chased steel of one of the handles.

"What about Heather?" she asked. "Is she going to Paraguay, too?"

"We haven't discussed it. If she's very good, I may take her."

"Otherwise, the canyon can hold three bodies as easily as two," Anne said, sending a desperate glance in Carlo's direction.

Despite his concussion, Carlo was alert enough to have realized exactly where she was standing and what she hoped to do. Perhaps Josh had mentioned to him that she had trained as a fencer, or perhaps he thought their situation was bleak enough to make even the feeblest hope worth trying. For whatever reason, when Anne looked across at him, he gave a tiny, almost imperceptible nod.

With tremendous strength, Carlo hurled himself and his chair sideways. He hit the wall with a resounding crash, at least six feet from where Anne was standing. Sebastian jumped, realizing too late that his quarries had separated themselves. In the split second that he hesitated before re-aiming his gun, Anne pulled the sword out of its wall mounting and, with a quicksilver movement that would have guaranteed her an Olympic gold, slashed the blade hard over the back of Sebastian's gun hand.

The sword was a stage prop, so its edge was blunt, but the sheer weight of steel was sufficient to inflict some damage. With a yell of mingled fright and pain, Sebastian dropped the gun. He lunged for it immediately, but Anne kicked it out of reach, holding Sebastian away from her and the gun with the point of the sword.

Panting, his teeth bared in a grimace, Sebastian grabbe the blade. His face contorted in agony as the steel cut int his palms, but he didn't let go.

"You don't think I'm going to let a damn stage prop de feat me, do you?" he demanded. He pushed against th blade, trying to shove it to one side, and was obviously sur prised when Anne's arms didn't immediately buckle. Hi eyes skittered sideways, searching for the gun, and Anne trained to take advantage of even the most fractional wa vering of her opponent's concentration, feinted by tiltin upward with her right arm. Then she leapt back an grabbed the other sword from the wall with her left hand While Sebastian was still off balance, she pressed bot points against his chest, just deep enough to prick the skin Sebastian froze, realizing that if he moved, she could pres the blades home.

"Put your hands on your head," Anne ordered desper ately. "Then walk backward toward the door. Other wise..." She licked her lips and swallowed hard, trying t moisten a throat that had become too dry for speech. "I you don't do as I say, this blade is going into your ribs clea up to the hilt," she lied. "I'm a champion fencer. I know exactly where to put the blade to do the most damage."

Sebastian followed none of her orders, but it was not be cause he actively defied her. He was temporarily beyond defiance. He had just noticed the wounds he'd inflicted on his own hands when he grabbed the swords, and he stared in horror at the blood welling out from between his fingers

"I'm bleeding," he whispered in disbelief. "My God, I'm bleeding to death. I need a doctor!"

His panic was so inappropriate, coming from a man with two murders to his credit, that Anne found herself smoth ering a gasp of laughter. *You don't have time for hysterics, she told herself. You're in a proper mess, Annie, my girl and you'd better do something useful—fast.*

Sebastian continued to stare hypnotized at the gush of his own blood. Feeling like a monster, Anne jiggled the sword a little to remind him who held the weapons. Sebastian screamed, although she'd barely scratched him.

So far, so good, Anne thought. But Carlo was slumped in his chair, dazed if not unconscious, and at any minute Sebastian was going to realize he wasn't likely to die of a cut hand. And at that moment, he would become extremely dangerous. The cornered rat always struck out hardest.

The only solution, Anne decided, was for her to get the gun, then run outside to call the police. Having decided what to do, there seemed no point in waiting, and she prodded Sebastian in the leg with the second sword.

"This way," she ordered. "Move it, fellow, or this blade is going right through you."

Dazed and muttering, Sebastian staggered across the room in the direction of Anne's prods. From the corner of her eye, Anne searched out the exact location of the gun. She had kicked it off the area rug, and it had slid across the parquet floor almost to the entrance. But where was it now?

Almost in the same instant that she spotted the gun, she saw Heather's hand snake out to grab it. Oh, dear God, no, Anne thought. Damn it, Heather, couldn't you have stayed unconscious for another couple of minutes?

The answer, apparently, was no. With the gun in her hands, albeit none too steady, Heather dragged herself to her feet. "Anne!' she exclaimed thickly. "What have you done to Sebastian? He's hurt!"

The sight of Heather regaining consciousness seemed to jerk Sebastian back to reality. Gambling that Anne would never plunge the swords into his body, he gazed at Heather, his lips twisting into a sick parody of a smile. "Give me the gun, Babe," he ordered. "Heather, I need you to help me. You must do what I tell you if we're going to be together."

Perhaps she was still too groggy to understand what he asked, or perhaps some subliminal understanding of the violence lurking beneath the command held her back. For whatever reason, Heather's only response was to retreat until her back was wedged against the front door. The gun shook in her quivering hands.

"Don't give him the gun," Anne pleaded. "Heather, swear to you, if Sebastian gets control of that gun, he's g ing to kill me and Carlo, and probably you, too."

"No!" Heather yelled, frantic with denial. "He would kill you. He'd never hurt anyone. You love me, Sebastia don't you? You won't hurt Anne and Carlo."

"Of course I love you, Babe. You're the greatest. A why would I want to hurt my own brother?"

"Heather," Anne said tersely. "Don't give this man t gun. He's a murderer. He killed Dom and Bertram Ke nedy, too."

"No," Heather said again, but this time her voice w little more than a pleading whisper. "Sebastian, y didn't—hurt—anyone, did you?"

"Babe, how can you ask such a silly question? Hey, suga don't you know I love you?" Sebastian's voice was silk caressing. "Be a good girl now, Babe. *Give me the gun.*"

Like a rabbit trapped in the glare of two sets of powerf headlights, Heather's gaze switched from Anne to Seba tian and back again. Finally, tears streaming down h cheeks, she turned toward Anne. "I'll give you the gun you promise not to shoot him," she said.

A thundering series of knocks hammered onto the doo and the bell buzzed insistently. "Anne! This is Josh! A you in there? For God's sake, open the door."

"I'm here!" she called out, not relaxing her grip on th sword by so much as a millimeter. "But I can't open th door. It's locked."

"Sebastian!" This time Anne recognized Shirley's voi calling from outside the door. "Sebastian, I beg of you! D not harm anyone. It's time to give up your mad scheme Sebastian, they won't work. We know what you've bee doing and we must inform the police even though you're m son."

Sebastian gave no indication he had heard his mothe "Heather, Babe," he crooned, his eyes fixed and gleaming "Babe, sweet Babe, give the gun to me."

Heather started whimpering.

"Heather," Anne repeated, in her firmest, most school-teacherish voice. "Please open the door for Josh and your Aunt Shirley *right now.*"

With inexpressible relief, Anne heard the girl draw back the lock, but her relief turned to horror when she saw the door burst open and crash against Heather's arm. The gun Heather held exploded in a cough of orange flame, and Sebastian tottered for a sickening second before doubling over and crashing to the floor.

Pounding feet rushed into the room. "Anne, are you safe? My God, did we get here in time?"

Josh's voice. Anne registered the fact without feeling any emotion.

"Ah, dear heaven, Shirley, don't look!" Ellen Kennedy entered the house immediately behind Josh, with Shirley Rossi following in her wake. She gently prised the gun from Heather's fingers, then gathered the weeping girl into her arms and held her tight. "Come into the bedroom, my dear, and we'll call your mother. No, don't look. There, there, my dear. Everything's going to be okay. Come with me now, you'll see. You'll be all right."

"Anne, I have to call the police. Can you hear me? Do you understand what I'm saying?"

Anne realized Josh was speaking to her. She nodded, although her head felt almost too heavy to move, then watched in silence as Josh went into the kitchen and picked up the phone. Like a spectator at the movies, she saw Shirley untie Carlo and start talking to him. Sound washed over her in an irritating, incomprehensible babble.

Anne walked to the empty fireplace and leaned her head on the mantelpiece. When she finally managed to turn around, Carlo had already taken a cover from one of the beds and thrown it over Sebastian's body. Shirley was crying, and he took her into his arms, rocking her gently back and forth.

Anne's weight suddenly seemed too great for her legs to support. She leaned on the gleaming jeweled swords and gazed around the room, her eyes seeing everything and absorbing nothing. Josh left the kitchen and came straight over to her. He hugged her tight, but Anne felt his strong arms and warm hands as alien intrusions in a world turned to ice.

"How did you know where I was?" she asked. Her tongue moved clumsily inside her mouth, and her body was so numb she wondered if it would ever respond normally again.

"Laurel called and warned us to start looking for you right away. When she came home and found you and Heather both gone, she was frantic. Apparently she suspected Sebastian had something to do with Dom's murder right from the beginning, but she didn't say anything because she was terrified her sister was involved. That's why she's been so brittle with tension these past few days."

"I don't think Heather understood what Sebastian was really up to," Anne said. "She was infatuated with him, but not obsessed enough to condone murder." She shivered, and Josh drew her closer. To her relief, his body warmth no longer seemed an intrusion. Instead, it seemed a lifeline leading out of the murky, freezing pit Sebastian had dragged her into. The ice encasing her skin slowly began to melt.

"He did it for money," she said. "Josh, can you believe that man almost destroyed an entire family because he didn't want anyone to discover that Bertram Kennedy had written a new will?"

"I have read my uncle's new will," Carlo interjected. "That's why I was so anxious to talk with you, Anne. I found the copy just this afternoon, tucked into the back of a photo album my uncle had prepared as a welcoming gift for you."

"So that's why Sebastian was so uptight about a photo album!"

"Yes. The will is a simple two-page draft, drawn up in Bertram's handwriting and not notarized, but I imagine it's legal. Sebastian must have been frantic to kill our uncle before the lawyers made dozens of photocopies."

"Is that why he trashed Josh's apartment? Searching for my grandfather's new will?"

"I'm sure it was. Uncle Bertram took the album to your hotel the night he was murdered, but apparently in the confusion following his death, the album got left in Dom's car. I guess Dom found the will and threatened to reveal its existence, so Sebastian killed him. But he still had no idea where Dom had put the album."

"How did you find it?" Anne asked. "Sebastian had already searched Dom's apartment a half dozen times, he said. And he literally tore Josh's town house apart last night, he was so desperate."

"Ironically the photo album never got taken out of Dom's car. I volunteered to clean his car this afternoon, so that we could offer it for sale. When I vacuumed, I found the album stuck way under the backseat. I was on the way to see you, Anne, to explain what I knew, but like a fool, I stopped off here to discuss my find with Sebastian." Carlo rubbed his eyes. "I guess, in my heart of hearts, I was already afraid he knew of the will's existence and had chosen not to disclose it, but that was the limit of my suspicions."

"None of you understand the full truth of why Sebastian behaved as he did," Shirley said. She clenched her hands into fists, her face so devoid of color that even her lips looked gray. "Sebastian wanted money because he believed it would buy him the love he could find no other way. My son never forgave me for the weeks and months I left him alone with a father who cared nothing for him."

"Mamma," Carlo protested, "you gave Sebastian all the love any child could have needed."

"Ah, no," she said. "If I had done that, he wouldn't now be lying over there, dead." Silent tears trickled down her cheeks. She brushed them away and drew herself up straight.

"In grand opera," she said, "the curtain rings down and the tragedy is ended. The dead bodies stand up and take their bow, and then the stagehands walk on to dismantle the scenery. In real life, we aren't so fortunate. We must rebuild our lives piece by piece and step by slow step.'' With hands that shook, she reached out and touched Anne's arm.

''I'm glad that you will inherit Bertram's money. I think that you will not find it very important in your life. And when money is not important to its owner, it can be used for good.''

''If Grandfather's new will stands up in court, I've already decided what I'm going to do with his money.''

''Let me guess,'' Josh said, his voice filled with wry laughter. ''You're going to give it all to Greenpeace.''

''Not quite. I'm going to set up a foundation to help protect and study the ecosystem of the tropical rain forests. That way, the wealth created by my father's research can be used for a cause he would approve of.''

Josh tightened his arms around her, then gave an exaggerated sigh. ''Darn it, and I'd already planned to marry you for your money. Now I guess I'll have to marry you just because you're beautiful and I love you.''

The ice encasing her had finally melted enough for Anne to feel the heat of Josh's body pressing against her entire length from head to toe. She still didn't turn to face him, but she laced her fingers into his, and welcomed the warm surge of life flowing back into her veins.

Shirley managed a small but genuine smile. ''Take her to a hotel for the night, Josh, before that dreadful Detective Goodine gets here and starts asking his eternal questions. Go somewhere you have never stayed before, somewhere you can work together to make the beginnings of your new life. Laurel's baby and your relationship are the only good things to be salvaged from this wreckage. Make sure you don't lose her.''

Josh turned Anne around within the circle of his arms, carrying her hand to his cheek and holding it there tightly. ''I love you,'' he said, and the words sounded as firm and solid as the body she leaned against.

Anne looked into his eyes, and what she saw there made her heart beat fast with hope. ''I love you, too, but is that enough?''

"The next few weeks are going to be rough, but I think we can make it. We'll never know unless we try. Do you want to try?"

"Yes," she said. "I want to try."

"Then let's get started," he said.

Holding hands, they walked out together into the starlit darkness of the Colorado night.

HARLEQUIN PROUDLY PRESENTS A DAZZLING CONCEPT IN ROMANCE FICTION

 One small town,
twelve terrific love stories

JOIN US FOR A YEAR IN THE FUTURE OF TYLER

Each book set in Tyler is a self-contained love story; together,
the twelve novels stitch the fabric of the community.

LOSE YOUR HEART TO TYLER!

Join us for the second TYLER book, BRIGHT HOPES, by
Pat Warren, available in April.

*Former Olympic track star Pam Casals arrives in Tyler to
coach the high school team. Phys ed instructor Patrick
Kelsey is first resentful, then delighted. And rumors fly about
the dead body discovered at the lodge.*

If you missed the first title, WHIRLWIND, and would like to order it, send your name, address, zip or postal code, along with a check or money order for $3.99 plus 75¢ postage and handling ($1.00 in Canada), payable to Harlequin Reader Service to:

In the U.S.	In Canada
3010 Walden Avenue	P.O. Box 609
P.O. Box 1325	Fort Erie, Ontario
Buffalo, NY 14269-1325	L2A 5X3

Please specify book title(s) with your order.
Canadian residents add applicable federal and provincial taxes.

TYLER-2

Janet Dailey ®
Americana

Janet Dailey's perennially popular Americana series continues with more exciting states!

Don't miss this romantic tour of America through fifty favorite Harlequin Presents novels, each one set in a different state, and researched by Janet and her husband, Bill.

A journey of a lifetime in one cherished collection.

April titles   **#29 NEW HAMPSHIRE**
                             Heart of Stone

                     #30 NEW JERSEY
                             One of the Boys

If you missed your state or would like to order any other states that have already been published, send your name, address, zip or postal code, along with a check or money order for $3.99 plus 75¢ postage and handling ($1.00 in Canada) for each book ordered, payable to Harlequin Reader Service to:

In the U.S.	In Canada
3010 Walden Avenue	P.O. Box 609
P.O. Box 1325	Fort Erie, Ontario
Buffalo, NY 14269-1325	L2A 5X3

Please specify book title(s) with your order.
Canadian residents add applicable federal and provincial taxes.

JD-APR

Following the success of WITH THIS RING, Harlequin cordially invites you to enjoy the romance of the wedding season with

**BARBARA BRETTON
RITA CLAY ESTRADA
SANDRA JAMES
DEBBIE MACOMBER**

A collection of romantic stories that celebrate the joy, excitement, and mishaps of planning that special day by these four award-winning Harlequin authors.

Available in April at your favorite Harlequin retail outlets.

THTH